THE
DISPLACED

a novel

THE DISPLACED

a novel

Rodrigo Ribera d'Ebre

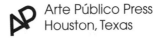
Arte Público Press
Houston, Texas

The Displaced is published in part with support from the National Endowment for the Arts. We are grateful for its support.

Recovering the past, creating the future

Arte Público Press
University of Houston
4902 Gulf Fwy, Bldg 19, Rm 100
Houston, Texas 77204-2004

Cover design by Brandon Francis
Cover art by Carlos Ramirez

Names: Ribera d'Ebre, Rodrigo, author.
Title: The displaced / Rodrigo Ribera d'Ebre.
Description: Houston, Texas : Arte Público Press, [2022]
Identifiers: LCCN 2021056529 (print) | LCCN 2021056530 (ebook) |
    ISBN 9781558859388 (trade paperback ; alk. paper) | ISBN
    9781518506987 (epub) | ISBN 9781518506994 (kindle edition) |
    ISBN 9781518507007 (pdf)
Subjects: LCSH: Gentrification—Fiction. | LCGFT: Novels.
Classification: LCC PS3618.I236 D57 2022 (print) | LCC PS3618.I236
    (ebook) | DDC 813/.6—dc23
LC record available at https://lccn.loc.gov/2021056529
LC ebook record available at https://lccn.loc.gov/2021056530

♾ The paper used in this publication meets the requirements of the American National Standard for Information Sciences—Permanence of Paper for Printed Library Materials, ANSI Z39.48-1984.

22 23 24   4 3 2 1

To my wife and children

PART I

ONE

MIKEY

June 18, 1999

This is my About page: I have sausage fingers. They're so bloated that I once went to the doctor because I had gotten into a fight and my left knuckles had two teeth marks because they went into the opponent's mouth. The doctor took one look at my right hand and said, "Whoa, your hand is so swollen, we need to get that down."

I said, "It's the other hand, doc."

I have a bubble butt. I can never get my belt to adjust at a comfortable level, so I wear my jeans a little low. Not like sagging or anything, but enough so that my belt doesn't cut into my stomach and heighten my ass. I have a slight gut, and partial man boobs. Maybe because I have two X chromosomes, like women. My father did always call me a girl, or a faggot, or a bitch. I have bad breath, maybe related to gingivitis or my lack of flossing, or my engorged gums. I have depression.

Sometimes I don't want to get out of bed. I've had suicidal thoughts about this. I used to cry myself to sleep in high school, but just like during winters. My facial profile sucks. My pudgy nose is a little wide and sits above my puffy lips. I have a Napoleon complex. 5'8" is average in Latin America, Asia, the

3

Middle East or some parts of Eastern Europe and the Mediterranean. But I'm American, and I'm from one of the vainest cities
in the world: Los Angeles. Short people are not taken as seriously
as tall people. We have to rely on other advanced skills. Hence
Adolf Hitler, Martin Scorsese and Maradona. And my skin tone
is like sand. Sure, there's black power and brown pride movements, I'm just not part of those. I get looked at a certain way
sometimes . . . by white people. It's a wild-eyed look, like they
have ownership over me because they're the "master" race, and
like I should continue skipping along my merry way, just happy
enough to be strolling along the streets of Anytown, USA. Lucky
that I'm even in this country. I get the look mostly when I jog. I
hate jogging, but I do it to help with my fat deposits. It's tedious,
but I don't want to spend the money at a gym or with a personal
trainer. But white people are more likely to give me a nod, a
greeting or head gesture on the jog. But when they dismiss me,
it cuts deep, because I need their approval. Black people always
greet me, though, they're the friendliest on the road. And visible
Latinos, like me . . . they usually ignore me. It means nothing
coming from them, we are nobodies in this great experiment
called America.

☙❧

I just graduated from UCLA, so a party is in order. When my
parents were together, they threw parties on the regular . . . to celebrate victories. This one is for the haters.

I call a bunch of people, some from the scene, others from
school. I want it to be packed. I want them to know what I did. It's
not easy being from the hood and getting a degree. Almost didn't
graduate though, because this professor, Koch, accused me of plagiarism in my last semester. In this class about War and Media.
She said I didn't cite outside sources. I said they were my own
words, my own ideas. She didn't believe me, she had that wild-
eyed look, and she was tall. A transplant from the South. Proba-

bly not used to people like me thinking critically. I never called her doctor either, like I did the other professors. She didn't earn it. We had to get a whole committee involved . . . to investigate my previous work. I guess I should've been flattered. I wasn't. I even cried a few times, not sobbing or anything, just watery eyes. But the committee had my back, specifically Professor Kunioka PhD, and Professor Andranovich PhD. Koch was forced to apologize in front of the whole department. She turned all crimson, or whatever. Victory.

I tell my friend Rick from down the street to call a few punkish garage bands—they agree to perform. They'll bring their own people too, hopefully they have a following. And girls, that's important.

July 10, 1999

My mom is out of town this weekend. I get two kegs from Bill's on Slauson and a bunch of cheap wine bottles. If people want other drinks, they can bring their own. Not going to waste money on other people, like last time. I'm still working part-time in customer service, nothing important. I can't do that much longer. I have a bachelor's in Political Science now. I'm supposed to be somebody. I wanted to run for office when I started college—city council or the house of representatives—but now I hate politics at that level. No real radical politician can make any formative change in this country, though, not with the electoral college, consensus-building or a bicameral system. I'm registered as a socialist. I'll probably end up on a blacklist somewhere. Had to give up the band too, have to grow up someday. Nowadays, I just want to work in civil service, like all those people in the Russian novels I read. A bureaucrat is enough, for now.

I'm unsure what to wear. I settle on a torn jean jacket, a New Order T-shirt from the "Movement" album, black Levi's and black Jack Purcell sneakers. I always wear these shoes with black laces 'cause they look less dirty when they're dirty. Plus, there's a lot of gangsters around here that wear white Converse, but with white laces. Never black. Black is neutral—punk rock. I don't want to get mistaken . . . for one of those *cholos*. Especially in this neighborhood. Never have though, because I keep my hair long.

I'm in the driveway, scanning and greeting people. So far so good. The partygoers have like a college-radio, thrift-store type vibe. Like they came out of Penny Lane Records. There's girls, and they're drinking. My friend, Stan Corona, is spinning Northern Soul records—oldies, but midtempo. The type nobody really knows. Nobody listens to this music, not really, but people like it when they hear it, because they think they recognize the sound. That's what we like about it. It's not played out, it's not popular, it's not on the radio. It's our own scene.

Stan's legs are both sleeved up—Posada *calacas* and all that—and he has a 45-rpm adapter tattooed on his forearm, and on his wrist that faceless character with a weird eye and a derby hat from "A Clockwork Orange." He's the only non-gangster I know that has that many tattoos. He wants to put a cactus on his forehead, like we say in Spanish, *Tienes el nopal en la frente.* Sometimes I get nervous when I'm with him on the streets. Like we're gonna get jumped or shot, and he has his head shaved down to a 1-clip with mutton chops as sideburns, like those British skinheads.

I'm posted up at a corner in my backyard with Rick. He's telling me about his ROTC program at UCLA. Getting ready for military service. Another way out of the hood. I spot another neighbor walking through the side entrance, Ruben Beltran . . . some tall-ass fool, and his nickname is Lurch. A Culver City gang member. He dances his way into my yard, arms winged, knuckles almost glued together, and he walks toward me looking in all directions. Red plastic cup in his hand with beer foam pouring out. He takes a sip. I don't like that he's here. Makes my chest thud, like a crow flapping its wings.

He says, "Damn, dog, that song's fuckin' hard!"

I say, "Joan Baker. . . . 'Everybody's Talking.'"

He doesn't know the song. I look at Rick on the side, he gives me that look, like the party's over.

Lurch shakes my hand, pats me on the back and says, "What's up." He gives a head gesture to Rick. Lurch shifts his head back toward the side entrance. A flood of his homies is there: sporty-looking dudes with red Cincinnati Reds hats or red bandanas hanging over their shoulders. They have a few hood rats with them with wet-looking hair and skanky clothes, like small shorts and low-cut blouses. Some of those girls chew bubble gum and look at everyone with attitude. My friends and acquaintances try hard not to stare at them.

☙❦❧

My guests start leaving, and it becomes a gangster party. Stan keeps spinning Northern Soul records, and these fools throw up C hand signs and yell out their neighborhood loud as fuck. I swerve around the kegs and head toward my house. I gotta call the cops. In secret though.

But Lurch pulls me to the side and says, "*Ay*, Mikey, trip out on this shit, dog. I seen this fool the other day, right. Some skinny white boy in tight jeans and he had a bunch of tattoos. He had a big-ass beard, too, like some old fuckin' man or something. You know somebody like that? I mean, you know a lot of weird looking people."

"I don't think so. I don't know anybody with a beard," I say. I take a drink from a plastic cup.

Lurch says, "He had a black military hat, too, with a star in the middle. Like a goddamn communist. That dude that was here earlier . . . your homie Rick from down the street, he's into military stuff, *¿qué no?*"

I reply, "Yeah, he just joined the Air Force. He has a cousin too, Robert, a skater that used to tag . . . he's in the Navy. But he doesn't have a beard. I'll ask around, see what's up."

I move a little closer to my back door. I want these fools to leave.

Lurch keeps talking. "I figured you might know him, because he had long hair like you. Thought he might be one of your new-wave homies. He looked sick, though . . . so like maybe he escaped from a half-way house, you know? Or he went AWOL, or he was like a homeless bum, you know what I mean? I didn't like him. Something didn't feel right about that *vato. Tú sabes.*"

"Yeah, I don't know. I'll ask . . ."

We're interrupted by Lurch's homie, Raven. Beer is overflowing from his plastic cup and pouring onto his hands as he staggers toward us.

He says, "Damn, Mikey Boy, why do all your friends look like a bunch of white people? Where'd they go anyway? You don't even look Mexican either, dog, with your fuckin' hairstyle and your clothes 'n shit."

He lets out a sharp-pitched laugh and pounds Lurch's fist. They smile and laugh. I want to ask what Mexicans are supposed to look like. Like them? Like *cholos?* Or like *paisas*—recent immigrants without papers? Matter of fact, Raven's not even Mexican, he's Guatemalan. I glance all over the place, then lodge my eyes on Lurch.

I say to Raven, "White people definitely think I'm Mexican." I purse my lips and pat Lurch on the shoulder.

I know I look different . . . I'm post-punk, and Lurch and Raven are pretty-boy gangsters. Lurch has short, slicked-back hair with a clean fade on the sides, and clean shaven. He's a light-skinned giant with green eyes, 6'5", and drives a Beamer. I wonder if they think that's some white people shit. Raven is dark-skinned with braces, and he sports a magnum mustache. His head is always shaved, but he wears a ballcap on the regular. And he's wearing a red, white and blue Nautica windbreaker. I wonder if he's aware that his maritime patriotic outfit is white.

Raven says, "But your hair, the way you talk, you're just . . . white-washed, like a fuckin' . . ."

Consecutive gun shots—*clack, clack, clack, clack.* They sound close.

I freeze up. My breath leaps out of me, heavy and rapid. I drop my plastic cup, beer splashes on my shoes. Partygoers duck and some run into my backyard through the driveway. Other people run toward the street, like Lurch and Raven. They're both reaching down into their waistbands. I see people getting pushed, and some girl falls on the driveway and someone tramples over her. Other people hide behind trash cans and my mom's Cadillac. I spot big curly hair and some red baseball caps just a tad higher than the car's hood line. I run inside the house with my head ducked and lock the back and the front doors. Nobody's inside. Good. Don't want those fools in here either, stealing shit or fuckin' in my mom's room. I peek through the curtain in the living room and I see two guys in ski masks sticking out of an '86 Oldsmobile, letting out some more shots—*dakka, dakka, dakka.* I see quick flashes of light and I hear a car window shatter.

Cross my fingers that it isn't my Jeep Wagoneer. I observe a body splayed out on the sidewalk.

Can't tell who it is.

Right there on my porch, I see this girl, Paulina, stuck between my mom's plants and the railing. Her boyfriend is that fool Raven, but he's not there. I open the door, just a little, while the bullets keep drumming.

She screams, "Help, help me, please!"

I lift her up with one hand and pull her toward me. I don't even know where I got that strength from. A bullet whizzes right by us and hits the stucco right next to the address. I fall back, she falls on top of me. She's crying and she's scared, and she throws herself into my arms. Her breasts are rubbing all over my chest, and she doesn't stop hugging me. Her body trembles, and it's soft and warm pressed up against me. Good thing I have a breath mint in my mouth.

I grab her by both cheeks with the palms of my hands, while her dirty blonde hair slithers between my fingers. I say, "It's okay, it's okay. You're okay."

"Where's Danny? Have you seen him?" She's referring to Raven.

I say, "I saw him running down the street or something. He should be back for you, you'll see."

"You're so sweet," she says. "But he's not that kind of boyfriend." She giggles.

She looks up at me with her emerald-green eyes, and the tears just hail out of her and she mashes her face into mine. I can taste her salty sweat. She has like a million freckles all over her pale cheeks, and she smells like coconut. She looks so fuckin' cute and fragile. I swear to God I have this semi-long one, and we just stay like that in that position, like a couple making up after a fight. I want to stick my tongue down her throat and graze all her tears away. I move my arm a little, and it slides right between her tits. She doesn't say a goddamn thing. She holds my hand, and it shakes. Oh man it's the best, the closest I've ever been to these types of girls.

⊙✖◎

When that Oldsmobile speeds off, I lift Paulina by the arm and take her out the back door. Some Culver City boys are right there, plotting inaudibly. There are dozens of red plastic cups distributed all over the dead grass—I have to clean this shit up. Paulina runs toward her friends and doesn't even say goodbye. Doesn't look back at her hero. She dashes through the driveway toward the street and vanishes. I bet you if she and I walked down the street together, hand-in-hand, people—white people—would think I was a somebody.

Stan's my only friend amongst the gangsters. We make eye contact while he's packing his records. He shoots me this weird glance, curious but like I fucked up. Shit, like he's never fucked up before. He pulled a gun once at some party in Gardena. He was all high. Almost got us all killed.

Lurch intercepts me before I get to Stan. He's slightly out of breath and his Reebok Classics look showery and have like dirt smudges or damp grass stains.

He says, "You all right, homie?"

I tell him I'm fine and ask if anyone from Culver City got shot.

"Uh, just some dude got shot in the leg . . . and Raven got shot in the stomach."

"What the fuck," I say. "We were just talking to him. Is it serious? Who was it . . . who shot up my goddamn house?" What I'm really thinking is: I hope that motherfucker dies. Maybe Paulina and I could start something.

Lurch says he doesn't know who it was. He offers to help me clean up. He feels bad about what happened.

"Lurch, man . . . you think I can go with you guys to get payback?"

He laughs at me because I pound a fist into my palm and brush my hair to the side. He can't picture me putting in work. He laughs even harder when I ask him for a strap, and he looks around like he has an audience.

He puts his arm up to my chest and says, "Calm down, tough guy. They shot one of ours, but we'll kill two of theirs. Straight up."

TWO
LURCH

July 15, 1999

I was born in West Los and I'ma die in West Los. You think I give a fuck that my neighbor's house got shot up, or that Raven got shot? I mean, I care that the homie got blasted, don't get me wrong. I'm just glad it wasn't me. That'll give him a rite of passage, like going to the joint. People won't think he's a punk anymore. Plus, me and Paulina had something back in the day, before he hooked up with her. I'ma tap that ass real quick, while he's in the hospital. Watch. For old time's sake. Shit, I was the one that even gave him permission to hook up with her. I introduced them. She invited me to her pad one day, and she had a friend, and I invited him over. And next thing you know, *bam,* he's calling her like . . . every day. Got her number on the side. Telling her not to tell me 'n shit. But she did, and I asked her if she liked him, at least a little, and she thought he was funny and charming and all that. I could see that she was into him, but she was sneaky about it. She's a player . . . a playette. And when I asked him about her, he acted weird like he was sprung or something. All stupid 'n shit. So, I said fuck it and gave him the green light and he was all like *gracias.* So, what I'm basically saying is that I fucked her first, and I backed off when they got together . . . but when he did some time in County, I fucked her again. Now that he's in the hospital, I have the right to fuck her some more, *¿qué no?*

☙❧

But like I was saying, people around here get lit up all the time. It don't change anything. I've been shot twice in the stomach by Venice, and once in the back by the Shorelines, in '96. And we killed like ten of those fools, so whatever. Everybody has to die sometime. You can't pick and choose when. You just do. That's how things are in West Los, home of the Mar Vista Gardens Housing Projects. We run the four corners. Not Venice or Santa Monica . . . or Sotel, we do: the Culver City 13 gang. The Little Locos clique—straight up. All day every day, since 1954, when the government tried to keep Mexicans from going anywhere. When they had signs: No Dogs, No Negroes, No Mexicans. Right there at the corner of Ballona Creek, the 405 freeway and Culver City. The only projects in the West Side. Not like Pico Aliso or *Maravilla* or some other housing projects in East Los or South Central that have like a hundred gangs inside. It's just us up in this piece, like Harbor City or Dogtown. I was busted with some of those fools. They run their program the way we run ours.

That's how it is inside the projects. A hood within a hood. And I don't even live there, I live a few blocks away. But I'm always in there, though. I love the projects. Got that shit tattooed all over my back. It's like a fortress, though. You could only drive in through Allin Street off of Inglewood Boulevard, and there's a kiosk with one unarmed rotating guard, a gate and traffic spikes. It's perfect for combat. Hard to catch someone slipping in there.

This one time, in 1988, a Venice boy called Loner mashed through the barrier gate. It was a suicide mission straight up because there's no way out. At the end of the projects are cul-de-sacs, and all the streets lead to like 20-foot high wrought-iron gated fences. There's no way to climb the bars, not even if you're a cop. That fool Loner made it to the rec center in a blue Chevy

El Camino, wearing a blue bandana over his forehead and his arm sticking out the window with a pistol. I recognized that he was an enemy from like a thousand feet away, and I shot that fool—*poomb, poomb, poomb, poomb, poomb.* I got busted for that like a few days later when I got pulled over and I still had the gun on me. I should've tossed it but forgot. The DA dropped it down from murder to self-defense. My attorney said I was protecting myself. Never trust a public defender, always get a lawyer. Especially if you're being charged with murder. That's why I always have like fifty grand stashed. I only did four years for that—from like 88-92. My first 187.

☙✦❧

Nobody else wants to be around the projects, the gangs, the beat-up apartments, the section-8 folks, the crackheads and smokers or the police department. Nobody. Except us, the Culver City gang. We love it, more than our own fuckin' lives. That's why we risk our lives on the streets daily, for the neighborhood.

For people like Mikey and them, there's no nightlife here like in West Hollywood or Santa Monica or whatever. No cool bars, bookstores, galleries, record shops, art centers or any of that shit. Things they like to do. Just burglar bars all over the goddamn place, and seagulls and pigeons flying everywhere—all over parking lots and alleys, fighting for crumbs like the rest of us poor folks.

And for sure nobody around here wants to be on Slauson Avenue, this dark ass street where we shot out the street lights. It's a leafy street, and could be all nice and normal, but things aren't normal in Culver City. Slauson is filled with trash, beer bottles, aluminum cans, used food and candy wrappers—drunk *paisas* posted up or staggering over, dogs bashing their heads into wooden fences, gardener pick-up trucks with tools flanked by plywood, old ass cars that fire up like they're missing a carburetor and of course flamed up Culver City boys. You don't wanna fuck with us, for real, in our clean white sneakers and red Cincinnati Reds ballcaps. The wetbacks and gangsters, we have that street locked down. You can't even use it as a short-cut. Never. Don't even try. Stay in your own goddamn neighborhood.

THREE

MIKEY

July 19, 1999

I got my diploma in the mail. It's written in calligraphy and my name pops out in golden lights: Michael Bustamante. It's inside a black leatherette cover. Bachelor of Arts in Political Science. I hang it next to a picture my mom blew up of me in my cap and gown. What this means to me is getting out of the hood. That's all people talk about around here anyway. Even the gangsters say it, but they leave in body bags or on that County Jail bus. I want to go to DC. In college, I wanted to run for the house of representatives and move to Sacramento or something, but now I'm just interested in a federal, state, county or city job. I want to come back to this region and run for city council . . . run the 11th District. Hopefully my PTSD is gone by the time I get back, and maybe I can move to Pacific Palisades or somewhere within the district boundary, so it'll still count.

My mom and I are at the kitchen table.

"I sent that picture of you to all my sisters, you look so handsome. My beautiful, handsome boy," she says. She gets up, hugs me and kisses me all over my head.

"Okay, okay, that's enough, okay." I push her off me, but I like it and I smile.

"Everyone's counting on you to do something special. You're our only hope," she says. "I told all of them that you're going to be a senator someday. *El senador.* You're my pride and joy."

"Oh, please don't say that. That's not what I want to do anymore."

"What do you mean?" she says. "You always talked about that before. You're like my shining star, like my little diamond. I have to polish you."

She rubs my head and laughs.

"One day I'm gonna make you real proud, *'amá.* I'm trying, I swear. I have that job interview tomorrow for the city of Santa Monica. Let's see how it goes."

She gets up from the chair again. "I'm already proud of you, *m'ijo.* You'll get the job, you'll see. They're lucky to have you. Who wouldn't want you?" She kisses my forehead and dashes through the door. *"Nos vemos, eh."*

I've thought about getting her out of here and getting a nice cottage or craftsman home somewhere in Pasadena, surrounded by greenery and birds. But not ghetto birds or pigeons or crows like the ones around here. I mean real birds, like bluejays or cardinals and hummingbirds.

⬦⬦⬦

I see Stan Corona with his skateboard on Braddock Drive. He's posted up on Berryman Avenue taking pictures of the ground. Right there by the fire hydrant and the red curb, and the no parking sign. He's subtle, like he's tying the black laces on his Jack Purcell's. I pull my Jeep Wagoneer over behind a Ford Expedition and hop out and ask him what he's doing.

He adjusts the lens on his camera, looks over his shoulder and down the street. He says, "You ever notice these cement carvings?"

"Not really. I mean. . . . I've seen them like in front of my house. Why?"

He says, "I'm like a crackhead following them all over the place. Like I'm looking for some dope to put in my crack pipe. They're just these old tags done by gangsters from way back when. When the cement was wet. Check this one out."

I walk over the yellow grass on the sidewalk and inch around a broken beer bottle.

He squats and points at the letters. As he looks up at me, he says, "See that? It says El Johnny, Randy, Jimmy Boy and Frog '72. Pretty gnarly, right? These cement carvings are like hieroglyphics. They're like history."

I trip out. Stan's always on some avant-garde artsy type shit.

A brown '79 Ford F-Series pick-up rolls up on us going westbound. It's lifted and has big tires, like an off-roading type. There's two dudes in the front seat and one in the cargo area. They stop in the middle of the street, and the dude in the back says, "Where you *vatos* from? *Aquí para Dieciocho.*" He maddogs us hard.

I lift my hands and say, "We don't bang, man. We're not from anywhere. We just live around here."

"They call me Pelón . . . 18th Street. Tiny *Malditos.* Remember that, rankers," he says as he surveys Stan head-to-toe.

Luckily, Stan is wearing pants and a long-sleeved shirt and you can't see his tattoos. But his head's shaved. Fuckin' Stan.

My heart rattles inside my chest plate before it leaps outside of me and rubbers down the boulevard. These fools are gonna kill me someday. Stan keeps his head tilted downward. Pelón shoots us a smug look and laughs as they drive off. I can see his head is shaved down to a zero clip and he has a black Champion sweatshirt. I can't see the rest of his body, but I think he was wearing some shrink-to-fits.

Both my hands tremble and I tell Stan to get in the Jeep so I can give him a ride. Stan scoops up his skateboard. His head hangs low. We remain quiet for a while.

When I turn right on Inglewood Boulevard, Stan says, "I haven't wanted to come back to your house since that one night, man. I didn't want to say anything before, but after I left, the Culver City boys followed me. I was going to my sister's house in Lennox, so I jumped on the freeway. I'm lucky I drive a fast car, dude, because I turned off the lights and hit the gas. I boned the fuck out."

I say, "What? Are you fuckin' joking? Who was it? You know the car?"

"That SS Monte Carlo. The navy blue one," he says.

"So that's it. You're not going to come to my house anymore? I'll talk to Lurch about it, don't even trip. That's Stranger's. He'll get this all sorted out. I'm sure it was a mistake."

Stan tells me it's too dangerous to keep living here. I can tell he's still nervous, his eyes bouncing all over the place. He glimpses at a Culver City boy near the gas station and nods. He says he's taking off to Rhode Island, to live around the greenery and snow, because his girlfriend, Sarah, got into Brown, in some graduate architecture program. She's from there actually. And her dad's there too. He invites me to go with him. I actually think about it. Me and my mom, in Rhode Island. Wouldn't that be something.

July 20, 1999

My mom gave me a prayer candle to burn and ask for help from Saint Cajetan, the patron saint of job seekers. I had never heard of him until last night. I placed the candle on a mantle near the TV, but the glass broke and I freaked out. I ran to the kitchen and got a glass of water and tossed it at the flame and it rose to the ceiling. Then I ran into the bathroom and got a wet towel and covered the flame. I almost burned the goddamn house down. My body was shivering for almost thirty minutes. Maybe that's a bad omen. Guess we'll find out later.

Sometimes when I'm in the bathroom, I lift my shirt up to my throat and look at my stomach. I suck my gut in and I don't feel that fat . . . until I take my shirt off and just stare at my body. At my little boobs and their shape like a snow slope. What I would give to have these stupid lumps removed. Good thing we ended the band too. Imagine if I'd have to be on stage and take off my shirt or something, in a crowd! I sit on the toilet. I developed irritable bowel syndrome in my last semester, and an ulcer or gastritis or something. My side always hurts, and I constantly have to shit, piss or fart. It's disgusting. It's because of stress and anxiety, they said, like now. I'm worried about the interview, there was no way to prepare for it. I reread some of my essays to sharpen up on vocabulary, but other than that, it's all about how I do in person. It's for an entry-level position in the Housing and Economic Development Department.

⊙⊰⊱⊙

I'm there fifteen minutes early. I've always been told to arrive at least fifteen minutes before. Chelsea boots, polyester Levi's, tucked in long-sleeved shirt and a black tie. Maybe I should've worn the gold one, or the blue one. I wonder if this one's too morbid. What if my pants are too tight, or my hair too messy? Do I look indie or rock n' roll, or like a Colombian drug dealer?

Goddamn, what was I thinking. I should've bought slacks. Fuck. The receptionist escorts me to a room. Thought I caught that wild-eye look from her, but I can't be certain. Fuckin' white people, they play the game well.

There's a panel across from me when I walk in—what the fuck? I sit down and greet the man and two women. All white. I knew it.

The man speaks. "Well, let me just tell you a little about what the job entails. It starts as an unpaid internship, for a few months."

My mind goes blank. *Unpaid internship?* That's for nobodies.

He continues. "Working with myself and my colleagues here on various administrative tasks, including creating spreadsheets, assessing budgets, um . . . developing and retaining job opportunities for our residents. . . . Oh . . . and reaching out to some of our more disenfranchised residents through a process of targeted activities and programs to assist in housing opportunities. You speak Spanish, right?"

"Yes, I'm bilingual," I say, but keep thinking about the unpaid thing.

They must have noticed that I made a face or something because one of the women says, "I know the whole unpaid internship isn't an ideal place to start, given that you've already graduated, but most of our employees started this way . . . interning while still in school and transitioning into full-time paid work upon graduation. We're just learning about you now, but we like your background and we definitely want to use your skills and abilities to help with these housing issues. It says here in your resume that you're interested in getting a master's in urban planning, is that correct?"

"Yes, I've looked into the programs at my alma mater, but I'm also looking into USC and Cal Poly Pomona, but I really need something quicker, before the student loans kick in."

The man makes a face, like he doesn't like what I said.

The other woman says, "Well, the city of Santa Monica pays for the master's degree, especially in a department like urban planning, so . . ."

The man cuts her off, "Well, Mr. Bustamante, do you have any questions for us?"

I get up and say, "No, thank you very much for contacting me. I look forward to hearing from you. This is an opportunity that I've been looking forward to for a while. I've always loved Santa Monica. My dad used to work here. I used to come here as a kid all the time. So, to be employed here, it would be a great way of participating in my civic duty."

They nod their heads and smile and make these faces like I have to bow down or something.

❦

Stan rolls up to my yard. He's with this white dude I don't recognize and says, "This is my friend, Mark Stahl. He's from Nebraska. He's your new neighbor, bro. He spins at KXLU after me, and he's in the film program at UCLA."

I say, "That's awesome, nice to meet you. So, you're in the film program, huh?"

"Yeah, I'm writing a screenplay about Joy Division," Mark says. "It's called *Control*."

"Are you fuckin' kidding me? Check this out," I say. The three of us smirk and smile.

I pull down my shirt from the neck and show him "Dead Souls" in handwriting across my chest. Then he shows me the word "Substance" tattooed on his arm. I tell him that I went to UCLA too.

"That's great," he says, "we're going to be neighbors! I just bought that house down the street. Come over anytime you want, I can show you my record collection."

"Which one?"

"The one with the orange door. The white one."

"Oh yeah, with that cool, horizontal wooden fence."

Mark nods.

Stan says, "Yo, Mikey, how'd that job interview go today?"

"It was all right I guess, but it's an unpaid internship, so. . . . I don't know. I need money, you know? I quit my job, so . . ."

Mark jumps in, "I think I might know . . ."

We're interrupted by sharp whistling. It's Lurch, and he's walking toward us. Stan and Mark start looking all over the place. They don't know what to do with their hands.

Lurch says, "Damn, Mikey, what's up? Who's this *vato*?" Lurch is staring hard at Mark.

"Oh right, yeah, this is Mark. He just moved here. To that house with the orange door. Mark, this is another neighbor of ours, Ruben." I say.

Lurch stares straight into Mark's eyes, sticks his chest out and Lurch says, "I go by Lurch, nobody calls me Ruben except my mom. Hey, man, you shave your beard off or something?" He rubs like this pretend beard.

Mark rubs his chin and says, "No, I've never had a beard."

Lurch gives Mark a dirty look, then one to Stan as well, and spits on the ground. He says, "Yeah, whatever, homes. I think I've seen your *máscara* before. I know you had a beard."

Looks like Lurch is gonna lift a hand up to Mark's face, but lowers it. Change of heart.

Stan wants to walk away. I can see it in his eyes.

Mark insists, "No, man, I can't even grow one. Sorry, wrong guy."

Lurch balls his fists ready for action, but walks away. Doesn't say shit, just takes off. I panic a little. My heart clunks. Stan and Mark take off too, to Mark's house. I see their bodies getting smaller in the distance.

I catch up to Lurch and say, "Hey, man, is everything cool?"

"Yeah, why?"

"Just wondering," I say. But I want to say this other thing to him. Do I have the courage, maybe make it playful? "You were a little mean to them back there, no?" I laugh a little. "He's just a new neighbor. He means no harm. He's just into rock 'n roll like me and Stan."

"Really? You think I was mean? Well, let me write them an apology letter, homie." He has this asshole look on his face.

I say, "Oh, you know what, Lurch? I think some of your homies, Stranger maybe, followed Stan that night after Raven got shot. He's a little worried about you guys, thinks you guys are after him, or that you guys hate him."

"So what do you want me to do?"

"Nothing . . . I was just wondering if you knew anything about that, or if you could talk to some of your homies and see what happened," I say.

"I have no control over what anybody does, dog. Especially in a situation like that, when there's blasting and a homie gets shot. Anyone we don't recognize right away is a suspect. That's just the way it is 'n shit. Besides, that fool has a shaved head and tats. Looks like a thug. You know what they say, 'If it looks like a duck, it's probably a duck.'"

Lurch takes a few more steps ahead of me and turns. "Hey, come to my pad, I got something to show you."

We walk together, pass up his Beamer in the driveway and I peek inside the car. I see a *Time* magazine riding shotgun. I pause. The front cover reads: *"The End of the World!?! Apocalypse Now! Y2K Insanity! Will computers melt down? Will Society? A Guide to Millennial Madness."*

"You like that shit, huh?" Lurch says.

"Oh, yeah, it's a dope-ass car."

"Anytime you wanna take it out for a spin, on a date or something, it's yours. I'm serious, Mikey. You can borrow it whenever."

Then we arrive at his backyard. On the ground there are stacks of water bottles and canned food. And there's a crate, like those army green ones with yellow letters. He lifts it slightly. It's full of assault rifles. He tells me about the enemy that shot up my pad.

August 5, 1999

Turns out that it was 18th Street, the Smiley Drive clique. Now I'm curious about them. I want to see how they live, how they party, how they dress. I want to etch their hang-out spots and their faces into my brain. I already hate that fool Pelón, anyway, the one that rolled up on me and Stan in that pick-up truck. What if it was that motherfucker?

I take my mom's '88 El Dorado Cadillac and head toward their neighborhood. I don't want to burn my Jeep. I remember that that dude Pelón saw me and Stan on Braddock Drive. I have to be smart, have to think about everything. I shut the music off and grasp the vinyl steering wheel as if I'm going to break it off the column. I sit as straight as possible and examine the radio dials, the turn signals, the odometer and the fuel meter. There are digital green numbers everywhere. I sport dark aviator sunglasses and let my hair fall onto my face. I wear a torn leather jacket with the collar flared up. My breathing is heavy in three-second intervals. I even count. I keep an eye out for that white Oldsmobile and that lifted Ford pick-up truck. Those are the only two 18th Street cars that I know about. Their hood is where La Cienega Boulevard, Adams Boulevard and Fairfax Avenue all meet, and further east, toward Alsace Avenue. It's like the border of Culver City and Mid-City. They probably go at it with Mid-City Stoners.

I cross over to Smiley Drive near Washington Boulevard. I notice a lot of the houses have iron burglar-barred windows, and some have enclosed walls around their yards with similar bars. It looks just like where we live in Culver City—they are just like us. They probably have a version of me and Stan over here somewhere. It's probably the same in other LA neighborhoods that I've never been to.

There's a doppelganger of me in all these places, a post-punk college graduate who can't find a goddamn job. I'd like to meet him someday.

I pass up a few businesses I've never seen before—modernist structures—one in a grey concrete tone, another in matte black and an art gallery that's all white with booming olive-colored cactus rising from the detritus. Looks fancy, looks out-of-place.

There's a big sign nearby, in aluminum on black. Reads: "Black-welder Los Angeles—Creative Campus coming soon!" I think: Those 18th Street fools live around these types of places? An Arts District? Here?

I take a right on South Spaulding Avenue, and it leads me straight into a dead-end and a park: The West Side Neighborhood Park. My heart runs a marathon, I should go back. I can't, I'm too curious. I pull into the parking lot, where pigeons and crows flock around cars and trash cans and scavenge for food, while some countless eucalyptus trees dot the cracked sidewalks. It's just like our neighborhood. I wonder why these fools hate each other so much. I look out for those cement carvings that Stan talked about. See one hit-up: "Crow X Eddy Boy 18." I spit on the *placa*.

I read more graffiti on some walls in blue spray-paint: "XV3," "Dieciocho," "18th Street" and just "18." "CEXCE Trece" is crossed out and circled, with a little "187" on the corner. I look the other way, don't want to know the results. Raven didn't die when he got shot, but someone from 18 did, or was going to get smoked. That's what Lurch said.

Then I see like twenty dudes in white T-shirts with bald heads near a basketball court. Not like pretty-boys, not like Culver City. They have long tube socks, tank-tops, white T-shirts, creased khaki and jean shorts. More hardcore, I think. They're looking in my direction. Probably because I'm staring at the graffiti. They throw up hand signs: a C with the thumb and index finger, the middle finger going right through the center. They mad-dog hard and proceed in my direction on foot. One dude runs faster and hurls a beer bottle toward the car. It smashes on the cement near a trash can. The shatter makes me tremble. I cow my head as a re-flex. I do a quick U-turn and go back toward Spaulding. I hear a few gun shots—*poomb, poomb*—one hits the car. Possibly the trunk. It feels like hail or strong rain coming down like a tragedy. I duck and tilt my body to the left, hit the gas pedal and head toward the 10 West. My breathing gets heavy. I look into the rearview mirror, but nobody is behind me. I almost careen into a parked burgundy Toyota Forerunner. The on-ramp is my sanctuary, and I feel like doing the benediction sign. My chest is beating so fast that I think I'm having a stroke or a mini heart attack. I think about driving to the hospital. But what I mostly think is, "Gotta go to one of those *paisas* on Slauson to get the bullet wound fixed on the car." Before my mom sees it. She already asked about that bullet hole on the house, and I made up a lie.

FOUR

LURCH

August 9, 1999

I showed Mikey the straps, but he didn't say shit about them or my supplies. Whatever, some people don't see nothing, especially what's right in front of them. I just don't want him opening his big ass mouth, telling neighbors about all the guns. I'm getting ready for the apocalypse, whether you do or not, I don't give a fuck. I'll go out like a *soldado,* taking my enemies with me.

I don't want that fool getting caught up in all of this, you know? He's a good kid, I guess, deserves better than what's here.

I spot that fool holding a water hose, staring at the blades of grass. The sprinklers hissing all around him—*fist, fist, fist.* I know what that's like . . . maybe he's on one, 'shrooms or something. That's how you describe it, like Kahlil Gibran, all poetic and lyrical. I read that fool in prison a few times. Probably sees ants crawling all over the place and up his skin. I don't miss that feeling, especially a bad trip. Mikey's hosing the sugarcane at the corner of the yard and then he stands on his toes. He's looking over the harvest and checking out that house with the orange front door. I stare at it too. I don't like it, and I damn sure as hell don't like that new dude, Mark Stahl.

I walk to Mikey's as I look down the street for unidentifiable cars—enemies. Nothing. They don't want none. We already took care of those lame-ass *vatos*.

I creep up on him, "C'mon, Mikey, leave that grass alone, let's get something to eat, yeah? I wanna talk to you about some important shit."

I can see that fool's shook, like I just gave him a heart attack. He drops the water hose and shuts off the valve. I know he doesn't wanna come. I see that look on his face, like he wants to say no but he can't. He knows I'll pistol whip 'im. We've never been anywhere together, not even the store. We don't walk or go for drives, we're just neighbors. We just talk right here on the block. And we damn sure as fuck don't talk about important shit. He's probably worried about enemies, about getting caught in a crossfire. I get it, I'd be worried too. But I need him to know what's going down.

So, I tell him, "Don't worry about it, homie. We'll be all right." I lift up my shirt and show him the gun tucked into my waistband.

"Ah, wait, look, Lurch, I . . ."

"We'll be right back, real quick. C'mon," I say.

I smile, but I get nothing in return. Just this look of horror. He's a fuckin' pussy.

We pass up ice cream trucks and *paleteros* near Berryman Avenue. I adjust my pants every now and then because of the strap, and I look over my shoulders on the regular. Got that fool doing it too. I think it's funny. On Slauson, street vendors are posted up with oranges, flowers, strawberries and mixed fruit bags. On the corner of Inglewood Boulevard, *paisas* are selling corn on the cob and tamales. A bunch of wetbacks storm these fools and buy *champurrado*. I buy one too. I like that smell, you know? This one lady even sells water bottles and soda out of a cooler, when the liquor store is just a few yards away. Gotta have a hustler mentality on the West Side. You ain't shit here without money.

As we turn right on Inglewood Boulevard, I say, "Remember when the neighborhood kicked out all those Shoreline Crips from the projects?"

He mentions that he does, and I remember that time I got shot and how I blacked out.

"We lost a lot of good homies back then," I say. "We lit up some of those *tintos'* cars. We even firebombed some of their units in the projects. I left notes on some of their doors, too. 'You got two days to move out, or else we're gonna smoke your ass."

"How'd all that end up, Lurch?"

"A bunch of people died, man. And a gang of good homies got busted. My road dog got a life sentence. Raven's older brother. It was a straight battle zone around here. All kinds of fools ended up in wheelchairs or crippled 'n shit. And I think it's gonna start all over, you know what I'm saying? But with white people. Not all of them. The sick-ass, weird-looking mother-fuckers. They're the new enemy."

I know it sounds crazy, but I had to get that off my chest. Felt good to finally say it out loud and tell somebody. I can't tell the homies yet either, I need more details. I've talked to the twins about the apocalypse here and there, but this is on a whole other level. Mikey's smart, he went to college, he'll understand as I explain it.

But he's confused, and almost laughs. "Why them? White people are just regular people. I don't understand. What kind of threat do they pose?"

Now for sure I'ma pistol whip him.

I never told anyone about these premonitions I've been having. All these dreams about doomsday 'n shit. About the locusts rising from below, devils taking over our streets. That's what Black rappers call them: devils in disguise. The new world order. I've seen white people with beards and weird outfits, walking their dogs, posting up on our blocks, taking over the wetland, the creek and the bike path. Spreading from Westchester to Santa Monica, all the way to Highland Park, to East Los and the Valley. Stealing our hoods. Taking our homes and apartments—even our stores, restaurants and food trucks. I even seen the projects get demolished, like they get blown up.

As I'm telling Mikey all of this, I see that he's clueless. Probably never heard of these books: *Apocalypse Culture*, *Holy Blood Holy Grail*, *The Mark of the Beast*, *Behold a Pale Horse*, *The Spear of Destiny*. I wonder what they were teaching him at UCLA, nothing useful, I guess. No survival skills. No preparation for the Illuminati.

So I tell him, "Look, basically, another war's gonna pop off. I can feel it. We're gonna need *soldados* for this one, though. I just want to let you know in advance, you know what I'm saying? Before it kicks off. It's gonna get messy. And this new neighbor that you hang out with, the one that . . ."

"Mark Stahl? The DJ that was here the other night?" he asks.

"Yeah, whatever his name is. He better watch his back. He reminds me of that white boy I keep telling you about. With the beard? The anti-Christ? I got a bad feeling about them. Just trust me on this, Mikey. If you want to keep that fool out of trouble, tell him not to show his face around here. I can't guarantee his safety. Better yet, tell Stan and all them that they should lay low for a while."

"*Ay*, Lurch, c'mon, man. He lives right there. What is he . . ."

"Don't fight me on this, dog. I'm telling you as a *carnal*. This shit's gonna get ugly. If I were you, I'd stay off the streets, *de volada*. Tell the rest of your homies, too."

I need this dude to understand. He needs to get out of here, before he gets confused for a 666. I won't be able to control him getting blasted on by one of the homies. Like I couldn't stop the homies from going after Stan. They're just collateral damage, if it really comes down to that.

August 14, 1999

I'm with a few of the homies—Rumble, Knuckles, Spy, Stranger, Wino and the twins, Noel and Leon—at the El Abajeño Restaurant on Inglewood Boulevard, near the ARCO gas station. The Little Locos clique, the popular fools.

I've been coming to this spot my whole life. Everybody knows us. There's something special about this place—the apricot colored walls, the circle top windows, the white wrought-iron bars. And the smell, like a real *cocina* from the old country. Reminds me of a restaurant in La Capilla, reminds me of my mom and dad. My dad used to bring us here all the time when we were kids, right after church down the street. We'd walk over here, then drive back home. He'd get a bottle of Siete Leguas from the liquor store next door, then get drunk and fight with my mom. Punk-ass motherfucker. I always got the *carnitas burrito*—still do. That's my jam. They have these rustic, hand-made chairs inside the restaurant and mosaic floor and wall tiles with little brown *paisitas* carrying flowers in their hands. Like a Diego Rivera painting or something. It feels like a Mexican home, for real.

One of the homies, whenever he goes out of town on a business trip, always wants a burrito from here. It's what we know. It's what we love. The chairs have tapestry patterns on the backs, like the ones my aunt has in Mexico. The tables are all scribed with Culver City gang hit-ups. You could sit here for hours and read the writing like a goddamn novel or something. I always look for my own *placas* . . . I gots many, you know what I'm saying? "Big Lurch," "CEXCE trece." As you enter, you stand in line and look up at the menu on the wall above the register. The line goes all the way to the liquor store next door. The food sits in warm trays, and most people just talk and look at other people eating while they wait to order. It's a weird setup, been like that for like forty years. But it's a safe place, no enemies have done a drive-by from the street. They know better.

As I'm sitting at the table, scoping out the outside scenery, I see that white boy with the beard, the one I'm always talking about. He's walking by with a girl that looks the same. Sick, the same. She has yellow shoes, black nylons, a black skirt and a tan cardigan sweater, like the one Mikey wears. Like I said, Mikey's gonna get confused for one of these people one day, I can feel it. One side of the girl's hair is fluorescent pink, another part shaved, and she has all these colorful tattoos on her chest— Americana flash images of an anchor and a jaguar. Like a sailor, like a fuckin' man. Like those fools in prison from the Nazi Lowriders. I feel a cold chill circulate throughout my body. The anti-Christ and a witch, right outside my doorstep. Gotta stab the dude with the spear of destiny and hang the girl like at Salem. They're the people in my nightmares. The couple turns the corner, quick-like, through the parking structure, and for a second, I think I'm tripping. I panic, really, more than anything. My heart beats like all crazy. Hope these fools don't notice. But they do.

Knuckles sees me staring and says, "What's up, dog, what's the matter, you see a ghost or something? Ha, this *vato*'s tripping, dog! Check 'im out, all spooked 'n shit."

"What's up, Lurch? You seen some sixth sense shit or what?" Leon says. "You see dead people?"

Everyone laughs hard. I was made. Gotta play it off. I say, "Nah, dog, I see white people."

I give them an awkward smile, a forced laugh, and I punch Leon in the arm without force. I put my arm over his shoulder and say, "Whata ya gonna order, dog?"

☙❦❧

After lunch, we walk to two different cars in the parking lot: Stranger's navy blue '88 Monte Carlo Super Sport and my '98 silver BMW. And just before I get into the driver's seat, I look around. Normally, I keep an eye out for enemies, but this time

I'm looking for that couple. Can't get their faces and bodies out my head.

I drive east on Culver Boulevard and see two white dudes in jogging outfits. One has a University of Oklahoma T-shirt, the other a Colorado Rockies baseball hat. They're just right there, like it's nothing. I can't believe my fuckin' eyes. The joggers aren't together, they're a few feet apart, but they have the same style. Like they belong. For a second, I think it's my homie Speedy . . . he's white and blonde too, and he has the same stature as one of those fools, but it's not. And the other one looks like us too, with that Colorado Rockies hat for CR—Culver, but he has a Dalí mustache instead of a *brocha,* waxed at the tips. Looking like an idiot. But it's not our people. The homies aren't stupid enough to get caught slipping, doing exercise in public. Nah, these fools are outsiders. Nobodies. I do a double-take and almost crash into the median strip.

Noel waves a hand over my face. "What's up dog? You've been trippin' all day 'n shit."

"Yeah, you know what . . . I'ma go to the pad and lie down or something. Maybe the food did me dirty," I say.

A pair of hands reach over from the backseat and massage my neck and shoulders, but not in like a gay way.

Leon says, "Leave us right there on Slauson and go handle your *pedo* at the pad, dog. We'll see you later on, homes."

I drop them off and drive quickly back to where I saw those fools. Those *vatos* have no business being in the hood. I'm so fuckin' pissed that they even exist. Do those lame fucks even know where they're at? What about the couple? Do they know? Why should these motherfuckers be allowed to walk around the neighborhood? Fuck that, they're not gonna get a pass. Would I get a pass walking through Bel Air or some shit? Probably not. They'd call the *jura* quick. We gave the Shorelines a pass once, and they tried to post up in the projects and sell dope. And that shit started a war. When I was busted with this Lennox boy—Grizzly from the Winos clique—he told me that they killed a few black pimps on Century Boulevard who tried to post up in their hood. And I know for a fact every hood has to look like it's controlled by the gangs at all times. That's how we have to represent.

I wait at the intersection of Culver Boulevard and Inglewood Boulevard, and it feels like I have a boulder on my chest. I spot that one fool with the Rockies hat cross the street. He takes a drink from a water bottle. He catches his breath, wipes sweat from his forehead and walks east down Culver Boulevard toward Kensington Road. I take a sharp right and park in front of an apartment complex. I reach for a strap from the dashboard stash and cock it back—*shick-shick.* Someone has to die.

From a few yards away, I observe that fool walk upstairs to the top floor of an open six-unit apartment complex. In the driveway, a couple of *paisas* are grilling *carne asada* and drinking beer. I greet them: "*Qué onda.*" They're playing a song, *"Un Puño de Tierra,"* by Antonio Aguilar. I think about my dead homies. Feel like joining them for a beer, but I don't. I can't be distracted. I walk to the apartment complex and see mail sticking out from several compacted boxes. I have my strap tucked in my waistband. I place my palm on the handle . . . just in case. I get up close and scan the last names: Guzmán, López, Castillo, García, Rosales and then: Kidd. That's the one, has to be. The boxes aren't locked, so I pull out some envelopes. Scott Kidd's name stands out. There's a credit card and a student loan bill, and junk mail. Kidd, an unusual last name for this part of town. What's this fool doing here, in our neighborhood? Is he an undercover cop or something? A representative of the new world order? If so, he's about to get smoked. These types of white people don't live around here, unless they were here a long time ago. Before they all moved out to the suburbs. But those ones were old as fuck, like the neighbor on our block who owns all those cats. If Kidd is a local, that's fine. I don't have a problem with that. But this fool doesn't fit the profile. I take his mail. I'm gonna study it at home.

FIVE

THE DOCTOR

August 17, 1999

People assume I'm conservative, because I'm a physician and I have my own health practice. Moreover, it sits across the street from the Mar Vista Gardens housing projects on Braddock Drive, which gives the practice an altruistic ring. What they don't know is that I put myself through medical school by selling dope. Back at USC, when I declared physiological science as an undergrad, I was making more money than actual surgeons—I actually researched their income. The crack epidemic was in full swing in LA, hence serving rocks and cocaine to the preppies and yuppies. Like "Less Than Zero." Until I was arrested in 1989. But I got leverage from a judge, so when I got out, I finished my program, finished my medical degree, did my residency in West Los Angeles and here I am, with my own practice in Culver City.

I like it here. It's where my roots lay. Everybody knows me, it's community. Not like back in those days when they called me "Gorilla Joe" from the neighborhood. I was lost. Now I'm "the doctor," or *el doctor*, and that carries a lot of respect. I make significantly less money now than when I was a street pharmacist, but it was never about the salary. It was about outflanking the system. Today, I care for underserved communities. *My* underserved community. That was the original goal, and I couldn't think about anything else in college. I guess it started long before then, at Santa Monica High, when a teacher told me I couldn't be a doctor. Because of the color of my skin. Who has the last laugh now, bitch?

Now I save people's lives regularly. Sometimes I grant people services even when they don't have the ability to pay. I'm a pillar of the community. And we just expanded to Echo Park. Plus, I speak fluent Spanish, and that helps with the non-English speakers and the immigrants. My parents are proud of what I've become. My mother brags to her relatives in Oaxaca. My father to his family in Texas. They both take credit because they pushed for the Ivy League at an early age. I was accepted to Princeton on a full-ride, but when I thought about it, the conclusion was always the same: What do I care about New Jersey?

൭෨ൟ෯

A nurse hands me a clipboard with a patient's antecedent form for me to survey. The first thing I notice is her name: Georgina Tweedy. It sounds like a joke. I don't recognize the name, and when I walk into the waiting room, the other patients are perusing her like she's a spectacle. Like they are paparazzi. Her pink hair, her pale skin, her head partly shaved, her bright green dress . . . I scan her from head to toe. An old Cuban lady scoots away from Georgina and covers her nose. I smirk. I saw people like this at USC, but not since then and definitely not in this neighborhood. They're the type that live off of their parents' allowance and spend too much time trying to find themselves. The kind that backpack through Europe and sleep in hostels. Entitled and fearless, like the world is their playground. They come from all over the country to reinvent themselves in Los Angeles, the end of the road. They usually end up in places like Hollywood, Melrose and Studio City. Most want to work in that industry anyway—screenwriters, actors, production assistants.

They're not supposed to be near the housing projects. Maybe they want to be here because of the Culver City studios.

Her hairstyle makes me uneasy. Like she's sick and infectious. I don't want to get too close; I have a little boy. I put on my gloves and snarl. I lead her to an examining room.

"It looks like your blood pressure and temperature are fine, so, how can I help you?"

"I wanna have a baby."

I raise my left eyebrow. "So, you need pre-natal care?"

"I just moved here from Kentucky with my husband, but he's from Denmark actually," she says, "and we're looking for a clinic. We don't like big, corporate, faceless hospitals. We want something intimate. We want to integrate into the community."

"Well, this is low-income, practically below poverty level. Do you belong here?" What I'm really thinking is, "This place is intimate for the people from here because they're from here. Not for people like you."

"I like this place. It's cute, it's charming."

Cute? Charming? That is disrespectful to people like us, but she doesn't know that. That's what white entitlement is all about. This is a business, there's nothing cute about it.

"You live around here somewhere? Near the projects?"

"Yeah, pretty close. My husband's a developer. He has a start-up, too. We moved here to start over—to the Golden Coast. We're going to help build up Silicon Beach."

I don't like what I hear. I'm caught off guard. Derailed in my own office. But I keep it professional.

"Do you need medical care for your condition?"

"Well, that's why I'm here. I thought you could help. This is the nearest facility to where I domicile, and I don't drive so . . . I like to walk. Sidewalking, you know? To be connected to the earth with my feet."

I practically roll my eyes.

She continues, "Like I did back home. Plus, I'm an artist. I have a studio by the creek. Ballona is untapped, it's a marvel. So gorgeous. I actually paint and I write. I'm in a PhD program at USC, in the creative writing program. I'm writing a novel about *cholas* from the hood . . . from Huntington Park and maybe here. Because they are badasses, you know? Do you know any?" She stretches a wide smile, like she needs approval. But I don't give her any. What I think is, "You need a PhD to write creatively? Another outsider to colonize our voice for entertainment?"

"Are you sure you want to bring a baby into this world . . . with . . ." I wave a hand from top to bottom, "The way you are?"

"I'm not a freak or anything! Didn't you take like . . . sensitivity training or something? Geez."

She sits upright on the stool and crosses her arms, then zooms in on my medical diploma.

"I'm sorry but I can't help you. There's a Kaiser Permanente nearby . . . on Cadillac." I point north. "They have better resources there for people like you."

She gets up from the stool and pushes the trash can with vigor. "You're such an asshole!" she yells before darting out the front door.

I walk to the front desk where the receptionist is sitting, crossing names off a clipboard.

"Was this some cruel joke or something?" I ask.

"What?" she asks.

"Sending that woman to me . . . with the pink hair?"

"Why? What happened?"

"Never mind," I tell her, then I shake my head. "Get back to work. I'll take Yvette and Serena González in room four. If you see that woman in here again, call security or the police."

The receptionist looks puzzled. I know she doesn't get it, but I don't either.

ᏉᏉᏉ

I close up for the day and walk next door to the pharmacy to give my farewells to the pharmacist, Kimberly Vuong. She has a sexy smile, and she's been touchy since her twins were born. It's the highlight of my day. I haven't been touched like that since before my baby was born. It makes things around here more interesting, more exhilarating than going straight home.

"I've been trying to potty train Mason and Joshua for two weeks," she says. "It's so hard. They just poop all over themselves, and my husband doesn't want to clean them."

"Yeah, tell me about it. The other day Nathaniel peed all over the bed, the pillows, all his clothes, the carpet. I mean, when are they going to learn? You like walking around with piss in your pants?"

We both laugh, she grabs my arm and her head dangles. My face gets warm and my heart beats quicker.

"Did you see that woman with fluorescent hair earlier? She asked for birth control pills without a prescription," Kimberly asks.

"She must be unstable because she told me she wanted to get pregnant," I say.

"Well, she *was* from USC, so she must be crazy. What'd you expect?" She laughs.

The pharmacist went to Stanford. We tease each other often about our rival schools. And just like that, my thoughts shift. I picture her naked, or me slipping off her lab coat. Right here among all the prescription bottles. But how does one start an affair? How do you make that transition? Kimberly understands me, she makes me laugh, unlike my wife, who just wants more kids. And the more kids you have, the deeper the trap. I'm going to get a vasectomy and not tell her about it. Or anybody else, for that matter. Then they'll test me, and I'll shoot blanks. Nobody will know except me.

"Ha, you got jokes," I say.

I really start thinking about asking her out. But I don't know how. Or where to take her. And if she rejects me, I won't be able to return here. I'll ruin it all. She touches my hand by accident, and I feel like giggling.

"I've never seen people like that around here before, and I grew up in Culver City. I remember they were all over Stanford, though."

My face lights up because I thought the same thing about USC when I saw her. Perhaps Kimberly and I are twin souls. I want to take her to the movies, where it's opaque and still. I'm nervous just thinking about it. I even tremble slightly. Like it's icy.

"I don't like those people being here, with their stupid dress codes and haircuts. Maybe that's how people will look in the new millennium, I guess. Whatever," she says.

I concentrate on the wrinkles around her eyes. She's absolutely stunning.

"Yeah, maybe we should do something about it. Put a sign on the door that says, 'Dear Weird-looking White People, if you don't belong here, don't be long here.'"

She laughs and says, "I read an article in the *L.A. Weekly* recently that criticized Mar Vista for all its free mental health centers and rehabilitation facilities. These yuppies are just here for the services. Tell them they're not welcome, tell them to go home. C'mon . . . " She air-shoves me. "What are you waiting for? Tell them. Go."

I think I might love her.

⟨∂⟩∞⟨∂⟩

I pull out of a parking space in my Mercedes Benz and almost reverse into a toy dog being walked by a man I don't recognize. The dog is on a long leash and I don't spot it in the rearview mirror. The man isn't alone either, he has a partner—

faggots. They let go of their hands when the dog scatters. "Bruce! Bruce!" "They call out. "You okay?"

They both have Australian accents. They're cadence is maddening.

I slam the brakes and step out of the car. I'm jumpy. The two gentlemen—in jeans, plaid shirts and sunglasses—walk toward me with their noses twisted. I ball my fists.

One of them says, "You should watch where you're going. Bruce isn't used to reckless drivers."

"Reckless?" I say.

"Yes, reckless. You scared him. Look." He points at the dog. The dog cows behind the owners.

The same Aussie says, "Now he's gonna get PTSD . . . he's not gonna eat and he's gonna be constipated for like a week. He's a rescue, ya know, he grew up with a lot of trauma, mate."

I think, "Fuck you and your dog and his trauma. It's a fuckin' dog. Everyone around here has trauma, bitch."

The one talking picks up the dog in one scoop and turns to his partner. "C'mon Liam, let's get out of here before this guy shoots us. You're gonna shoot us, huh? Menace to society. He looks like trouble, doesn't he? Shoot me? C'mon, Scarface, I fuckin' dare you!"

They continue through the parking lot. I glance all around me, more vexed than when I took the MCAT. I look at myself and my clothes and wonder if I look like a gang banger. It's been such a long time since that life. I touch the scar on my face, from the time I got stabbed in County Jail. They probably think I'm a drug dealer or something, because of the Mercedes. I'm tall and my skin is dark, but I don't look like a *cholo*. I know that for a fact. They probably can't tell us apart, though. That's typical. I can't help but wonder what these Aussies are doing near the clinic. I live a few blocks away, off Braddock Drive, right on the other side of the freeway. Maybe they live there. Then I see them walk into the Mexican grocery store. They even take the dog inside and carry it in a little handbag like a purse. A stupid little dog, like in those movies where pretentious artists carry them around inside of art galleries.

⦿⦿⦿

My abode has a well-manicured lawn that's split down the middle because of the walkway. There are two Agave Americana plants on each side and a few rose bushes underneath the windows. The exterior color is Odessa pink and the inside has a flat white finish. There's a three-piece sectional in the middle of the living room. That is where I lounge. Always on the right-hand corner. I read, watch TV and make phone calls from my favorite spot near an end table. My wife, Cecilia, sits on the opposite end, if she even shows up. We can't ever watch a movie together because she falls asleep early or she's just drained. She spends a lot of time in the baby's room. She acts like I don't care about him. She makes me feel as if I'm unfit as a parent. I feel like snapping her neck sometimes. Most days I loathe the sight of her. I dream that she's not home when I return from work. Like she's gone missing or she got kidnapped. I pray for that miracle. And maybe someday I will actually pay for that miracle.

On my off days it's worse because we're obliged to spend all day together. I'm forced to maintain diplomacy and show a united front for the sake of my boy, but something always triggers an argument. I'm always doing something wrong. If I tell her the truth, or if I lie, or if I suppress certain feelings, it always leads to a fight. There's always something. She probably can't stand me either, but we're both afraid to say it out loud. But I'm getting close. With absolute certainty, I can honestly say that marriage is a sham. It's a contract of the absurd—Camus and Sartre knew this too.

That's why they had numerous affairs. And to think that Sartre was married to the most feminist woman of all, Simon de Beauvoir!

I don't talk to my wife about my practice anymore. She doesn't know I took out a loan to expand to Echo Park. I file head-of-household anyway. She talks about going back to school, to get a masters in whatever interest she has that week—sociology, landscape architecture, geology, whatever. You can't do anything solely with a bachelor's nowadays. That's an end-of-century phenomenon; the millennium requires new skills, computer science or information technology perhaps. I don't know what those skills are just yet, but they're definitely not what she does.

We mostly talk about food choices or baby concerns. I can't share my creative aspirations with her: to write a philosophical work about something modern-day. Something before the millennium shift. If I bring it up, she always interrupts and changes the conversation when I go abstract. I bet Kimberly Vuong would listen, perhaps even Georgina Tweedy. That's why I read. Because I'm an escapist. I find answers in the characters' lives. I pretend their choices are mine. Both fiction and non-fiction, doesn't matter really. I just wish I could live out some great adventure someday. And contribute something great to civil society.

I love my son, but I picture my future without his mom. I don't know how to reconcile that. He's in my future somewhere—a boy needs his father for guidance. Especially around here. And I know he needs her too, but I just don't know anymore.

My freedom is at the second office in Echo Park, on Alvarado Street. Commuting back and forth and getting that office up and running before the New Year. I'm hoping that all the time away from home triggers my wife to ask for a divorce. Then I reconsider, because she'll take my business. What I really hope: That she dies an unusual death. But since we're stuck together for the time being, I decide to be cordial.

"Have you seen any weird-looking people at the pet store?" I ask Cecilia. "This woman came in today with fluorescent hair, and a part of her head was shaved. Then there were some gay

Australians with a little toy dog at the grocery store next door to the office."

"What, did you like that woman? You think she was hot?"

I just laugh. I'm livid, but somewhat nervous, only because I actually want to start something with Kimberly Vuong. I can't believe Cecilia asked this, she's getting bolder.

Cecilia serves me a plate of mixed vegetables and chicken and then dashes to the bedroom, saying, "I'm not hungry. You can eat."

I'm ecstatic to be alone, so I grab *Invisible Man* by Ralph Ellison.

She returns a few minutes later and says, "Are you going with me to the wedding in Orange County?"

"You know, my business partner is out of town," I answer, "so I'm sorry but I can't."

Standing at the end of the hallway with a hand on her hip, she kisses her teeth and says, "This better be the last time you do this. I'm tired of going to family functions without you. Everyone thinks we're getting divorced."

"I don't care what everyone thinks. Is that what you want, a divorce?"

I look at her with inquisitiveness. I can't believe we're finally going to have this talk. If so, it needs to be amicable. I need to be civil to get the best terms possible.

"You always bring it up. It must be on *your* mind. Family is important to me. . . . I care what they think. You know that."

I look up at her and say, "And the clinic is important to me. It's my life."

"We are your life, too. Don't forget you have a family."

She always gets me into a jam. I can never get my words straight. A simple disagreement turns into a tornado. The baby crawls from the nursery room to the hallway while Cecilia and I are exchanging blows. She scoops him up and they disperse to the bedroom. I internalize these words: Fuck you bitch, fuckin' die already.

I finish dinner and resume the novel. I can't get passed the first chapter, though. My thoughts are on the woman at the clinic. She's going to USC, like I once had. Maybe I was too judgmental about her. I could've handled that encounter differently. She's a fellow Trojan, in need nonetheless. I'm also bothered by what my wife said, about liking her. I mean, do I? I picture her naked, but I'm a little grossed out by her shaved head. Like a man or something. And you never know, maybe I'll reject her and she'll say I tried to rape her like what's-her-name in Chester Himes' book, *If He Hollers, Let Him Go*. No, can't take my chances with a girl like that. She probably has gonorrhea.

Cecilia walks back out and says, "We need to talk."

Again she has her hand placed at her hip. I think it's sexy and cool in an uncanny way. I even think about having sex with her for a quick second, but nah, I'd rather not. I don't want to insert my penis inside of her anymore.

"For what?" I say, and close the book and set it on the table.

"Why are you mad, or irritated, or upset, or whatever you are? Fuck."

I take a long sigh. "I'm none of those things. But you're badgering me now and making me upset. Now I'm mad, because you keep asking if I'm fuckin' mad." I raise my voice and pound the table with the book.

"Wow, you go from like zero to a hundred, just like that."

I place my hands over my face and slide them down. In an escalated voice I say, "I can't do this anymore. I'm so sick and tired of you. All these fights, they're all you. Everything is you. I can't even talk to you about anything."

And not once do I look in her direction. I can't. Like I said, I can't stand the sight of her.

"What, you want a divorce? Just say the word, and I'll sign the papers. Say it, c'mon, fuckin' say it!"

I remain quiet. I hate when she cusses, it's unbecoming. I pick up the novel instead. Go back to reading. I shift my lips to the side.

She waves her hand to dismiss me, rolls her eyes and goes back to the bedroom.

I roll my eyes too and flip her off behind her back. I think about the PhD candidate instead. I think about Kimberly Vuong, then back to Georgina. I wonder if beneath all that junk that she wears she might look decent. Like a normal woman. I'd probably fuck her if it came down to it, if pressed. If she was the last woman around, I guess. But I'd never admit that out loud, oh no, not that.

I get sleepy contemplating how I will get rid of my wife.

August 18, 1999

I have a patient waiting for me in the clinic. I secretly wish that it's Georgina Tweedy. It's not, but I recognize this gentleman: Lurch from the Culver City gang. My old hood.

After Lurch is weighed by a nurse and she takes his blood pressure, I walk into an exam room where he's sitting on a chair.

"Mr. Beltrán, what are we doing today? Same as always . . . the ear flush?"

I remember that he has a ringing in his ear and he gets wax build-up periodically. We both have eager smiles on our faces. We even shake hands. I don't do that with anybody else. But Lurch and I have a shared experience from County. It's a mutual respect.

"Yeah, same thing, just trying to be proactive."

I like that he uses good verbiage. He's always tried to better himself. He could've been a good politician, if he wasn't a gangster. Matter of fact, there's a lot of smart dudes in the hood and in jail, but they chose a different life. I'm the only Culver City boy that went to college, that I know of. And I have a medical degree. That's something right there.

I grab an otoscope and look inside his ear. "Yeah, looks like there's some buildup. Let's get you cleaned up. Anything else?" "No, that's all," he says. "Just trying to prevent my ears from getting plugged up, you know? Gotta keep my ears clean for the ladies." Lurch kicks his legs around as they dangle from the position he's sitting in, and he smiles and laughs.

"Good man! If only everyone else had something this simple. The nurse will be right in. She'll get you squared away."

I start toward the door, when Lurch says, "Hey, Doc, have you noticed anything weird around here? I mean, any weird people coming around? People that don't belong?"

I pause for several seconds. Another person, like the pharmacist and me, who sees beyond these peoples' fakeness. He's sharp, this guy.

"Now that you mention it, yes," I answer. "I encountered a few yuppies recently. They seemed to have been from somewhere else. Some girl with pink . . ."

"Yeah, that's her, that's the one! I saw her too." Lurch hops off of the exam table, arms flailing all over the place. "With the side of her head shaved. I've never seen people like that around here before. I wonder what she's doing in our neighborhood. It's like a conspiracy or something."

"I think something should be done to stop them. These yuppies coming here from different states and even different countries. A lot of them are here because of the free mental health facilities in Mar Vista. They're like a disease spreading all over, right?"

I plant these specific words on purpose, because I know that he'll make sense of them. Somehow.

SIX

LURCH

When I take off from the clinic, my head is all like, *wham, wham, wham, wham.* It's all spinning like that, and I don't know what to think. I'm not gonna lie, I don't want it to be true. I didn't really want the doctor to say all that. Now what am I supposed to do about these people? I've gotta do something, right? I drive around the projects and Del Rey and Culver City, not knowing where to go. It's a Thursday morning, and none of the homies are around. I keep thinking about what the doctor said— that they should be stopped. Something has to be done. It's like he put it in my hands, you know? I have to protect the neighborhood.

All these rappers talk about it, so I'm switching CD's—Wu-Tang Clan, Goody Mob, Soul Assassins, Sons of Man, Mob Deep, Cypress Hill, Killer Army, Nas, Kool G. Rap, Psycho Realm. There's answers in them somewhere, just gotta look. The new world order, the apocalypse, the mark of the beast—that's all I keep hearing about. And Y2K. I even tattooed a bar code on the back of my neck, like I know some shit's going down. The end of days is near. Those that aren't prepared are gonna suffer. That's why I have all those canned foods and bottled water. And I have all types of batteries, flashlights and rifles. Those FEMA mother-fuckers are not gonna take my shit away. I'll kill them first. There's gonna be blood on the streets, watch. I'll take like a hundred of them with me. Like in "Scarface." I wonder why nobody's taking this shit seriously. Then again, I haven't talked about it with the homies as much, not in detail or anything.

People don't even know, man. In the future, after Y2K, barcodes are gonna be stamped on people. It's the final prophecy. In the new millennium, people won't carry cash anymore, they're gonna be scanned like barcodes in order to make transactions. That's why I have that stash, around three-hundred Gs, because when the shit comes down and people lose everything and the Federal Reserve Bank decides to take everyone's money or freeze their accounts, I'll have my shit right here so I can trade on the black market. In the underground, like those Europeans in Paris or London. People think I'm playing, but watch, this whole world is gonna exist in the sewer. It's the only way to survive all this. Like my homie Spy said in one of his raps, "Neighborhood watch, it don't stop, governments plots, the beginning stages of a war—want all and have-nots." *Guerra*.

And I keep listening to "Lost Cities" by Psycho Realm. These fools are just like us: Mexican Americans from the hood . . . Pico Union to be exact. And this fool, Duke, says that the empire is going to strike back at Rampart, that he's part of all that. It's like a call-to-arms, and they encourage gangsters to unite and fight the police and the system. These yuppies, like the doctor said, they're coming into the hood like nothing. They represent the system and the new world order. They're like informants watching every move we make, but I'm a keep my eye on 'em. They're like Big Brother, but I'ma be like Little Brother, you know what I'm saying?

That Psycho Realm song even starts with a verse from the Bible: the Book of Revelations and the four horsemen of the apocalypse. It says to kill with sword and hunger. Mark my words: there will be war. In this other song by RZA, he says that the government's gonna release a new virus in the western states. B-Real says that ghetto birds are gonna hover over Los Angeles and drop deadly warheads on civilians. B-Real also says something about a plague that's gonna wipe out humanity. These people are like a plague . . . like a disease that's spreading all over the West Side. Psycho Realm and their followers wear gas masks and call out gangsters for continuing the death cycle in the barrios of Los Angeles.

NWA said, "Fuck the police," but Psycho Realm is telling us to shoot police captains. Everybody talks about the destruction of Los Angeles—fires, riots, floods, earthquakes and plagues—like it's just around the corner. This one dude, Mike Davis, predicted a riot in Los Angeles in his book *City of Quartz*. And then '92 happened. Somebody's right about the millennium. I even read that California's gonna separate during the big earthquake, and Los Angeles will sink into the ocean, like it had in the past. Like it did in San Pedro back in the day, when they called it Sunken City. Los Angeles will be remembered like the lost city of Atlantis. If so many people talk about it, and there are so many predictions, there's gotta be some truth. I can feel it in my bones.

Damn, bad times are coming, and my palms are getting sweaty as fuck. Gonna grab my pistol from the stash and look for a target on the street range. That dude with the beard. We're already living in a city that's lost, and like the homie Knuckles always says, "This is Lost Angles, the city of Lost Angles."

෧෧ඁ෧

When I get home, I remember that I have Scott Kidd's mail. He's definitely a 666 and a yuppy. I open the student loan bill and the pay-off balance is around $60,000. There's a minimum due of $294.36, and it's late. Broke-ass motherfucker. I could pay that shit off right now, you know what I'm saying? Ha! I open the credit card statement and examine purchases. There's a bunch of local restaurant charges, some from Best Buy and others from

Macy's and that sort of thing. One charge came from a university in Australia. Maybe this dude is from down under, and maybe *I'm* gonna place that fool *down under.*

One last charge stands out: something from Cal Arts. Like supplies or something. So I'm thinking, "This guy works there or he went to that school." I don't even know where the fuck that is, never even heard of it. But that's a good thing. I can kill him there, and it probably won't get back to me in Culver City.

I drive back to where I saw him at that apartment complex. I park nearby to monitor him. Like I said, I'ma be Little Brother. I wait about one hour, until I get so bored and restless, I have to take off. At the corner of Culver Boulevard, I see some dude on a bicycle with a pant leg rolled up and a helmet. I can't see so well because the Green Culver City bus passes and blocks my view. When it moves, I see this fool in a V-neck sweater with a diamond-pattern over a short-sleeved button-up shirt, suspenders and he's wearing a tie. Looks like a goddamn Mormon. A wolf in sheep's clothing. Watch, when the new world order comes for people in the hood, they're gonna use these types of decoys. I observe my target walk upstairs, lock his bike on the rail and remove his helmet. He's a dwarf, like 5'5", and pasty, and he twists his mustache at the tips. And he looks goofy, like a damn dodo bird. It's Scott Kidd, for sure. This fool needs to be stopped, and probably needs a good beat down. I point the gun through the car window. He can't see me. I fake-squeeze the trigger, but something tells me to wait. I don't know why.

If this motherfucker has the mark of the beast, then I should smoke him, or run him out the hood. Not today though. It's his lucky day. At least I know where to find him.

August 26, 1999

I've just parked in my driveway, when I see Mikey driving down the street in his Jeep, probably on his way home. I reverse real quick and pull back toward his pad. I park behind him and signal for him to approach with my index finger. He gets close to the car, squats and rests his elbows on the door so we're both eye-level. My eyes pierce through his, but he doesn't blink. He's solid like that, and I respect him for it. He looks down both sides of the street like I indirectly taught him that day we rolled around the hood. Like he's watching his back and looking out for enemies. I can't help but smile, but I don't say anything.

"Get in the car, man," I tell him. "I want to show you something."

"I just got home, Lurch, I have some work to do." He turns to walk away.

"Like what? You graduated from college already, so I know you don't have any homework. C'mon, it'll be just for a second, homes."

I know he's thinking of an excuse to get out of coming, but he's not sharp enough. I don't give him any time. Instead, I reach over to the passenger seat and push the door open. He looks in several directions, like he's not sure. He better get in voluntarily, or I'll make him. I'll put the gun to his face if I have to. But then he gets in, and I'm relieved because I don't wanna seem like a bully to him. He's had enough of that from other homies, but not from me. I always treat this *vato* with respect. I admire his dedication to always do the right thing. Since he was a kid, just trying to survive all this madness.

"I told you that some shit was going down around the neighborhood, right?" I say.

He nods.

"About some suburban type warfare or whatever? . . . Well, I want you to see some of these changes for yourself . . . see what I'm talking about."

I take him to the empty Ballona Wetland, where the Playa Vista housing community is going to be built.

I lower the music and say, "You know how many bodies we buried down there?"

"Wait—what?!!"

"Nah, I'm just fuckin' with you. Look at your face, ha, ha, ha!"

We laugh like that for a while. Like I almost gave that fool a heart attack.

He says, "Feel my chest, no c'mon, really."

"Nah, but for real, I'm telling you, it's polluted," I say. "You know the doctor right . . . my homie, Gorilla Joe?"

He nods.

"He's noticed the same thing I have. Weird-looking white people, yuppies that don't belong here. All up in the hood. Playa Vista is going to be built for people like them. Not us. We're gonna get this entire community of outsiders with homes on top of a polluted wetland. And they're gonna be right here: our next-door neighbors, all sick 'n shit."

"What type of people? I don't know what you're talking about."

"C'mon, let's drive around the hood so you can see with your own eyes."

We drive down Inglewood Boulevard, and I pull out the *cuete* from a dashboard stash.

His eyes zoom in on the handle and he says, "Hey, what's up with that? I don't want to be part of this. Just take me home."

"It's registered, man, don't even trip. I got you. I'm just bringing it out in case we gotta cap somebody."

"I don't wanna cap anybody, man. Just take me home. Please. C'mon, Lurch. I just graduated from UCLA. I wanna start my life. I'm probably gonna move to Rhode Island with Stan in a few months."

I roll the tinted windows up. I like what I hear, so I say, "That's smart. The smartest thing I've heard you say all summer. Now you're starting to make sense. You *should* bounce, homie.

There's gonna be a war soon. It's the apocalypse, big dog . . . World War Three."

He squeezes the front seat, and I can see that I'm making him nervous by driving around with a gun in my hand. I guess it's not normal to him. I pull the car over near Culver Boulevard and Kensington Road. I turn off the ignition and roll the windows down. He's still looking at the gun.

I point and say, "There's some fool that lives right there in those apartments. I know for a fact he has the mark of the beast. And you know what? Even the doctor said that these fools should be stopped. Before they spread around like a disease."

"A disease, Lurch? Why do you keep telling me stuff like this? Why me? I'm just some regular guy. I don't know anything about the mark of the beast or the new world order or whatever, man."

"You should," I say. "You went to college . . . you should know about shit like this. Besides, I'm telling you because I don't want your people, or you, to be mistaken for these sick-looking motherfuckers. They already look like you. Or you look like them, I don't know. When it comes down to it, it's gonna be weird-looking motherfuckers versus regular-looking people . . . people from the hood. And you, my boy, are a weird-ass looking motherfucker."

Then that bald-headed white boy comes out the apartment— Scott Kidd—and he has on that same V-neck sweater. He looks like a skinhead, like Stan Corona, so I wonder if Mikey knows this dude. I need him to understand that these people and him and his friends all look alike. Mikey says he doesn't know him.

I reach toward the glove compartment to pull out Kidd's mail, and Mikey gets all jumpy and almost hops out the passenger seat.

I'm like, "Damn, dude, I ain't no fag or anything like that. I'm just getting some paperwork."

I hand him the stack of mail and look up toward where that dude is standing, smoking a cigarette on the balcony. Trying to be all cool or whatever. Playing with his mustache.

Mikey says, "You stole his mail?"

"Yeah, so? Gotta know who I'm dealing with. I think he might be Australian or something. Check it out. He wears those sweaters that you and your friend Stan like to wear. What brand is that? Izod or some shit?"

"Fred Perry—elite British underground stuff," he says with attitude.

I laugh and say, "I'm gonna keep an eye on this guy. Maybe you should too. This fool doesn't belong here. That's why I don't want him in the hood."

I point the gun in the direction of the balcony and say, "I'm gonna kill that motherfucker. Watch. The doctor said something should be done about it. And that's what I intend to do."

"So why am I here?" Mikey asks. "What does this have to do with me? Can we just please go? I gotta get back to the house. I'm serious, Lurch."

I start the car. I'm glad I told him about all this. Whatever he decides to do with all this information. It's on him. If he tells that new neighbor, Mark, to pack his shit and bounce, then cool. If he doesn't and we smoke him, that's on Mikey. I decide that from here on out, I don't gotta tell him anything anymore. I did my duty. So, if he's leaving to Rhode Island, then that's dope. He'll miss the whole *guerra* and won't get caught up in the crossfire. But if he sticks around, despite everything I've said, then he's stupid. And he deserves to die, if it comes down to that.

That song "Doo Wa Ditty" by Zapp and Roger comes on the radio. I say, "That's my jam—straight up!" I turn up the volume and swing my right hand up and down and bob my head. He looks at me all weird, and I smile while I dance like that in the car. He smiles and loosens up a little. He even does a little dance move. I didn't know he had it in him. He's always so serious and uptight. So, I'm thinking that we're good and Mikey's gonna be straight. I'm glad, you know?

I bust an illegal turn on Culver in front of the ARCO as a cop pulls out of the gas station. He mad-dogs us and throws on his siren. Fuck. I panic a little and think about speeding up. I look at Mikey. He has his hand on the door handle like he's gonna jump out. I slow down.

"Don't trip, dog." I tell him. "Calm the fuck down. You're making me nervous, fuck."

"You have the gun, man. I don't want any part of this."

He's nodding his head, and his long hair is shaking. I think he's gonna cry.

"There's a warrant on me. I'm gonna get busted. Don't worry about anything. You don't know anything. So just relax. Hang back, man."

"For what?" he asks. "What'd you do? What about the gun?"

I lower the windows as the cop approaches the driver's side and says, "License and registration."

"My name's Ruben Beltran," I tell the cop. "I have a warrant for possession for sales. The car's registered to me."

The cop pulls out a strap and says, "Step out of the vehicle . . . with your hands up."

I look at Mikey and say, "Take the car, take it to my house. Borrow it, whatever, you're in charge. And remember what I told you about all this."

I pull the door handle from the outside and I place my hands behind me, interlocked so he can cuff me. He walks me backwards to the backseat of the squad car. Then he starts typing in some info into his monitor. I know Mikey is all worried now, but he's gonna be all right. I'll do some time and, who knows, maybe the new world order will happen when I'm in the joint and the outside world will go to shit. I'll be inside, not knowing what the fuck.

SEVEN

MIKEY

August 26, 1999

The cop returns to the BMW a few minutes later and asks for my ID. I can hardly move my body. My hands tremble and are clammy, so I rub them on my pants before handing him my driver's license. Hope he doesn't make a big deal about my hair in the picture, since it was shorter when I took it. When the cop leaves, I look toward the dashboard stash. The gun's right there—a chrome .45. I want to run out of the car, but my IBS is creeping up. Might shit on myself if I make a run for it. I wonder how far I can get before the cop actually shoots me. Maybe just a few yards. I keep my eye on the cop through the rearview mirror. I see Lurch in the back seat of the patrol car. Is that a smile on his face? I wonder if the cop is going to search the BMW. If he does, I'm straight fucked. I'm looking for a warning sign, like if he walks differently or calls for backup . . . something.

When he comes back, he just says, "Get this car outta here. Move it, NOW."

"Yessir," I say and slide toward the driver's seat. I bone the fuck out.

I've never driven a BMW before. My heart is still pounding. But I feel like somebody important in this car. Maybe this is how rich people feel, like everyone should notice. I roll down the windows, let the wind penetrate my hair and switch the radio dial to KXLU. I think Stan or Mark Stahl might be spinning records on campus right now. I consider waving at people, presidentially of course. Maybe I should go to Melrose, or Penny Lane Records, park right in front so the world can bear witness to my arrival. This car will impress the ladies . . . I might be able to get a couple of phone numbers. But the more I think about it, the more I can't continue.

That gun's still here, and I want to get as far away from it as possible. Who knows how many shootings or drug deals have gone down with that gun. I think about master's programs in Rhode Island again. This type of shit can't be happening to me, I'm a college graduate. We're supposed to be better than this.

I don't want to drive Lurch's Beamer to his family's house. I don't want my mom or my neighbors seeing me in this ride. I don't want the association nor the questions. As I'm driving down Culver, I realize I know where the twins live, near the exit off Sawtelle Boulevard.

Leon is the only one home when I pull up. I remember the house because they always have a bunch of toys in the driveway and the yard—dirt bikes, jet-skis, sand rails, quads, whatever. I park over yellow-brownish grass, weeds and dirt. They have a big family too, with at least four brothers from CXC—Leon, Noel and two older ones. And they're cousins with Raven, I think. I don't actually know who lives here, but for some reason, I think Paulina might be inside, visiting Raven's relatives or something. That's the real reason why I've come, if you want to know the truth. I think about her daily. All the songs remind me of her, in every genre. Northern soul, post-punk, shoe-gaze, Britpop, whatever. My favorite: "Alone Again Or" by The Damned.

I spot Leon in work gear: khaki shorts, construction boots, striped navy-blue Pepsi button-up and a Colorado Rockies ballcap on backwards with an embroidered C/R. He's busy cleaning the rims on an International Scout. I recall that he's a beverage distributor and drives one of those big semi-trucks. They make like $60,000 a year, and he didn't even go to college or anything. It's a cruel world. All the entry-level positions I applied to start around $40,000.

"What's up Mikey, why you have the homie's ride? I thought you were Lurch," he says.

"He was giving me a ride and we got pulled over. He said he had a warrant, so they took him in. I thought the car would be better off with you guys. You'd know what to do with it."

"Did he say anything to you about some Australian dude?" Leon smirks.

"How'd you know?"

Leon's face shifts, his pointy noise curls and his fair skin heightens his ruddy cheeks. "He's been talking about that for a minute. Said he wanted to chop it up with you about that. What'd the dude look like, anyway? Did Lurch tell you his name?"

"Scott Kidd, I think. Lurch had his mail, so . . . maybe that's his name. Short, white boy with a stupid mustache."

Leon hands me a business card with Scott Kidd's name on it. I'm confused.

"Lurch's been on some new world order shit lately, huh? Thinks white people are gonna run us out of the hood. What do you think about all that?"

"I don't know, man," I answer. "I really don't know. I'm just dropping off the car." I hand him the keys and say, "Would you mind giving me a ride home? I gotta get back to the pad."

We hop in the International Scout. The old leather bucket seats are cracked and noisy, like a vintage leather jacket. I like the smell, reminds me of my Wagoneer. The center console is minimalist, and the engine fires up after some hesitation.

"That's fuckin' weird, dog," Leon says. "You think it's a coincidence? Lurch mentioned some white boy with a beard, but not this guy. And then I run into this one wood at Von's on Centinela. This fool seen my tats or something . . ." Leon lifts the sleeves on his shirt and shows me lowercase shaded Old English letters "CXC" on one arm, "LLS" on the other. "And you know me, homes, I represent the Culver City Little Locos clique. All day every day. And that fool says, 'Excuse me, can I ask you a question?'

"I almost socked that fool up. I said, 'This is Culver City Gang!' I got into a fighting stance, you know what I'm saying?

"Then he said, 'I was just curious about your ink.'

"I was like, Ink? 'The fuck you mean, ink? Who the fuck're you? What the fuck you want, *ese*? This is my hood, ya know what I'm saying?'

"He covered his face and was like, 'Nah, nah. I'm a novelist. . . . I'm writing a story about the race war between Hispanic and Black gangs.'

"I said, 'Why? So you can make us all look like a bunch of savages. We got a truce going on, we don't need you writing about us.'

"And that fool said, 'Interesting.'

"And I was like . . . 'Interesting? You think Blacks and Mexicans killing each other is interesting?' I laughed my ass off, you know what I'm saying, Mikey? And then he was all apologetic and said I was getting the wrong idea. And I was like, 'Where you from, anyway, you're not from around here, huh?'

"Then the dude says, 'Iowa, by way of Colorado, but I feel like I can relate to you guys. I've had my own personal experience with violence too.'

"I told that fool, 'So, just because you had an experience with violence, you think you relate to us, and the South Side? Who the fuck are you, really? You ain't nothing like us, homie.'

"Then he says, 'I'm just trying to write a cool book about Los Angeles gangs. I wanna study . . .'

"'What? You wanna study us, like a bunch of monkeys or some shit?' I said. 'Get the fuck outta here with that bullshit.

Write about your own goddamn city, you know what I'm saying? LA is for real motherfuckers, homes. You don't know shit about West Los.'

"That's when the *vato* said, 'I know . . . that's why I want to be here! This is Hollywood, the land of sunshine.' Then he named off some writers or some shit. Lebowski or something, and some other fools. I don't know.

"He didn't get the point, though. He still handed me his business card. Fuckin' lame, dog. *¿Qué no?* He tried to shake my hand too, but I was like, '*Chale, ese.* You don't know me. Don't fuckin' touch me.'"

"This is my stop," I interrupt. "Thanks for the ride, man." I bone the fuck out of his International Scout, quick-like.

⊙∂ℯ⊙

Stan and Rick roll up to my pad, it's nighttime. I hear Stan's '69 Camaro rumble in the driveway. I had told him I don't like that shit, it's ghetto. It was a good thing they were there because I had dealt with Lurch all afternoon and then I heard all of Leon's bullshit. I just needed a break from stupid gang talk. I just need to stop thinking about those dudes because they're all up in my head. And Stan and Rick are like, "Let's go to Spaceland, let's go out. Mark Stahl's going to DJ tonight too. In between bands."

My face lights up, but I don't have the luxury of spending unnecessary money right now.

Rick's like, "Hey, man, I got your back. I got you covered. We're all gonna be gone soon, anyway, let's just have this last hurrah."

I lead them toward my room. Stan posts up at the computer desk, Rick at the corner of the sleigh bed. I should go. This is what life is all about anyway, right? . . . Good friends and a good time? Plus, Stan's leaving to Rhode Island, and Rick's getting stationed in New Mexico. This might be the last time we're all together for a while. My eyes get watery.

"So, Mikey, you think about Rhode Island or what?" Stan asks.

"I mean . . . I've looked at the University of Rhode Island and some other places," I say, "but I just don't know. It's far, and I'm still waiting to hear back about that job for the city of Santa Monica."

Stan looks through my bookcase and says, "You said it's an unpaid internship, right? Well, Sarah can get us both jobs out there in the meantime. She already said so. Her dad's a famous architect, bro. You could do urban planning out there, or something gnarly like that, you know? We just need to get out of here, dude. At least for a few years. Rick's leaving too, fuck it."

He picks out *A Clockwork Orange* from the shelf and smiles.

Rick puts in his two cents: "I think it's a good idea, Mikey. I went to basic training in San Antonio and now I'm getting stationed in Alamogordo. Soon, they'll send me on temporary duty assignments all over the world. And you know, I don't think I'm gonna miss this place. Not for a minute. Maybe later, but for now it's just good to be away from all this hood BS, you know? Gang shit, crime, all that. I'll miss you guys, but we'll keep in touch."

"But what about my mom?" I say. "I'm just gonna leave her here?"

"I don't mean to disrespect or anything like that," Stan says, "but you gotta live your own life. She wants the best for you anyway."

"If Sarah's dad can hook you up in government in Rhode Island, you should do it," Rick says. "You need to man up. If things aren't happening here, then maybe you have to look somewhere else. But in the meantime, let's go to Spaceland. Let's just listen to some music, dance a little and have a good time. Maybe go to the French Quarters after to eat. You love that place, right? Throw some tunes on, yeah."

I say, "Fuck it! Let's do this!"

෨෴ඏ

I'm literally having a heart attack. I can't believe who I see at Spaceland. Paulina! I was like: What the fuck is she doing here? In our scene? We're standing around the bar having a few drinks, letting our eyes wander. Even Mark Stahl is with us, talking about obscure bands and growing up in Nebraska. It's dark and smoky and dense, and a gang of people slither all around us as we move up toward the stage. Stan and Mark are planning a trip to New York City, before CBGB, that famous punk club, closes down, and before Stan moves to Rhode Island. They invite me on the trip, keep pressing on about it and for me to move to the Northeast. After a few drinks, I decide I'll go to New York, but I'll have to pull money from my last emergency stash. I toast them, "To New York!" After this, though, I'll be completely broke. I have a few thousand dollars saved, and that's for like rainy and soggy days. Like gap money before I find another job. A plane ticket is around $300, hostel is like $150 for a week and spending cash like $400. If I can keep it under $1000, I'll be all right. I'm calculating all this math in my head and how much I can allow myself to eat per day. But then I remember that New York is like double the price of whatever's in LA and I get depressed by how frugal I have to be. I think about having another drink, but I'd have to ask Rick to buy me one.

My peripheral shifts toward the tables near the restroom, and I notice Paulina again with two other girls posted up with a couple of drinks in front of them. I can't believe my eyes. My heart thumps and thumps like I don't know what, and my face goes all weird and hot. It's like this flaming energy that crawls from my throat to my forehead. Like my face gets numb and crimson. I pick up my vodka tonic and down it in one gulp. My hands tremble.

Rick says, "Damn, Mikey. You all right? We have the whole night ahead of us."

"Yeah, I'm cool," I swear. "Order me another one, yeah? Please. I'll be right back."

I start inching forward and turn to say, "I'm going to the bathroom real quick."

I snake through tons of people, bumping into a handful of them. I keep my eyes fastened on Paulina. She hasn't noticed me. I'm not surprised. She's just sitting there in a white flowered dress, her hair covering part of her face, cascading down toward the beginning of her breasts, where a small amount of cleavage pops out. Damn, she's so beautiful. I can't stop staring. When I get really close to her table, I look right at her. She still doesn't bother to look up at me. I keep walking, straight into the bathroom. I throw water on my face and look at myself in the mirror. I'm so nervous and I holler, "You got this! Don't be such a pussy. You got this."

I pop a breath mint in my mouth. I walk back out, stomach going through a tempest, chest almost imploding. I pause at their table and look right at her. I point and say, "Paulina?"

She stands up and says, "Oh my God, you're the one that saved me!" She looks at her friends. "He's the guy I told you about. At that party."

She throws her arms around me and says, "Sit down, please. Have a seat, honey."

I don't know what the fuck is going on, but it's already more than I had expected. I sink into the booth and she scoots close to me. I mean, my leg is pressed up right against hers. Our bodies are touching, I can't believe it. And she smells like coconut, like that night at my house.

She pushes up her face really close to mine, and I say, "What are you doing here? You like this kind of music?"

"Yeah, we go to all types of venues," she says. "We go to artsy places with cool music. These are my friends from Occidental. It's over here in Eagle Rock. This is Jessica and Marcy."

I look at her friends' faces for the first time since I noticed Paulina. I don't recognize them from the hood. I smile at them. They look indie and hip, like some girls me and the guys would go for. One has a black leather jacket and a short bob cut, the other has dark hair, glasses and a Ramones T-shirt. But they are still invisible to me. Paulina is radiant, with her blonde hair and her bright dress and the halo hovering over her head. She's a ray of sunshine in this dark place. I'm wearing dark solids, too. And Paulina just brightens everything up.

"I don't know," I say. "I just pictured you differently. I pictured you with the Culver City boys and going to like sports bars and house parties."

"That's funny, I pictured you the same." And she cracks up. I do too.

She pulls my face close to hers, and my cock gets stiff. I'm all elated.

"So, you go to Occidental?"

"Yeah. I'm in Cognitive Science. It's my second year. What about you, you go to college?"

"Not anymore. I just graduated from UCLA. Political Science."

"Oh, congratulations! What are you going to do now?"

"I'm moving to Rhode Island in a few months. Going to work in urban planning up there and do a graduate program. It's all lined up already."

She lowers her lip and grabs my hand. "Oh, I'm never going to see you again?"

She looks genuinely sad. I get all warm and weird inside and regret telling her that.

Just then, her friends excuse themselves to use the restroom. As they get up to go, Paulina places my hand on her thigh, right where her dress cuts off and her leg starts. Just like that. I don't know what to do, I just look around all embarrassed, hoping nobody is watching. Then she moves my hand underneath her dress, and I slide it toward her vagina soaking through her underwear. She moans and her body jerks. My heart explodes. I just keep at it like that, and she licks my ear and kisses my face and bites my bottom lip. When her friends come back, I stop. But she doesn't move my hand away and places hers over mine and keeps it on her leg. Her friends don't sit back down, saying they have to go. They get all smiley and wave goodbye at me and Paulina.

"What's that all about?" I ask Paulina.

"They think you're good for me."

"What do you think?"

"We'll see." Then she whispers in my ear. "Let's get out of here. Let's go to my place."

She hastens me out of the booth and takes me by the hand. I feel like the luckiest man on earth, like I've just won the lottery. I even sing that one song from The Verve in my head. I purposely walk toward where the guys are to let them know I'm taking off with Paulina. When we approach the bar, Mark's back at the DJ booth and Rick is on the dance floor. I place my hand on Paulina's lower back, and she's cool with it. I wish I could jump in the air. As soon as Stan and I make eye contact, he shifts his head horizontally and gives me that same look as when those dudes shot up my pad. Like I fucked up. He turns away when we get close. No need to converse. I know he doesn't approve, but what else can I do? I'm a grown-ass man. He doesn't know what I feel for Paulina, nobody does. And I know it's dangerous, she knows it too, but I guess we both feel something for each other and we're just responding to our mutual attraction.

We make it to her car, a Toyota Camry, and we drive from Silverlake to Eagle Rock. All the while we fondle each other and laugh and take vodka drinks from a flask she has stashed in her purse. We go inside her apartment and shut the door.

ⓢⓧⓢ

I wake up. Paulina is gone. No note, no coffee, no nothing. I look around at her stuff: a Cincinnati Reds cap on the dresser, probably Raven's. I spit on it. There are pictures of her and her friends and family. Her mom (I presume) looks really pretty, same dirty blonde hair and green eyes like Paulina's. Her jewelry is spread out on the dresser. Clothes are thrown about on the floor. I see a pair of black panties and snatch them up. I smell them and place them over my face, then insert them into my pants pocket. I want to take a bra too, but I can't stash it in my pockets. Fuck it, I slide it inside my jacket sleeve. It rubs against my arm, and I picture all the things she and I did just a few hours ago. Her legs over my shoulders, my hands snapping off her bra, my body splayed out on top of hers, my stiff boner inside her. Thrust and repeat, thrust and repeat. I find a pen and write my number on a piece of paper. I almost write "I love you" too. *Fuck, I'm such a pussy.* I throw my clothes on and walk out of her studio apartment. It's the upstairs unit of a small business, which is closed. I memorize her address and walk toward the street corner. I emblazon the street name into my heart. I would tattoo it across my chest if it wasn't such a lame thought.

September 10, 1999

I finally have the chance to go to New York. Home of The Ramones, The Velvet Underground, Talking Heads, Sonic Youth and many other great bands. I'm wearing my olive green parka with a fur collar, black Dickies and my black Jack Purcell's. Stan has a red Herrington jacket, navy blue chords and some Tiger Asics sneakers. Mark has a black military jacket, black pants and black Doc Martens. I feel like we're in a band and I get nostalgic about playing music. We take a picture like that right outside of LAX, on a bench outside of departures. With our legs crossed and our sunglasses on. Some people stare at us, like we're somebodies. Like they want a picture or an autograph. Maybe that would've been the case if we had continued playing music. Now I'm just a groupie.

We're at an airport bar. Stan's had three vodka tonics back to back at about $15 a pop. Mark and I have one each and we're drinking slowly.

Mark says, "So, you guys have been friends since middle school?"

I say, "We went to the same middle school, but we weren't friends back then. Not until high school, actually, when we played in the same garage band. What about you, you play? Or just DJ?"

Stan is boisterous and slurring. I tell him to take it easy. In an amplified voice he announces, "You know how us Mexicans do!"

I lower my head and try to tuck it down into my parka. Stan almost falls off his stool, and I turn to look in a different direction, away from Mark and the crowd. I take a small sip of my drink. I catch two older, well-dressed white men staring at us, and I apologize with a hand gesture and a half-smile. Mark smiles at them too. I want to tell them that I just graduated from UCLA, to perhaps encourage them to look at us in a different light.

Suddenly, apropos of nothing, Stan asks, "Did you apologize to Raven for fuckin' his lady?" He laughs like a motherfucker and spits some of his drink out as he does.

People stare at us harder.

Mark gets up and says, "I'm gonna use the bathroom," as he walks away.

I hop off the bar stool and trot to the bathroom too. Stan follows suit, stumbling and laughing at the same time.

Stan catches up to me and says, "What? You can't take it?"

In a low-pitched tone as we walk, gritting my teeth like how my mom used to scold me, I say, "What the fuck is wrong with you, man? You're acting like a goddamn idiot. I'm gonna go check on Mark."

Stan says, "He's a grown-ass man. He can grab his own dick when he pisses."

He shrugs and tells me to calm down. He segues into a story about Paulina, about how she fucked this dude from Carson Skinheads on their first date. He says that that's why he was bothered by this whole thing with her and me to begin with. Not because she's with a Culver City boy, but because I have feelings for this girl. The wrong type of girl. And he knows other things about her that I didn't. He keeps rambling as we walk.

She hasn't even called me. Not since that night. I'm embarrassed to tell Stan that. Can't even get a girl that I had sex with three times in one night to call me. I wonder what she saw in me in the first place, and what I did wrong. My heart is crumbling as we speak, and my face turns warm. I thought about waiting outside of her apartment numerous times, but if Raven is there and he sees me, I'm through. I get pissed at Stan for telling me that story and I storm into the bathroom so I can wash the shame off my face. I feel thousands of needles threading all over my body. I get IBS too, real quick—I have to shit everything out of my system. I think about not boarding the plane. I should just leave this fool with Mark right now. They'll be all right.

Stan's in one of the toilet stalls, while I stand around the sinks washing my hands and staring at my ugly face in the mirror. When he comes out, he has white powder all over his nose. Like a goddamn clown.

I'm so pissed, I yell, "You're so fuckin' stupid, bro! What the fuck is your goddamn problem?"

He laughs and dances, then walks languidly toward the sinks before washing his face off. He stares into the mirror and laughs some more.

I say, "We could've got busted at checkpoint, you fuckin' idiot!"

He says, "But we didn't."

☙✲☙

In New York, I don't find anything unusual. Not the cold and rainy weather, not the bands at the Bowery Ballroom, not the smelly train stops, not the way people pronounce Houston Street like House-ton, not the Swiss woman at the hostel who doesn't leave the facility and doesn't shower, not the endless tourists in Chinatown, not the German tourists from Cologne who drink 40 oz. Old English beer and dress hip-hop, not the numerous project buildings and tenements, not the crowds at the Met, not the people and lofts we visit in Williamsburg, not the entrance fee at the Guggenheim, not the trendy and hip restaurants in Brooklyn and Midtown, not the mafia-looking goons in Little Italy, not the skyscrapers and tourist spots like the Empire State Building, Times Square, the Twin Towers or the Statue of Liberty, not the brownstones, not the graffiti-plastered walls, not the bar at the Beauty Salon and certainly not the Korova Milk Bar like from *A Clockwork Orange*. But around CBGB, in that neighborhood, things are out of the norm. I mean, the Lower East Side, known for gritty streets and alleys and trashy music venues, is lined with yuppies and preppies outside of cafes and restaurants and art galleries. They look like they're not from New York. It's like what Lurch keeps talking about. These people are just right there, next door to bums and sketchy neighborhoods, like Culver City or Echo Park back home. And there's a bunch of people in tents on streets, like Skid Row in Downtown Los Angeles, but they look like regular people. Young white moms and teenage kids, Blacks and Latinos, even some grimy Asians. They're everywhere, even near the music venues. Just regular-looking people that happen to be homeless. Asking other young people for money. You can see them from CBGB's entrance. I think about the Velvet Underground and that heroin song, and if someone offers me smack right now, I'll do it in a heartbeat. I know Stan would. That's the kind of place this is.

I order a drink at the bar, and I ask the heavily sleeved-up bartender why the venue is closing.

"Yo, rents are getting too high," he answers. "Fuckin' displacement. Just look outside. New York is vanishing as we speak. Fuckin' gentrification."

I don't say anything, but suddenly my stomach churns and my IBS just creeps up. Oh no, not here. I run to the toilets while holding the back of my legs. People don't get out of the way, and I'm just bumping into them. I reach the bathroom, and the toilets are filthy and smelly and stained, graffiti and stickers all over the place, and there aren't any liners or toilet paper. I'm like, "Fuck!!" As I'm pulling my pants down, a small trickle of shit shoots out of me and lands on the inside of my pants in a splash, and when I sit down, the whole world just tumbles out of me. Like an explosion. I remove my parka and toss it on the floor, then my T-shirt, which I use to wipe the shit off my pants. It's then I realize I don't have anything to wipe my ass with. I'm thinking, "No, no, no."

Man, I'm so embarrassed. My face is red, and I almost want to cry. I don't know what to do. Then, through the crack in the door, I see this dude walk in and use the sink. I ask him if he could please bring me some napkins from the bar or something. He does. Just a few minutes later—cool-ass dude, you know? So, I clean my asshole up. I have to kick it at CBGB for a while longer without a shirt under my parka, knowing that I have literally just shit my pants. That is what is unusual in New York.

Like at four in the morning, while me, Stan and Mark wait in the subway station all alone and drunk, this Black dude, a street bum, walks toward us with a bat in his hand. He's muddy and stinky and has snot dripping from his nose. It's so gross. I'm not gonna lie either: I'm a bit scared. But my fear is suppressed under my intoxication. Stan's beamed up, finds it comical. He's ready to squab. Mark too, I can see the chords bursting from his neck. But I would never fight a dude like that. What if he has some disease?

The bum says, "Yo Bee, are you motherfuckers ready for the battle zone?"

We ignore him. I look around the train station and confirm we're alone.

The bum continues, "There's a war goin' on ta-night. 'N every other night till the New Year. It's the new world order, and white boys like you gonna die. You can't be comin' up in here and takin' our shit, son!"

Mark says, "White boys designed this subway you're living in, chief."

I'm tripping out because I didn't think Mark was like that. I'm also tripping because he thinks we're white. Nobody thinks I'm white, only white-washed. I think I might love New York. Stan gets into a fighting position, like he's going to kick him into the tracks. He even rolls his sleeves up and laughs and pounds fists with Mark. The bum stares at Mark's combat boots. But just then, the train arrives with fury, and the noise rattles all through my gut. We board quick-like, and all I think about are these goddamn Yanks being displaced and living in tents on the streets . . . and, of course, the shit stain inside my pants.

September 16, 1999

There's a bunch of mail waiting for me at home from last week. There's a letter from the DEA, from the California Alcohol and Beverage Control, Caltrans, the City of Santa Monica and the County of Los Angeles. They are all rejection letters. Even the internship. Not one single callback. No emails, no telegrams, no postcards. No nothing. And nothing from Paulina either. I don't want to sleep with her underwear resting on my pillow anymore, but I can't throw it away either.

Nobody tells you in college that you should find employment while you're still in school. I should've gotten an internship before, like the lady in the interview said, or I should've applied to law school in the summer. I thought there would be a surplus of organizations lined up to interview me. But now I'm just another beaner with a college degree who doesn't mean anything to anybody except to my mom.

I even applied to the LAX Police Department, the Sheriff's Department and Culver City PD. The Sheriff's Department wouldn't take me because I lied regularly about drug use and I didn't remember what I wrote on different questionnaires or applications. I failed the physical exam for Culver City. I did well on the run, but I couldn't do pull-ups and I struggled with the sit-ups. I got a 100% on the LAXPD written exam, but they disqualified me because I had once been arrested for trespassing. I lied about it, though. I considered the Air Force because Rick had joined after he graduated and went in as an officer. Everybody's moving on to bigger and better things, except me.

I keep wondering what I'm doing wrong. It's like everyone has their shit in order while I'm stagnant. I think about that Syl Johnson song, "Is it Because I'm Black?" Yes, it is, the fuckin' man is keeping me down. At least that's what I tell myself.

There's a knock on the door, it's Mark Stahl. He says, "Did you like New York?"

"It was so dope. Best trip ever, right? At least for me it was."

He says, "Yeah, I love going there. Gotta go back soon for this DJ thing. But listen, I wanted to talk to you about this other thing. I've been meaning to tell you about it. One of my students works at the *Argonaut* newspaper. He said they're looking for a writer to cover the news and politics section. Stan told me you studied political science and that you're a pretty good writer."

I'm embarrassed by this and say, "I'm okay. I got accused of plagiarism because a professor said I didn't cite outside sources, but there weren't any because they were my own words and thoughts."

"Dude, that's so awesome. They were just trying to fuck with you, ignorant-ass academics. Give me a sample and I'll pass it along. Hey, you wanna come over my house and check out my record collection? I also wanna show you these letters I got from Debbie Curtis, Ian's wife."

"No fuckin' way!"

"Yes fuckin' way, bro."

Mark and I walk over to his house, and that orange entry door is no longer a mystery.

September 21, 1999

I'm at this interview for the *Argonaut News* in the industrial part of Playa Del Rey. All this time trying to get out of this place, and now I'm interviewing for a job here. This woman, Sandy Schwartz, comes out to greet me and just starts talking about how my writing reminds her of Marshall McLuhan because it's a fresh take on media discourse. She goes on about the media's role in abandoning a philosophical outlook on societal trends. Right away she wants to put me in News because of my writing in the War and Media class. Just like that she offers me a job, says I can start next week.

Of all the professors I asked, and friends and relatives, and anyone I could think of in my circle, and submitting profiles on CareerBuilder and Monster, who helps me? Mark Stahl, the outsider, the transplant. The person Lurch thinks is an enemy of the state and is going to displace me in my own hometown.

September 27, 1999

I walk through the front door of the *Argonaut* and I'm immediately greeted by the receptionist, Gila Gould. Maya Jones, the editor, comes out to get me right away. She's with a coworker, Christina Chan. They walk me to a desk and introduce me to other writers: Shelby McKenzie, Steven Alonso, Mike Rendon and a few others. A guy named David Trinidad approaches me. He has an EZLN pin attached to his collar and says a few

words in Spanish, calls me *compañero*. He mentions that we need
to write from a leftist perspective because it's part of the solidarity movement with our comrades in the Third World. At lunch
time, Maya and Gila take me to Dina's. They speak fluent French
and Hebrew and have traveled extensively throughout Europe
and the United States, so I feel out of place. But then the conversation turns into relationship talk, and I tell them how I'm in
love with this girl Paulina who I haven't heard from for a while.
They sympathize and get all mushy because I expose my vulner-
ability. Then the dialogue switches to work-related writing, and
the new Playa Vista development on the endangered wetland
pops up. I tell them I might have an angle, and Maya gives me my
first assignment.

EIGHT

LURCH

September 29, 1999

I keep thinking about this dude that was in the holding tank before I got transferred to County: Peter Ramírez, aka Pelón from 18th Street. He lived in the hood for a little while back in the day, but then moved to the other side, the *enemigo* side. Ramírez was trying to be all cool 'n shit in the cell, like we were homies or something, but I got a bad taste in my mouth the first time I saw him. "Drug addict lame fuck" is all I thought, probably broke into our house that one time. When they stole my *jefita*'s jewelry. I kept it cool with him in the station, from the holding tank to the bus, to County. You never know who's watching—the South Side is like Big Brother.

I'm on the top bunk, Stimey from Echo Park is on the bottom—dark-skinned fool, darker than dark, black almost. I think they should've called him Crow, or Blackie, or Moreno, or Shady, or Shadow, but then he tells me Stimey was that black kid from Little Rascals, and I trip out because this dude's named after a *mayate*. But whatever, it ain't my neighborhood, so I don't give a fuck. He's been here longer, that's why he got the bottom bunk. I'm up here tripping out like I'ma fall off or something. I'm just staring at this WF13 carving on the ceiling. Looks like it's been

painted over a gang of times but it's still there, can't be erased. I
wonder how many people have seen it. More importantly, I wonder how many Culver City boys have seen it. It's cold up here.
Only got these state-issued blankets. The orange uniforms don't
do shit, or the white T-shirts underneath. They're not the Stafford
brand. They don't have that same thickness. That's what I wear
on the outside. Counting the minutes 'til morning, 'til workout.
Burpees, dips, water bags. I'll be good then.

   I can't get Peter Ramírez out of my head. Something didn't
feel right about that fool. Usually when you come across a South
Sider, he's either cool or not. You can just tell. The way they talk,
what they talk about, how they dress, that sort of thing.

   Peter Ramírez was dressed lame: white Levi's and dirty
Cortez's, typical low life. He ain't no baller. No style but trying
to look hard and clean, you know what I'm saying? Not like us.
No Lucky Brand or Polo or anything sporty like that. But there
was something about the way Pelón kept looking at me. I keep re-
playing it in my mind 'n shit. That's all you can do in here anyway, think and think, and when you're done thinking, go on and
think some more. And don't forget to shank an enemy if you have
to. I keep thinking about him on Purdue Avenue. I should've recognized his grin and the way he asked me how things were on the
block. It was suspicious. All smug 'n shit, like he knew something that I didn't. And then it hits me. That fool knows about the
blasting on Mikey's house and the hit on Raven. Maybe he knows
exactly who did it, or maybe he was involved. It all makes sense
now, and when I get out, and the end of the world is like just
around the corner, I'ma find out where that *vato* lives and smoke
him in front of his mom. Watch. I know his brother Martin got
smoked not too long ago, some regular Joe. I think he got car-
jacked for his white Monte Carlo.

   Either way, that fool Pelón is on the list.

NINE
THE DOCTOR

October 4, 1999

There's a cub reporter from the *Argonaut* waiting in the lobby. It's about time someone is interested in my thought process. Perhaps you can't imagine what it's like to interview yourself in the mirror at home or while driving in the car. Out loud. Maybe you don't have a wife like mine, who turns every intellectual exercise into an argument. I have something to say, and the world needs to hear it. I've finally been granted an opportunity and need to present it with alarm and accuracy.

The paper is following up the petition I organized against the new housing master plan, Playa Vista, set to begin construction early next year, where the Hughes Aircraft Company was once located. The land previously belonged to DreamWorks, and to some extent it was protected, but now it's up for grabs. The Friends of the Ballona Wetland non-profit keep putting pressure on the City of Los Angeles to preserve the wetland, but developers and investors have other plans, and deep pockets. My concern is that there's methane in the soil and the construction workers, who will mostly be Mexican or other Latinos, are going to get sick in the process. So many families will be destroyed as a result. It's enough to wipe out an entire generation. The women who'll clean the houses and facilities will get sick too. Kids will be left without parents. And when the development is finally built, all these people who live there will get sick too, and they'll just pour out into Culver City with their sickness and into my clinic.

I invite the reporter in. He looks rock 'n roll, kind of gay, I guess. Not what I expected. And he's young—a rookie. I don't like what I see. But he says he's from around here and that he's genuinely interested in the wetland. I don't entirely believe him, but then he mentions the name Rubén Beltrán and how they're neighbors, so I let my guard down slightly.

"If the *Argonaut*, Friends of Ballona Creek, you and Rubén are all concerned about the wetland and this new Playa Vista development, I shouldn't ignore it. I need to understand this from a social-political perspective," he says.

"Look, I don't know how truthful you'll be or if the newspaper will censor you, but this is all related to gentrification. Haven't you noticed all the new people moving here? Transplants from out of state? They're all over the West Side now, taking over the 11th District. I don't know why people aren't taking this more seriously. We're all going to be gone soon."

"Can you elaborate? I'm a little vexed," he says.

"It's the return of the gentry," I say. "The bourgeoisie. . . . It's white-flight reversal. These people are moving back, in a metaphorical sense, into working-class urban communities. And they're changing the dynamic of the place. But not just any ol' white people, not like working-class whites or low-income ones. Young urban professionals. Stylish ones."

"What's wrong with that? Don't we need change around here, anyway?"

"It's not going to benefit people like you and me. They're going to jack up real estate and drive people out of here. They're going to displace working-class people, people that look like us, our parents, neighbors and friends."

"So where are these gentrifiers you're talking about? Where are they coming from?" he asks, leaning back on his chair.

I move forward and place my elbows on the desk. "They're creative types. From New York, Boston, Iowa . . . wherever. Not from here, that's for sure."

"Yeah, I saw the same thing happening in New York recently, in the Lower East Side. The gritty coolness is vanishing over there too. And those people are coming *here,* right?"

"Exactly!" I hammer the desk with the bottom of my fist and slide back on my chair. "And they're going to fill up Playa Vista and spread out to Del Rey, Westchester, Mar Vista, Culver City, Marina Del Rey, Inglewood, Venice . . . the entire West Side. You'll see."

"Why? What's the point? What's here that's not there?"

"I don't know yet," I tell him. "That's the problem. Can't be just for the weather. It's probably related to Y2K and the tech bubble up in Silicon Valley . . . in the Bay Area. Those techies are going to come here and ruin the city, you'll see. Someone should do something about this, fast."

TEN
MIKEY

October 4, 1999

When I walk out of the doctor's clinic, I bump into two white dudes, like in their 30s. One is wearing a blue Brooklyn Dodgers ball cap, the other a beanie and a flannel—in warm weather. The one in the flannel looks grunge almost, but cleaner. They're talking about some technology employer and something about start-ups. They don't even notice me or say excuse me. I mad-dog them, but they don't notice that either. I'm invisible to them. Both are wearing nerdy glasses, and they sound cocky, like some of the white boys at UCLA who thought they were all bad-ass because they did rowing or lacrosse. Like the ones you see in Manhattan Beach playing volleyball or whatever. The ones that I wish I looked like. The one with the beanie turns back and hits the chirp on his keychain, and the lights blink on a stupid-looking electric car. Something about those guys bothers me. Like they're showing off privilege, or something else, but I can't figure it out. And, they're not scared to be in the neighborhood. Not even *I* dare go into certain places in Los Angeles, and they're just right here across the street from the projects like nothing. I thought about what the doctor and Lurch said about these weird people being all up in the hood and not giving a fuck. And pushing us to the side.

I cruise down Braddock Drive by the projects. I notice a home with a six-foot high horizontal wooden fence I hadn't seen before, like Mark Stahl's. Cacti are being planted by some wetbacks, and they're putting down mulch and gravel. The car in the driveway has an out-of-state license plate: Minnesota. Further down, I see a grey house with bold white trim and a blonde couple playing with a dog and child in the yard. Throwing a ball around. Some dude with a heavy beard and a netted trucker hat walks a dog. His pants are dirty with paint marks. Was this the guy that Lurch has been worried about? What are all these new people doing in the hood?

I turn left on Centinela toward the 90 and I see two apartment complexes with For Sale signs. Working-class Latino families are packing belongings into cars and tending their yard sales. I even see two mom and pop shops with "Going out of Business" banners. What the fuck is going on? I nearly crash the Wagoneer into a parked car because my chest is throbbing.

ELEVEN

THE DOCTOR

October 7, 1999

There's a Del Rey Neighborhood Council meeting at a senior living complex off Culver Boulevard. The building was renovated recently—in a phony Mission Revival Style. Perhaps it's an attempt to promote the region as Mediterranean living. Like the booster campaigns used to do to promote WASP migration. The right type of transplant. The people at the meeting are mostly older baby boomers, like my parents' age, old school homeowners. They look beat and leathered with a respectable temperament. The backbone of the community. I feel embarrassed because I've never been to a meeting before, but then again, I do live on the Culver City side. But as a business owner in Del Rey, I do have a vested interest in the area. I *should* be allowed to voice my concerns.

After the meeting is adjourned, I corner the president of the board, Jonathan Newman, near a table with coffee, fruit and donuts. He has a shaved head and a chiseled face, and he's wearing a fleece jacket and hiking boots. He looks like a bird-watcher, like those that go to the wetland. He might be an ally.

"Mr. Newman, you're the president of the board, is that correct?"

"Yes, that's right. How can I help you?" He half-smiles.

"I was wondering if it would be possible to address the Land Use & Planning and the Health & Wellness committees." I zoom in on the strawberries. I think about grabbing a few.

"What about?"

Jonathan Newman takes a bite from a donut and doesn't look at me. I'm nothing to him. People like him don't know what it's like to think about race and skin color all the time.

"Well, to start off," I say, "I'm a physician and I have my own practice. . . ."

"Oh, good for you," he says, looking surprised, his eyebrows raised.

"Several of my patients have complained about these transplants . . . these outsiders that are invading the neighborhood. Just a few days ago, a journalist told me he saw entire families packing up their personal belongings and selling stuff on the street. I saw one apartment complex get torn down, and immediately it was rebuilt with mixed-use luxury housing. The rents are now much higher there. Hardworking people are getting evicted in exchange for boutiques, cafes and whatever else. All for these people that are not from here. . . . "

"New businesses and storefronts are coming in to help revitalize the community, sir," Jonathan says. "There are a lot of changes happening as a result of the Playa Vista development. It's good for property owners and good for businesses. You're gonna do well."

He grabs another donut and elbows me playfully.

I'm bothered by that and I say, "Most of the apartment and property owners who rent to families . . . they don't live here. How do they know what's good for the community? I've lived here my whole life. . . . I don't think people getting kicked out of their homes is good business."

I think, "Where are all my patients going to go?"

"Well, I apologize, but who the fuck are you? That's not up to you to decide. This is America. People can do whatever they want with their property. Or move wherever they want."

I get up all in his face and say, "But there's an ethical concern. Community and business decisions should be made with empathy. They're destroying people's lives, and people are being kicked out of their homes." I also think, "False. Mexicans, Blacks and Asians in Los Angeles were not allowed to live wherever they wanted, even if they had the money. There were housing covenants against us and the repercussions are still felt today."

"Says who? You a social worker or something? You said you had your own practice, right? You stand to make a lot of money from all these new clients. I don't understand." He pauses and ponders for a moment, then says, "You know what, I get it. You're like them. You've made your case. I'll put you on the agenda for next week."

"Excuse me? Like them? Like who?" My blood is boiling. I ball my fists.

"Never mind, I'll see you next time."

Jonathan takes another donut to go and walks away. He laughs and doesn't even look back at me. His demeanor is very superior, privileged. I think about that time I knocked a guy out with one punch in County—the one who shanked me in the face, the one who fell on his back and convulsed. I picture Jonathan convulsing the same way.

TWELVE
MIKEY

October 12, 1999

The doctor invited me to a neighborhood council meeting at the Mar Vista Family Center on South Slauson Avenue near the projects. He said he liked my story, said I'm on the right path. Two Culver City boys are sitting outside of the facility on a bench. Both wear Cincinnati Reds hats, one smoking a cigarette, the other eating sunflower seeds. They mad-dog the crowd as it enters, especially a Black couple in their 40s. The Black dude is wearing a black jacket and a Raiders hat. Maybe he's a Shoreline Crip. The woman he is with is chewing gum. She rolls her eyes at the CXC boys. Her long and loopy gold earrings clack as she walks. The boys laugh at the couple, then at me as I dash through the entrance. They probably have guns and don't know about my relationship with Lurch. Doesn't matter, I hate most of those fools anyway. They always have some dumb shit to say, just like in high school. But I don't care anymore, I have a job to do. These illiterate fools probably can't even spell their own names.

I notice a well-dressed white lady near the entry door. She's writing something down in a notebook. She looks important in her corporate suit. There's a tag on her lapel: "Nicole Anderson."

The doctor is talking inaudibly to Jonathan Newman near the podium. He's in doctor scrubs and a lab coat. Almost looks like a superhero. I'm way in the front in order to hear everything and capture it on my recorder. I turn around to look back at the people trickling in. Mostly middle-aged white people, *paisa*-looking Mexicans with young kids and a handful of Blacks that look disabled. A few Asians are walking in too, men and women that look retired. The two CXC boys post up inside as well.

As soon as the doctor speaks, Nicole Anderson quits the writing and marches down the aisle. She announces, "There are going-out-of-business signs everywhere because we're trying to replace low-producing, cheap-paying retail tenants with new ones that are willing to pay more. By changing these buildings cosmetically, they attract new clients who want to make their home here in the community of Del Rey."

The doctor counters her speech: "What about rent-control? The City of Los Angeles protects these types of people from getting evicted. Affordable housing has served local labor and low-income people since the 1920s. My parents moved here in the '50s and they worked nearby in Santa Monica. They eventually moved to Santa Monica, but we have roots here, like many other people."

His lab coat sways behind him, like a cape. I get goosebumps all over.

The audience applauds, but Nicole Anderson speaks up again: "As a real estate agent, my job is to get the best price for my client. I know it sounds greedy, but there are clients that are willing to pay more for the same storefront. Also, many of these apartment complexes are going to be torn down and rebuilt, anyway. The new owners are going to want better tenants who can pay more. It's perfectly legal . . . it's called the Ellis Act. We can overturn rent control by selling the property or rebranding it. Again, we're not doing anything illegal. This city is changing . . . people are going to start coming here once again from all over the world, like in the Roaring Twenties. There is a renaissance going on in this city. Information, the arts, technology…. these things are key for the millennium. Not cheap labor or gangs. Nobody wants guns being waved around in their faces anymore."

The audience does a combination of clapping, standing up, booing and shouting. It looks divided: whites on one side, pockets of Latinos and other people of color on the other.

I'm saying to myself, "What's wrong with trading some dirty *paisas* and gang bangers for cafes and bookstores, anyway? Why the fuck not?"

☙❦❧

Later that day, my mom shows me a letter she received from the Keller-Williams Real Estate Group.

Dear Resident,

   Have you heard about the great opportunity going on in your neighborhood? Have you thought about selling your house? Look no further. When you list with Keller-Williams, you get a bottle of world-famous Jameson's Irish Whisky. And if your home sells, you get two round-trip tickets to Ireland!

What the fuck? I've never seen anything like that in my life. I wonder why anyone would want our house. It's nothing special, just a three-bedroom with one bathroom. The front entrance has unpainted stucco on the side from that bullet hole when Raven got shot. And we have burglar bars all over the windows. The front gate is falling over, too. It's like a house you'd find in any ghetto. And I'm curious about the Ireland excursion. What's that all about? I've never been to Europe before. Always wanted to go to the UK to catch a bunch of bands I like. Why do these realtors want our little dump?

Another letter arrives:

Dear Neighbor,

We thought you'd like to know a little about our client list. These are all the people who are very eager to move into the neighborhood. As a highly coveted area in the Silicon Beach region, we are personally reaching out to you to secure housing for our clients, due to the low inventory in the West Side.

Courtney from Boston, a single mother and counselor at Kaiser Permanente, is interested in buying her first home. Jason and his two dogs are moving to Los Angeles in two months from Brooklyn; he works for a technology company in Santa Monica. Edwin, a software engineer from Oklahoma who now lives in El Segundo, is looking for an income-producing property. Audrey, an artist from Idaho, is looking for a small home where she can have a studio. Janice, a single, middle-aged woman from Ohio, wants to relocate to Culver City.

Silicon Beach? . . . What the fuck is this all about? Where the fuck is that? And these people . . . they all sound like a bunch of white yuppies, none of them locals. All transplants.

I take the letter and crumble it up, flush it down the toilet. Now I'm super-pissed. Why do these people want our homes? Lurch and the doctor are right: they're trying to take our neighborhood.

I sit my mom down and tell her, "Don't you even think of talking to an agent, okay? Ever. We're never gonna sell this house. Never!"

She has this really worried look on her face. Like your father or dog has just died. I think about that song from Leonard Cohen. "Everybody Knows." He said that a plague is coming. Maybe everybody did know about it, and *I* was just finding out. My mom knows something's up, but she won't say it out loud, she just seems depressed and gloomy.

I make her repeat it: "This is our house. Ours."

"Yes, son. Ours. Our house."

She looks defeated. She turns away from me to look out the window. She's hiding something. The same way a mother knows her son, a son knows his mother.

☙❧

I keep seeing transplants in Culver City and all around the 11th District. They have this certain look: trendy and all types of art-school cool. Or like they play in indie bands. Like my new neighbor Mark Stahl. On NPR, a host calls them hipsters. I like transplants better. Hipster gives them too much credit. Black people were the original hipsters—hep cats. But trendy whites stole that from them too, just like they stole jazz, rock 'n roll, the whole beat thing, dignity and whatever else from Blacks. Transplants aren't the new hipsters, we are—marginalized folks. We've been carving out an independent identity in the city for the longest time. Going against the grain. Getting our hands dirty. Punks, goths, emo kids, new wavers, skaters, skinheads, stoners, whatever. Even *cholos*, ever since they started as *pachucos*. We have a bunch of subcultures here in LA—it's all fusion. Like the band Pulp sings about: the mis-shapes, the mistakes, the misfits, the ones who use style as refusal—we fought for that right to exist. Side by side with the gangsters. Mexicans, Blacks, Whites, Asians, whatever. But the ones from here, not outsiders. One of my friends walks with a cane because he got shot in a crossfire between Venice 13 and the Shorelines, not because it's cool to use a cane or act like a wannabe thug, or because it's artistic. He swings that stick with pride. A symbol of survival. And now these transplants are coming out in *Sunset Magazine* and the *Los Angeles Magazine* and talking about alternative lifestyles and new fashion in Southern

California. Like they brought *us* style. Fuck them. The underground scene is ours.

◎◌×◌◎

You know what else is happening? Construction is booming in the region, that's what. For those fuckin' people. Not for us. No new developments have sprung up in like two decades. In my entire lifetime: the '80s and the '90s. Then suddenly—*bam!*—I swear to God, it just happens overnight.

And some of those people are buying small plots of land and putting up tiny homes. In places like Topanga Canyon and Mount Washington. It's a trend: micro or simple living. They claim to live light, and that less is more, saying that the middle class has become superfluous. That is definitely some white privilege type shit. A company out of Canada, New Frontier Homes, specializes in sustainable, aesthetic and affordable houses. It manufactures and ships houses all over the American continent. Small homes that look like boxes are popping up everywhere. A do-it-yourself spirit is in the air, related to home improvement, construction and livability. They even have a reality TV show about it, set in Westwood. Damn transplants are invading everywhere. Los Angeles is losing its soul: the grittier and grimier side, our side, the *best* side, where alternative cool and the hood intersect. In places like Mar Vista and Silver Lake.

Anywhere you look . . . in the grocery stores, walking down streets, in playgrounds, jogging down Culver Boulevard, in cafes, at the taco stands, at Ballona Creek . . . all you see are transplants.

I don't know exactly what it is, but I'm not a fan. They just keep spreading like a goddamn virus and they think this place is theirs. On all streets, I see yellow license plates with blue letters, or white ones with light-blue letters. In grocery stores I hear people with weird accents. Even at the Mexican grocery stores. And a lot of them drive those new electric cars. I made a correlation between the two and suggested to the newspaper that someone should do a survey on that. David Trinidad said he would do the research. The Department of Motor Vehicles in Culver City is always filled now with people turning in their home state license plates for a California one. The line orbits all the way to the UCLA Hospital. People have to go to other DMV's now, to other neighboring cities.

⊙∿⊙

My friend Stan says to me, "The Culver City boys should just smoke anyone with an out-of-state plate. They could set up a checkpoint, like off of Inglewood Boulevard. That would be so sick, right? They're easy targets anyway. Look for white belts, trucker hats and beards on the guys. But not the girls, though, they can stay. . . . You know I like me some white girls."

Stan tickles me as I drive.

He blows a kiss at a white girl with tattoos who is swaying down the street with her dress swinging all over the place. He does some hand moves in the passenger seat to the "Manifesto" track by James Lewis bumping out my speakers. The girl ignores us. She smiles a little though.

I pound his fist and say, "For sure, man! I'll take one of those fuckin' chicks any day."

"*Ay,* by the way," Stan says, "whatever happened with Paulina? What's going on with her? You seen her since we got back from New York, or what?"

My chest caves in. I've tried not to think of her for a while. I haven't spoken to anyone about her outside of the girls at work. I turn a corner and I'm all nervous, my heart pounding like an anvil.

"I guess she's all right, man, I don't know."

"What, you haven't talked to her?" He looks out the window, away from me.

I register that gesture keenly. Like he's too embarrassed for me, or he doesn't want to see the discomfort on my face.

I bite my bottom lip and, with all the pride I have, I just let it go and say, "You were right, bro. She's a fuckin' bitch. She never called me back."

"Fuck her. She's a snake anyway. Who cares?"

That cuts right though me . . . him disrespecting her like that. I pull the Wagoneer over near the DMV parking structure and ask Stan to take pictures. I'm trying to get Paulina out of my mind. The newspaper gave me a small budget for photos, so I offer Stan some work as a colleague. We become a writer/photographer team, especially because we're real West Siders and probably know the region better than my co-workers.

Before we get out of the Jeep, Stan says, "Guess what, man?" He turns the volume down on the music.

It sounds serious. I say, "What happened? What's going on?"

"You're not going to believe this. We're getting evicted, bro." And his eyes get moist.

"Are you serious? What the fuck?"

"My parents got a notice the other day," he says. "The owner's selling the duplex, so we got a letter. They gave us thirty days to move out so they can renovate."

"Oh, man, I'm sorry. This is bad . . . much worse than I thought. That's how they're getting rid of people. Overturning rent control. Sending eviction notices to everyone. What are you guys going to do?"

"I don't know . . . I think my mom's going with my sister Luz, and my dad, well . . . back to Mexico, or something, I guess. You know he goes to TJ all the time. They even have an open house at the duplex today. I can't believe it. Someone's gonna go into my room and look through all my shit . . . judge my skinhead paraphernalia, my *Playboy* magazines. Probably look around for some dope, too."

"Let's go over there," I say.

"Why?"

I tell him what the doctor said about gentrification, that it's gonna jack up real estate prices in the neighborhood. Then I tell him about the letter we got, about the transplants who want our house.

He says, "Well let's go then, to Ireland! Fuck it, whatcha waiting for?"

We laugh all the way to Louise Avenue, where Stan's childhood home is on the auction block. On the way, I play him a CD that I took from Lurch's BMW: "Lost Cities" by Psycho Realm. I get goosebumps all over my arms and the small hairs tiptoe on the back of my neck. I even shiver for a quick second and my teeth chatter.

Stan shoots me a look I can't read, but his eyes open wide as he says, "What the fuck? Who are these guys?"

"I don't know, man, but they're from LA, and they're just like us. It's like they understand our people and our struggle, and they empathize. You heard what that one fool said, that the beasts of the earth and the angels in our city commit violent crimes because we are lost? Dude, that shit's deep. They also use 'We' a lot, not 'I'—like a collective consciousness rather than individual ego or whatever. That's unusual for rap music, no? It's like that dystopian book, *We* by Yevgeny Zamyatin. And they're always talking about the 'Sick Side.' I guess that's our side. The South Side. It's a call-to-arms. Lurch said that the government installed spy cameras on TVs, so he threw his out. I put my TV in the garage, bro. Swear to God. I'm getting a little worried, you know? Especially now, because you have to move too. This is all too real."

Stan is startled. "What the fuck is going on around here, Mikey?"

"I don't know, man, but I felt something similar in New York, by CBGB. It's just eerie. It's not normal. Welcome to the 'Sick Side!'" I say in a raspy voice, like Duke from Psycho Realm did in one of his songs. And I throw my hands at Stan, the way some rappers do.

Then we come up on the For Sale sign on his block.

Stan sulks and nods his head. There are a bunch of cars driving on the block and stopping right in front of the property, causing a traffic jam. The lawn has recently been dug out and now has cacti and sand near the driveway. The duplex has this concrete-colored finish, a red door and yellow lawn chairs on the porch. Mark Stahl's house has the same feel, like a transplant look. It's as if all the houses that are being sold are getting a facelift right when they hit the market.

"What did they do to this place?" I ask.

"I told you. Hey, look, why's there so much traffic? Did something happen?"

We see a bunch of cars piling up on each other.

"Hey, man," I say, "look at their plates . . . all out of state."

"You think they're here for the duplex?"

"Of course!" I yell.

"They're all white people. Hey, man, check that out." Stan sticks half his body out the window and announces, "Asians . . . what do they want over here?"

I say, "Asians are cool . . . it's no big deal. But what do all these white people want in our hood?"

We can't find parking on Louise, so we park on Inglewood Boulevard. A bunch of potential buyers pass us up on foot or drive by us. The girls are hot in an exotic, plain-white-girl way, and the guys look trendy: European hairstyles, modern jeans, new tattoos.

Stan stops before we reach the duplex. "I can't go in there. I just can't. You go take a look."

He lowers his head and starts walking back to the Wagoneer. He runs a little.

☙❦❧

I get my stroll on, keep looking at the street, at cars slowing down in front of the duplex.

I grab a flyer at the front entrance and zoom in on the price: $675,000, for a two-unit, 1,800 square foot lot. I'm only twenty-one and nowhere near interested in buying a house. But more than half a million dollars for this unit near the projects sounds excessive. I think it's a typo.

I must look confused because the agent at the door says, "No, it's right. It's the right price. Silicon Beach is an up-and-coming community. It's the next hot spot."

She's tall and hot and has a heavy accent. Eastern European. Maybe Scandinavian. Thin and blonde, like a movie star or singer. Like a model. Her name is Vanessa Lipstein. I assume more like an Eastern European Jew. Or an Israeli.

"'Up-and-coming?'" I ask. "What does that mean?"

"It means that it's a sellers' market. Playa Vista is going to drive up prices. If you have a property here, now would be a good time to sell. You live around here?"

"Yeah, closer to the projects." I stare at her heels and up toward her white skirt—legs for days. I'm embarrassed to keep looking, but it's hard not to.

"This neighborhood's a gem. There's going to be a bidding war."

I think, "Gem? Bidding war? What the fuck?"

She hands me her business card and says, "If you know anybody around here who wants to sell, they can make a lot of money in this market."

☙❧

I tell my mom about the duplex and how much it's listed for. She's in the kitchen having coffee. She looks tired. I see a few grey streaks in her wavy hair that I haven't seen before. She has dark rings around her eyes and her hands look decrepit. Wrinkled and shoddy. Her hands tremble, and not once does she make eye contact. She's in pajamas and her white robe envelopes her. Looks like it fits her baggy, though, like she lost weight.

"Did you hear what I said, mom?" I ask. "That's more than half a million dollars. What . . . are you considering it?"

"We couldn't even if we wanted to," she says ominously.

I sit down next to her and grab her hand. "What's that supposed to mean? What's going on, mom? You're not telling me something."

Still not looking at me, she starts sobbing.

I grab both her hands. "What is it? What?"

She pushes away, gets up and walks toward a kitchen drawer, pulls out a stack of letters. "I thought I could fix this. I really did." She saws her nose with her wrist.

I open one of the letters from the mortgage servicer. It says the mortgage hasn't been paid in months. I open another, from the County Assessor, an increase in property taxes.

My mom says, "They just keep on coming. Year after year, they keep getting higher. I don't know why. One was a supplemental one, another said that property values were rising . . . and I had to take that leave-of-absence. . . . I haven't been able to catch up on the payments. I just can't afford it anymore."

I wrinkle my forehead and grab another letter: A Notice of Default and Election to Sell under Deed of Trust. My mom squeezes my hands, her tears run down to the table. Her sobs reach a climax.

"What is this?" I read aloud: "That if we 'don't take action to protect our property, it may be sold at a public auction?'"

I turn to her, hold her by the chin. "What the fuck is this, Mom?"

"It's a foreclosure letter. They're taking our house."

For the first time since we started talking, she looks into my eyes. Her look, shameful and scared, pierces my entire soul. I run my hands through my hair.

"Who's taking the house? They can't do that," I say.

My mom points at the letterhead: Bank of America. "We're going to have to move. You should've gone to Rhode Island."

My heart sinks to the floor. I look up to the ceiling and focus on small specks of what appears to be tomato sauce. Miniscule ones. I push myself back from the chair and stand up quickly. With vehemence, I grab the stack of letters and say, "I'll take care of this. I promise."

She tells me that it's too late and that it's too much money. I storm out of the kitchen toward the living room. I look back at her when I reach the entry door and yell at her that I will handle this problem. She sinks her face into her palms.

ᕙ᙮ᕗ

I fire up the engine on the Wagoneer and keep the windows down, crank the A/C all the way up. I scream, "Fuck! Fuck! Fuck!" and pound the steering wheel with my palms. I say aloud, "I shouldn't have to deal with shit like this. I'm only twenty-one."

I bone out down Braddock Drive west. Need to run someone over. I tell myself that I'm a pacifist, though. On the corner of Culver Boulevard and Inglewood Boulevard, there's a well-dressed man, a *paisa* maybe, with a sign that says, "God is coming." I think about the millennial change, Y2K, the new world order, the plague. I drive down Centinela, looking at possible stores to rob. Perhaps the Mexican restaurant or the jewelry shop. I have to do something—quick. Something gangster. A car with out-of-state plates cuts me off, almost rams me from the side on Short Avenue. I honk my horn, wave my hands all over the place. I yell, "Fuckin' stupid-ass cocksucking, cracker-ass transplant motherfucker! You should die! You should all be murdered! Die, motherfucker!" I know he is. I can just tell he's a goddamn transplant. When I get to Venice Boulevard, I dial it down a little. Breathe in, breathe out. Deep long ones. Like yoga or something. I scroll through radio stations in search of KUSC classical music, but I pause on KCRW because the author Mike Davis is talking about his newest book, *The Ecology of Fear*. The host says that the book is about how Los Angeles is portrayed in the media as the American epitome of apocalyptic doom. Davis comes on and says that in the 11th District of the City of Los Angeles, which stretches from the LAX airport to Pacific Palisades and Brentwood, there's a steady wave of new and incoming transplants that hasn't been seen since the booster campaigns of the 1920s.

It's the same thing Nicole Anderson said at the neighborhood council meeting!

Between then and now, our city has suffered a depression, fragmentation, wartime hysteria, juvenile delinquency, white flight, suburbanization, the Watts Riots, the radicalization of minorities, the crack epidemic, the warehousing of people of color, the rise of the industrial prison complex, the proliferation of street gangs, the '92 Riots, the '94 earthquake in Northridge and now the Y2K threat. In that order. His prediction is that if the New Year comes and goes without a hitch, the booster campaigns will begin all over. It will be a reversal of White flight. Just like what the doctor said. And he says that it isn't the fires, mudslides and riots that people have to fear. He says, "The real decimation of the city will come from urban planners, developers and powerbrokers. Urbanization will destroy the city."

If Mike Davis is saying this, then it's true. I have to get that book, and I have to get one to Lurch after he gets released from County. Or send it to him in there. There's this whole thing about zoning and urban planning that I don't know about. Makes me think more and more about that master's in urban planning. The City Council is rapidly changing the city, right under our noses.

I pull up to the library in Mar Vista to do some quick research. I find out that young, white, urban professionals all over are on the hunt for up-and-coming working-class communities where they can rent or buy. That's the new thing. That's what's causing homelessness and tent communities in New York City and in other places. These yuppies can't really afford to live in suburban enclaves like their parents, and they don't necessarily want to. They're attracted to neighborhoods that are considered edgy and interesting and operating under property value speculation. Which basically means that investors and people with money are able to profit from the difference between present and expected future value. In other words, Del Rey, Culver City and other parts of the 11th District West Side are en route to becoming cool urban communities that are marketable to young professionals willing to pay more than they are worth. Hence, Stan's family's rental duplex. Hence, our house. Lawyers and zoning laws can't do shit to stop it either. Lurch said something dramatic had to be done—something criminal. Something related to urban warfare.

He's right.

⚜

As I pass by the Bird's Eye Tattoo Shop on Venice Boulevard on the way home, I see Leon running down the street holding his nose. Blood is oozing out of his pointy snout and in between his hands. I'm like, "What the fuck happened to this fool?" His white T-shirt is all bloody below his chin. I want to ignore him, just pass him up like whatever. But I can't. Something guides me to be a humanitarian or some other bullshit like that. I swoop up on him and lower the window.

I yell out, "Leon! It's me, Mikey. You need help? What's going on?"

He runs to the Wagoneer, hops in and yells, "Drive—bone the fuck out!"

"Where to, man—where should I take you?"

"I got jumped, man, I got jumped! Take me to my pad. I'ma get a strap and my brothers."

I keep looking at my tan leather interior. I don't want it to get smudged or stained with his DNA.

I recall that the lobby of the tattoo shop is dark and stale with stuffed birds: eagles, crows and ravens on the walls. There's a glass coffee table in the center of the lobby with dozens of tattoo magazines, and there's a water cooler nearby.

"I had an appointment with that fool Ritchie Bird," Leon starts. "I was getting that barcode on my neck, like Lurch."

Leon takes a minute and wipes his nose with his T-shirt. I'm grossed out.

He continues, "So, when I'm finished, I step outside, right? And guess who's out there? That faggot-ass fool, Scott Kidd, that fool that looks like a Mormon. And he's just right there smoking a cigarette. And he says to me, 'Hey, what's up, man, you remember me? From the grocery store?' I'm like, 'What the fuck are you doing here?' An' he tells me that he has an appointment with Bird, to get a surfboard tattooed on his back and like beach waves and shit. In black and grey, our style.

"And I'm like, 'You're just some phony-ass motherfucker. Didn't you say you were from Iowa or some shit? You been in surfing for what, like two months?' And he says, 'I'm LA-based now. I'm basically from here now.'

"I ask him for a cigarette real quick, right?" Leon laughs as he's telling me this. "An' then, I get all like fuckin' frustrated, and I think about why this fool bothers me so much, trying to claim LA. I remember what Lurch said, so I just take off on that *vato*. A straight jab to the chin. Then I go crazy—hook, hook, hook, hook. Right jab, cross, two right jabs, cross. Then some fools came out the tattoo shop and jumped me. So, here I am, dog. *Gracias*, Mikey, for real."

THIRTEEN

LURCH

October 14, 1999

S timey wakes up, it's like six in the morning. The sun is just creeping in through the window, just like a fourth of it, because the rest is covered with newspaper to keep the cell dark. He's all like doped up.

Suddenly, he yells out, "Global warming . . . global storming, red alert, red alert, this a global warning!" And he hops out of his bunk and starts doing push-ups.

I look down at him and I'm like, "What's up, dog, you okay? What's going on, *perro?*"

He's sweating and all that, and he says that the world's gonna end soon. I start tripping because me and this *vato* haven't chopped it up about anything like that yet.

So, I ask him about it.

"The shit's gonna hit the fan, *ese,*" he says and looks up at me with this real sly look, all menacing *a toda madre,* and says, "We're gonna have a civil war in this country. We gotta be in tip-top shape, *carnal.* You hear me? This is a war against the government of the United States of America."

Now he really has my attention. So I start talking to this *vato,* like how I've been talking to Mikey and the doctor, hoping someone gets it. Stimey's big thing in here is to stay off the drugs and eat healthy, because we gotta be fit and ready for them when they come to our doorstep. So I tell him that one of the homies from West Los, some older fool, works in the cafeteria. I offer him this hook up for him and me. He's cool with all that and tells me he'll make me a list of foods to eat and which ones to avoid. Then he tells me we gotta be more militant, we gotta follow a strict regimen. Our bodies need to have endurance, and we have to be flexible. We gotta read and be sharp and set the example. The South Side workout is the best, but we gotta apply it on the outside as well, make sure that the rest of the homies follow suit. If we can get the *soldados* on the outside to maintain military form and train them to look out for government spies, or cameras on the streetlights and in trees, or outsiders who look regular but are really spies, and straight smash on them fools and shoot out the cameras, then we'll be fighting the system at all levels. Use all of our gang experience for real combat, for urban and suburban warfare, because a lot of barrios aren't even in urban centers. Look at Santa Monica or like North Side Redondo, those ain't urban gangs. Not for nothing. Los Angeles isn't all urban like New York or Chicago. *Chale*, our city is horizontal. And who knows it better than us, those of us who know all the ins and outs and secret passages and all that. Us, the gangsters from the *calles*, that's who. We're the ones who gotta step up and fight back the government, because it's World War Three. To protect our neighborhoods from outside invasion by transplants and the new world order. Who else is gonna do it . . . the *paisas*, the Blacks, the Asians? If anything, we're gonna reclaim this land for our people. We share it with other groups and races, especially gang territory, but the cracker jacked us for this land. And we're gonna take it back and reclaim it for Mexico, or just to establish it as something of its own, independent of the federal government. Like how California was its own republic for like five minutes. But maybe Los Angeles can break away and be free like that too, how it used to be. When they called it Sonoratown because of our people all over Los.

Our people hold a heavy grudge, and we will tax Uncle Sam. You *vatos* wanna tax us? *Chale*, we're gonna tax you . . . all up and down the city, so don't even bother. This is West Side Culver City 13 gang, Little Locos clique. That's what you hear before your ass gets hit—*plop, plop*—straight up in your face. Mar Vista Gardens housing projects, that's what we represent. So, it's on, and me and Stimey got a plan to go against the system and fight back like those fools are striking back at Rampart. Corrupt cops, secret government agents, transplant devils—we will bring the holocaust to you. Deliver it right up to your *máscara*.

FOURTEEN
MIKEY

October 16, 1999

It's the great Ballona Creek clean-up today. It goes down once a year, put together by the Friends of Ballona Wetlands. The event is sponsored by REI, Patagonia, the City of Santa Monica, the City of Los Angeles, the 11th District Council, Loyola Marymount University, some local businesses and a bunch of other for-profit organizations. Flyers were distributed on people's windshields, on home doors and at business establishments. Email blasts were sent to people on a mailing list. NPR promoted it daily for like two weeks. It's the day everyone goes out to restore the glory of the once fluvial stream, which is now just a concrete channel filled with waste and graffiti. I have personally never been to a clean-up before and don't really care too much for the nonexistent water. But the *Argonaut* covers it every year and they asked me to keep an eye out for anything unusual.

Hundreds of volunteers from the 11th District are here to pick up trash from the concrete beltway in hopes that one day the water will return as a fluvial canal and rejuvenate the city, perhaps like the Isar River in Munich, Germany, they say. That's the problem with Los Angeles, and throughout California. Boosters always try to compare it to Europe. They never compare it to Latin

America or Asia, or the Dark Continent. I mean, why can't it be like the Tigris-Euphrates River in ancient Mesopotamia? Or like Tenochtitlan? Why Germany? And this goddamn heatwave here, in this godforsaken desert, is more like Chile. Why don't they compare the region to the Atacama Desert or the Amazon? Playa Del Rey and the Marina Del Rey Harbor are about three miles east from the creek and the projects. Our spots. The sea brings in the cool Pacific to Culver City as it passes the swaying boats and palm trees, while the starbursts creep through the tall masts. Some people say, "There's no life east of the 405." Some people even say, "East of Lincoln or the 1." White people, probably, because I never heard anyone I know say that shit. Man, we love the ocean breeze, and we ride our bikes, jog and drive to the beach within minutes along the creek. But right now, there's like a severe drought, and that's causing famine-like conditions in certain parts of Southern California. It's nothing new. After all, this place is a desert, and water has always been scarce, which is why we stole water from the Owens Valley. Boosters can call the area "Mediterranean" all they want, but this isn't Santa Barbara. Los Angeles is like the Sahara.

The drought and famine are signs of the apocalypse. The militias in the outskirts—Bakersfield and Death Valley—are getting ready to fight. You hear that sort of thing on the news every now and then. But it's so far from here, nobody ever thinks it'll happen in their towns.

ⓈⒹⓔⓈⓞ

Stan and I are in the creek, tripping out on how many transplants are here. You can identify them easily if you pay attention. Their university T-shirts, their hairstyles, their pasty skin. The white people from here look different from the transplants. Simpler. Not as pretentious. Not as jumpy and eager.

It smells like a dumpster down in the creek. Used condoms and syringes are mixed in with seaweed. Some bums left tarps

and their shopping carts with clothes and blankets inside. I spot
a Latina woman washing her clothes in the trickle of water that
still runs in the ditch. I think about the Lower East Side. I wonder if these bums have recently been evicted, like the people back
East. Stan and his family, and to some extent my mom and I,
we're now in the same boat.

I haven't had much time to think about a plan. I have to do
something to stop the eviction, though, ASAP. I think about that
angle for the newspaper: tent communities popping up everywhere. I observe food wrappers all over the place. Burger King
and Wendy's bags. Stale-looking French fries. Half-eaten oranges
with black on the inside. Some sections smell like piss, like the
elevators at the metro stops. I hold my breath.

Several of the transplants look upbeat amongst the foulness.
What are they so happy about? That shit bothers me. Maybe
they're just glad to be in Los Angeles—in the sun, in the metropolis, out of their goddamn farms and hideous towns. They remind me of those kids that hop on trains and eat food out of
dumpsters for sport. What the fuck is so cool about picking up
trash?

Stan says, "Why do they gotta lie to kick it?"

"I don't know, man," I answer. "They're just phonies or
something. This place is fuckin' disgusting."

"What do they think, that they're like doing God's work?
Saving the planet?"

The transplants keep trickling in and filling up the creek, with
their bags and gloves and sunhats and smiles.

Stan says, "What the fuck? These people don't know anything about the 11th District. Why are they even here? It's the
same thing like out in the water, all these wannabe surfers coming from butt-fuck Egypt, trying to be all Dogtown or whatever."

"Somebody should do something about that," I say. "Bring
that locals-only flavor back, you know? Straight smash on these
fools." I think, "Damn, I sound just like Lurch and the doctor."

I approach this white girl who is most definitely a transplant, what with her Florida State University T-shirt, visible tattoos on her arm and the palest legs I've ever seen. Like straight up bone color. She's wearing a red bandana on her head too, but she damn sure isn't from Culver City 13 or a Piru Blood. Her tattoos are black and grey, like prison-style images, like Lurch's. Looks like Mister Cartoon did them. I think there's a proper term for that: cultural appropriation. I tell her that I'm with the paper and that we are running a story on transplant culture.

"Oh, I'm from the South," she says. "My name's Anna May. I moved here a few months ago."

I ask her why, and she says, "I was hoping to make the trek out West. . . . I thought either the Bay Area or here. I read several online chats that suggested that this area was one of the top ten coolest and hippest places to live in the country. It was the cheapest too . . . on the West Side."

"Do you surf?" Stan mocks her. "Have you been to the ocean? It's so gnarly, right? I can take you out there sometime if you want. I can teach you."

He steps into her face and says, "'Cool and hip,' huh? Must be talkin' about me."

She moves back a little and wipes the sweat off her face with her handkerchief. She cringes.

I interrupt and ask, "What kind of work do you do?"

"I'm a graphic designer. I couldn't find a job back home. I had to move."

"What do you think about the gangs and the crime? I mean . . . we're standing right across from the housing projects. You live around here?"

"There's some dodgy spots around here," she says, "but it's not all like lily-white back home either. There's a lot of new neighbors around here who drive these new hybrid electric cars. It makes us feel more comfortable that the community is changing. . . . I don't mind the projects."

"White people," Stan growls. "You said new neighbors . . . you mean new white people. Just kicking us cactus-eaters out. That's what's changing."

"I understand," she says. "I'm not trying to offend anybody." She throws her hands up. "But maybe some people around here don't know how lucky they are. I moved from extremely humid weather, and my boyfriend there . . ." She points to a red-headed, freckled white boy with a green bandana wrapped over his head, who turns to walk in our direction. "He moved here from Minnesota—extremely cold weather. Southern California is just the right touch. And with the vegan restaurants popping up nearby, this area is definitely a place we can call home."

When the boyfriend joins us, I ask, "How's it going, man? I'm doing a local story. I was wondering what kind of work you do."

"I'm a bartender. I manage a few bars around here."

He sticks his hand out to shake it, but I'm not interested. I step back so his hand doesn't make it to mine.

"They have bars in Minnesota, don't they?" I ask.

He doesn't get my joke, just gives me a puzzled look.

With that, we just turn our backs and leave.

I put my arm over Stan's shoulder and say, "Like that book, you know, *They Shoot Horses, Don't They?*"

He nods and I go on, "They turned it into a movie, too. The dude that wrote it was also a transplant."

Stan still looks confused.

"Man, you're a dumb fuck. And you claim to know Hollywood? You're not from Los Angeles," I say. "Hold up. You a transplant too?"

Stan pinches my stomach playfully, and we look for other people to bother.

☙❧

It's late, the apricot sun is setting behind the Pacific Ocean. Clean-up day is over. A street vendor in a faded and torn felt sombrero selling bacon-wrapped hot dogs out of a cart leans over to catch his breath. His face is leathered and his course hands are swollen. He has thick hollows around his eyes and forehead, and I remember seeing him earlier in the day, walking in a low hunch as if his whole body sagged. A handful of transplants crowd around him, but simultaneously tip toe backwards. Someone that knows him says to give him space, because he has high blood pressure, arthritis and asthma. He places his hands on his thighs and bows his head, wheezing and coughing several times. He has shortness of breath and he pants repeatedly. Now and then, his legs buckle. I've never seen anyone sick like this before. I genuinely feel bad for him. He looks frail, then he spits out blood.

The whole Ballona Creek is in shock. People talk inaudibly in small groups. I see a woman drop gardening tools and walk away backwards. Others point fingers toward the vendor, and their eyes pop out. Some residents walk quickly toward home, while others are uncertain of how to respond.

They're just stuck there. Nobody wants to help, not even me. The doctor would, if he was here. I hear a Spanish-speaking couple say that possibly the dirty water made him sick. That maybe he drank it or bathed in it. Stan catches people on camera with their mouths open wide as they dash along the concrete beltway.

A helper notices the vendor dragging his feet. His head is ducked down, his arms are splayed out and his dry cough is increasing. The helper stretches the sick man out on the pavement, pounds on his chest. More people panic, some are pushed out of the way. The helper touches the vendor's forehead. Seems like the old man is blazing with a high fever. His dark skin looks moist. His gums are engorged, his eyes bloodshot, his lips clustered and his body swelling up. I'm so disgusted, I want to vomit all over the goddamn place. The vendor beats me to it. He regurgitates uncontrollably and has a seizure or something. He falls into the creek. He tumbles all the way down. Nobody can stop him. People cover their noses at the repellant odor. Stan throws up too. It splashes all over his red, white and blue Tiger Asics.

"Do something, do something!" a woman in the crowd cries out.

A few people run into the creek. But it's too late, the vendor takes his last breath.

People run in fury and almost trample over each other. A kid falls into the creek, and his mom gets him out immediately. Dozens scream as they sprint. Stan snaps pictures of the running mob and of the dead street vendor. I think that he could be an immigrant from the same town my grandparents came from.

FIFTEEN

THE DOCTOR

October 19, 1999

I should have read the climactic signs earlier. They were all there. The sweltering summer of 1999 broke record numbers. Climatologists looked at data to analyze the unstoppable heat wave. A new term circulated around the world, "global warming," which referred to atmospheric temperature changes and anticipated the warming of regions, rising sea levels, expansion of deserts and fluctuating precipitation. Experts claimed that in the past three years in Los Angeles, the average temperature had risen four degrees, including the beach cities. Downtown and other industrial concrete belts rose about five degrees.

Researcher said that in a few years Los Angeles would look more like Jacksonville, Florida, not like the Los Angeles of the past few decades. There were more fires in 1999, too: Malibu, Topanga Canyon and Pacific Palisades got hit the hardest. With constant car use and increasing smog, the valleys saw a rise in wildfires as well. There was a spike in lung damage and heart disease related to air pollution, and rising sea levels along the coast contributed to a higher storm surge, bigger waves, and extensive flooding. Hermosa Beach and Manhattan Beach budgeted for millions of dollars to replenish sand and upgrade piers. The international community has agreed that reducing greenhouse gases is what needed to be done around the world. Electric and hybrid cars are being spotted all over Los Angeles.

☙❧

Everybody's talking about the end of the world and looking for solutions to slow it down. But we also have gentrification to worry about in Culver City. That's where the militia comes in. I have visions of it, of the gangsters fighting back on the streets. Claiming what's rightfully ours. We can introduce a new conversation about resistance in order to fight this problem from the bottom up. We can play on people's fears and use religious prophecy to get them involved. Use all the natural changes and disasters as metaphors for the apocalypse. That article that the journalist wrote, *Death at Ballona Creek,* really stirred an outrage here: the images of all the transplants running away from the sick vendor, yet simultaneously cleaning up the area. Nobody wanted to help, or get dirty. Get rid of the mattresses, tents and people down there, but let the flora and fauna flourish. It reminded me of people who care more about dogs than humans. As a community, we let the street vendor down. As a society, we failed him.

I need to get Lurch out of jail, though. Maybe I should bail him out. There has to be a way.

The gang members are the only ones who can instill fear into the heart of the general public, law enforcement and public officials. They can be used for something valuable, something they've been preparing for their whole lives. There was a peace treaty among the Black gangs in 1992 after the Rodney King thing, and one in 1993 for the Mexican American gangs, although it was more about power and money for the mafia. But this is about community and neighborhood. If the gangsters don't stick together now, there won't be a neighborhood to protect. They won't be fighting in the abandoned streets that will become white-washed or removed. There will be no more street life. There will be nothing left to claim. It will all be gone and stolen and subdivided and piecemealed to outsiders. I need to do something. I can't just sit back and witness the execution of Culver City, the projects or the 11th District. I can't just wait for someone or something to spark change. Like Che Guevara tried to start a revolution in all of Latin America, where all those people were united by background, region, tongue and conquest, I too shall attempt to bring together all the barrios in Los Angeles that are united; we all experience disenfranchisement, disillusion and social disorganization. That's what we have in common. Fuck it, this is my calling card.

SIXTEEN

MIKEY

October 23, 1999

I wake up to boatloads of racket. The sun is just coming up and the light creeps through the bars on my window and lands on my pillow. My eyes squint, I stretch out my arms, let out a few yawns. Sounds like someone is moving furniture or something outside. I peer out the window, it's my mom. What the fuck? She's dragging a wooden bench with a wool blanket underneath it. I look further down the driveway. She has a bunch of junk sitting on tarps: lamps, DVDs, decor, whatever. I storm out of the house in boxer shorts, a t-shirt and sandals.

"What the heck is all this, Mom?"

"We're moving, remember? We've to get rid of all this stuff. It's not going to fit in an apartment."

"I just gave you my entire paycheck. Didn't you use it to pay what we owe?"

She adjusts her robe. "Of course I did. It wasn't enough. I talked to someone at the bank . . . she said we haven't caught up. The interest keeps adding up, too. They're going through with the foreclosure."

Neighbors start coming out of their houses. They've heard us screaming. I see Mark Stahl, his cat and daughter on their porch.

My mom covers her face with her palms.

"We need more time," I say. "At least 'til the New Year. 'Til January. Can't you get an extension?"

"It's too late! Don't you understand, Mikey? I've prayed to God for answers. There's nothing. We have to move, son. Maybe to Inglewood . . . or South Gate. I don't know. That's it, Mikey, it's over. You should start packing your things up, too, and get rid of things you don't need."

"I'm not moving to fuckin' South Gate! Fuck that!"

My mom gives me this dreadful, sarcastic look, like it's all my fault. Maybe it is. Maybe I'm a leech and I shouldn't be living at home, using her electricity, water and gas. Demanding that she cook for me and eating all her food. Or maybe not. Maybe it's still partially her responsibility to take care of me, I don't know. I feel like I'm still a kid. I see all these people around here, much older than me, still living at home with their parents. And they bring their spouses and children with them. And they have all these new cars. Not me. I'm working the beat, getting stories, getting leads, trying to stay out of the house as much as possible. Maybe my mom just needs to be alone now. Maybe she needs a boyfriend or wants to get remarried but is embarrassed because I'm still around. I think about some of the people at UCLA. They lived in the dorms, by themselves or with roommates, and when they graduated, they went back home. Not all of them, some got jobs, got apartments and stayed in Los Angeles. But still, parents helped. I was a commuter. I drove back and forth from here. Parents are supposed to help, but mine didn't. I'm not supposed to be worried about my mom losing her house. Not right now. That's not my jam. I just started being a reporter. I have a career now. What does she expect from me?

I walk back into the house. I notice some open mail on top of the washing machine. It has my name on it. It's from the *Los Angeles Times*. It's an offer of employment, as a staff reporter. I can't believe what I'm reading! I almost jump. I can't believe my mom opened it and didn't tell me. I read it, then reread it. The amount they are offering per word count, the sliding scale, the signature from the editor, their praise for my previous writing . . . I almost sob from happiness. I've never been presented with this much money before. And I didn't even apply for this position. It's just landed in my lap. Fuck the civil service, it's all about journalism! I want to go outside and tell my mom everything is going to be all right. Tell her that we're keeping the house. I want to thank her for everything.

But I think about scolding her instead for opening the mail and not telling me. I don't even know how long that letter has been sitting here. All week? A few days? What if I had to send something back in a timely manner? Now, I'm not excited anymore. I'm pissed, actually, trying hard not to be. I can't help but think that my mom is trying to sabotage this. All these different thoughts run through my head. Maybe she doesn't want me to leave. That would be like divorcing her. She told me so. She's demented, thinks of me like a husband. If I leave, I'm abandoning her. But if I stay and we get an apartment, I'm stuck with her forever. I have to make a run for it. Maybe she's saying and doing all these cruel things to push me away, but in fact she wants the opposite. I don't know, I just don't know anymore. All I know is this: I need to get a loan for her ASAP or do something extreme to get her out of this mess. I need to find a way to get money, fast.

☙❧

All afternoon I've been thinking about it. Rob a bank? Rob that restaurant owner? Hold up a liquor store? Break into someone's house? I don't even know anyone who has that much money. I don't even know how much money we need, but I know it must be in the thousands. And I'm going to need a gun to do this hit. I think about movies in which someone needs money. They usually follow someone's routine, and then they have a safe

or something and they figure out the combination . . . and then—
bam!—they get the money. But this is real life. I needed this
money yesterday. I can only think of one person who for a fact
has that much money or has something I can sell to get that much
money. Lurch.

I know I shouldn't even be thinking about this, but I am. He's
in County, and he's worried that the world's gonna end. He's actually expecting the world to explode or something. What does he
even need money for? Not for things like the rest of us, who have
real world problems. My mom isn't thinking about the apocalypse, she's thinking about mortgage payments, property taxes
and apartment searches. What about Stan and his family? They're
thinking about eviction. And who knows how long Lurch's gonna
be busted for. A month, a year, several years? Last time, he did a
few years, and when he got out, everything was the same. He's
still gonna have a home, a car, a family and his homies. But not
us, we won't have a house or a neighborhood to come back to.
We'll have to find a new home. Lurch said the warrant on him
was for possession and selling. Of narcotics, I guess. He probably has all that money lying around his guesthouse in the back .
. . and drugs, definitely. Weed, coke, heroin. I need to find a
buyer. Maybe those dudes from 18th Street. That guy Pelón that
hit us up that one day. Or, I could take some of those rifles in that
crate, sell them to those same fools from 18. I could tell them that
I jacked a Culver City boy, and they'd be all happy and excited
by that. But how do you pull off something like that? When I get
t   h   e
merchandise, what do I do? Drive my mom's Cadillac to their
neighborhood? Definitely not gonna drive my Jeep. Do I wear
a disguise? Tell them I have something to sell, all cloak and
dagger?

They're probably gonna think I'm a cop. They'll probably
want to kill me. Nah, I can't just roll up on them. I don't know

any of those fools from Venice or Santa Monica either. Maybe Stan does.

I'm probably gonna have to let him in on this. But that's risky. Stan likes drugs. What's he gonna do if he has all these drugs to worry about, and measure and count and weigh, and all that? Nah, it has to be someone else. I think much harder, even rub my face like people do when they're deep in thought.

☙❧

I start getting ready at eleven at night. Everything happens at night. Black Doc Martens, black jeans, black sweater, black Harrington jacket, black fingerless gloves, black baseball cap. Wrap my hair real tight and grab it from the back. I place the cap over my new hairstyle. I think about cutting my hair. That's the better option, so the hat can fit better and I'm in a better disguise. I look at myself in the mirror. I just don't know if I can go through with it: cutting my hair. My teeth chatter in the mirror, and my hands get moist. I stare at my eyes, my chin, cheeks and profile. I haven't shaved in a few days. Doesn't matter. I need to concentrate on the plan, but I have none. Just take my empty duffle bag and fill it with what I can. Start with the rifles, that way I don't have to break in. Or, take a little of everything: drugs, money *and* guns. That's the gangster way to do it. My heart is ready to implode. Perhaps I should rethink this. Maybe living in an apartment with my mom isn't so bad, maybe I'd get used to it. It's better than getting caught by Lurch's family in the middle of a heist . . . against him! But what's the big deal? Lurch can make whatever I take in like a minute. He's resourceful. Or, I'll pay him back. I hadn't even thought about that. I'll save all my paychecks and give them to him, make monthly installments. I wonder if he'd accept that. He can charge interest if he wants. I don't mind.

Fuck it, I've made a decision. I have to go through with it. I'm at the entry door. I have the military duffle bag strapped over

my shoulder. There's no turning back, only looking forward. I
have to do this. For my family. I take a few steps out the door. I
look up the street and down the street. Nothing. The lights at
Lurch's house are turned down. Hopefully his family's asleep. I
make it to my yard. The earth is moving so slow, it's slowing my
legs down. I probably won't be able to run if I have to. It's like
I'm dragging my body. My heart is pounding, and my sweaty
palms are about to drool all over the damn sidewalk.

I make it to Lurch's house. I pause in the driveway. Fuck it,
I dash through the corridor. Branches from the tree brush up
against my shoulder. Kind of damp. I duck and head toward the
backyard, looking in all directions. If anything, I'll hop over that
wall toward the other neighbor's yard. Just a big empty concrete
slab. I stay behind Lurch's BMW and lower myself to sit down
on the ground. Better to scope out the scene and hide for a little
while, study the household's movements. There's nothing. It's
quiet, it's lonely. Almost too quiet. But then again, I don't know
their routine. I don't actually know who lives there. His mom,
grandma, maybe some sisters and their kids. I don't really know.
I do know that Lurch lives in the back by himself. Then it occurs
to me: What if someone is housesitting for him while he's in
County? Damn, didn't even think about that. But it doesn't look
that way. I'll take my chances. I inch forward a little, I can see a
crate from where I'm posted up. It's not that far, just a few feet
away. Just a few feet from freedom for my mom. That's all this
is. Or, I could have just asked Lurch to help me out. Maybe he
would've said yes. Damn, I fucked up. Now I have to live with
my decision. I take a step, then another, then another. I'm standing right over the crate. I can almost smell the guns . . . like ma-
chinery, like an auto shop. I reach for the handle. The crate has a
latch. I undo it. I lift the cover and see all these rifles right there.
I almost can't believe my eyes. Each one has to go for at least
$500. They're brand new. Even if I just take like five or six, it
can put us back into our house. But before I even pick one up, I

see a light turn on in the guesthouse. I slam the cover down on the
crate. The sound is loud, *so* fuckin' loud. I back off and pause in
my tracks, like a goddamn dear in headlights.

I see a body at the entry door, in silhouette, and I hear a voice.
It's Lurch's.

"Mikey? Whatcha doing here? How'd you know I got out?"

And then I see Paulina standing behind him.

SEVENTEEN

LURCH

October 24, 1999

My ex and her new boyfriend are in the driveway dropping off my son. I was actually thinking a lot about my little homie when I was busted. Like I wanted to see him more often, you know? Like all these things I'm about to do are so that he has a better future. Aurora thinks I'm a dick, though. I mean, it's basically why we're not together anymore. 'Cause I fucked around on her with her friend and I got caught. So, I can't really say shit about her being with someone else. I gots to be civil. And that new fool she's with is just a security guard, but he's all judgmental 'cause I'm a gangster. But I need to play nice and pay child support and stick to our agreement outside the court. I got a criminal record, and that shit don't fly. They'd probably never let me see my son again. I give her plenty of loot for whatever they need: car, apartment, clothes, whatever. But if I ever find out that the *vato* is a child molester or that he hit my son, or Aurora, or some other crazy shit like that, I will blow his motherfuckin' head off.

I don't really talk to her when she drops him off. My mom and sisters go out there. That dude's scared of me, maybe 'cause I'm so tall. My family calls me, *El Alemán*, the German. Don't let the homies hear that shit though, they'll clown for days. Or maybe he's scared that I carry a gun tucked inside my pants. You never know, right?

But I'm looking through the window and I see Mikey's mom, so I start thinking about Mikey. What the fuck was that fool doin' at my pad last night? If I didn't know any better, I'd think that Mikey was trying to jack me. But for what? Drugs? Guns? That fool took off like a bat out of hell when he saw me. Said he just wanted to say what's up real quick. But nobody knows I got out. The doctor is the only one that knows. It's literally been like a few hours since I been home. And I doubt that Mikey and the doctor even know each other like that, enough for this dude to have the inside scoop. Here I am trying to warn this little motherfucker about the battle zone, and he's all up in my pad trying to figure something out. The doctor told me he's a reporter now. So I'll guess we'll use him to our advantage. Little Mikey Boy, who'd ever thought?

Maybe he's following a lead for a story or some shit, about gangsters in County. I'll go with that. Call me naïve or something, but I just gotta look the other way. Put a padlock on the crate for now. Or, I could walk over there, put a gun to his face and ask him what the fuck he wanted. That *vato* better tell the truth, or, like the white boys say, that fool is 'toast'. All right, last time Mikey. I'ma let you slide this last time, but after this I'll let you know what time it is. You're not gonna get a pass next time. I'ma invite this fool to the big meeting, so he can see what's up.

EIGHTEEN

MIKEY

October 24, 1999

Anybody who's anybody in the region is inside the Mar Vista Gardens gymnasium, in the projects. Hundreds of Culver City boys, other gangsters, local residents, militant-type anarchists, some dudes from the Shoreline Crips. Even the doctor is here. Lurch's at the podium with Raven. I haven't seen him since that night he got shot at my house. I guess he got released from the hospital and he's doing better. I think about Paulina. I imagine my naked body on top of hers. But then I can't help but picture Raven inserting his prick into her. He should've died that day, swear to God.

Raven has a pistol tucked in his waistband underneath a Navy peacoat, and he has his dog Grumpy on a leash. It's a grey pit with a red handkerchief around his neck on a tight chain. Grumpy's mad-dogging everyone, like he was trained. He has a mouth muzzle and looks like a masked wrestler, his coat is tight and he's chiseled as if he works out. He pants and salivates and almost drags Raven off the podium. I think about other dogs in the hood, in people's back and front yards, sometimes in small crates. The ones that bark at everything, including wind . . . but this one is quiet. Can't trust a dog like that. I think Raven catches me staring at him, because he looks right at me while I search for his shit bag underneath his coat. I don't see it.

Lurch grabs a microphone and taps it a few times to generate sound. He has a Cincinnati Reds ballcap and a red handkerchief wrapped around his neck. He begins, "Recently, I was busted with a *vato* from Echo *Parque,* and we both agreed there were a lot of changes going on in our neighborhoods. What's going on there is going on here.

"Most of you . . . like me, were born and raised here in the West Side. Our relatives started the Culver City gang to keep outsiders away from the projects and our neighborhood. Now, we're starting to see a lot of changes around here and a lot of people that don't look like us. And they're not moving here from places that we know, like Santa Monica or West Adams or whatever. They're coming from far off places: Minnesota, New Jersey . . . or some other fuckin' place. A *vato* from Drifters said it's happening in Jefferson Park too. Some dude from Avenues described similar things in Highland Park . . . like these fuckin' people taking advantage of the low-income clinics and changing the look of their houses. They tattoo their bodies in our black and grey style to fit in or whatever. They're trying to steal our neighborhoods, infecting us with their outsider bullshit. Some fools from Echo Park contaminated a lake where all these people rowed little boats 'n shit. They tried to put a library in the middle. Dumb fucks. He told me they smoked some of these people at a cafe too. He got busted for that *pedo.* We have to do the same around here . . . show them they're not welcome. We need to show them the flag."

Lurch removes the red handkerchief from his neck and holds it above his head. "*¡Aquí para Maravista! ¡Aquí para Los Angeles!*"

The crowd roars, and soon there's a flood of red rags flowing above people's heads. People are making C hand signs everywhere. Other gangs, too. Venice, Lennox, Inglewood, all of them. I catch Lurch staring at me, the way Raven did. They know something's up with me. This isn't good.

I'm probably the only person here not throwing up a hand sign or shouting.

After about a minute, Raven says, "All right, all right, *calmados*, let the homeboy finish."

And the crowd settles down slowly. Grumpy barks a few times.

"Thank you, thank you. We appreciate your support," says Raven.

I mad-dog him, but he doesn't notice. I wish I could do it while he's looking, show him I'm not scared of him.

Lurch continues. "I was listening to some music the other day and heard something about lost cities, like ours . . . in danger of vanishing. They talked about beholding a pale horse. It's a metaphor for these outsiders. The Bible, B-I-B-L-E, stands for Basic Instructions Before Leaving Earth. That's what Killer Priest from the Wu-Tang said."

Lurch pulls out two books from a backpack and holds one in each hand. "These two books—*Behold a Pale Horse* and the Bible—they describe what the end of the world will look like. It sounds a lot like what we're seeing today. It's supposed to happen at the end of a millennium. And we're seeing it in Echo Park, Venice, around USC and now here in Culver City. Technology is going to crash and bring this motherfucker down. All these stupid fucks with their internet stuff. It's another way for them to monitor us. They have built-in cameras on the computers and TV's. The locusts are coming: its these transplants. And they're bringing *la plaga* with them. It's our duty to stop them. Who's got my back?"

The crowd goes through a second uproar. I feel goosebumps all over and, for a second, I wonder how it would have been if I had joined the CXC gang. Stan is standing right next to me and he's getting teary-eyed. Raven pulls out the gun from his waistband, removes a silencer from his peacoat pocket and fastens it on. Lurch looks at him with approval. He points it toward the ceiling of the gymnasium. The crowd goes still.

"Normally we would shoot this motherfucker up," Lurch says, "but we have to protect the projects now. Or else they're gonna become ruins like Tenochtitlan. In the future, they'll say . . . Culver City boys used to live there."

8:15 p.m.

A handful of Culver City boys are on South Slauson Avenue, including Lurch and the twins. They're standing in a circle. Raven isn't there. Maybe he isn't as down as he comes off, or maybe his wound makes him incompetent, I don't know. I'm glad he's an absentee gangster.

It's dark and quiet, and fog floats above cars and trees. It's almost romantic. These fools let me stick around for a while as the night descends, because I'm with the *Los Angeles Times* now. They want me to write about the good stuff. Most gangsters, I think, want to be recognized for their efforts, regardless of their crimes. They want their neighborhood to take credit. They just don't want you to make them look bad. Nothing like their gang accidentally shot a little girl or some grandparents. Oh no, not that.

"We gotta set an example . . . we gotta do it tonight," says Noel to the crowd.

"Did everyone bring a strap?" Lurch asks the group.

Some people nod in agreement, some in disagreement.

Leon whispers into Lurch's ear, "Remember that fool I told you about . . . that punk-ass writer from Iowa? The one I got down with?"

Lurch nods and says, "Scott Kidd," then smirks as he looks at me.

I think, "Damn, they're gonna shoot that dude they think is Australian, the one with the Fred Perry shirt." How could they do that, just shoot someone on a hunch? Then I think about Mark

Stahl. If they bring him up and put a hit on him, I'm walking away.

"I'll handle that. Me and my brother will," Noel volunteers.

Leon walks right up to me and whispers, "*You* should write about *this*. Don't let anyone else tell our story. Not like these fuckin' fake-ass transplants trying to be all up in our business. This is all you, homie." He pounds my fist with his.

"We need one volunteer to . . ."

Before Lurch finishes, Rumble lifts his hand. "I'll do it, I got a TEC-9," he says.

"All right . . . it's settled," then, Lurch says. "Me, Rumble and the twins will lead three different groups. It needs to be quick and savage . . . make them fear the neighborhood. The rest of you can tag up their homes or burn their businesses . . . whatever you want. I'll give you some locations."

Rumble is Italian American. I always thought he had a dope-ass name too: Enrico Zanetti. Real clean-cut, he comes from money. His parents own a few pizzerias in the region. He drives a black Grand National with a banging sound system. He got Lurch into slanging because I heard he has connections in Lawndale and Redondo Beach. Now that I think about it, I'm glad I didn't rob Lurch. It'd probably be this dude I was jacking too. And this guy's a loose cannon, the type to chop your hands off with a butcher knife. Like real mafia. He has short, dark hair with a fade on the sides, Patagonia blue eyes—and his arms are sleeved up with a bunch of girls and devils. Not too many of these guys are sleeved up like that. It means you don't have an alternative plan in life and you don't really give a fuck about nothing. It also means you carry the flag at all times.

There's also a dude named Wino right here. He's thin, short and dark-skinned. I remember seeing him wear football jerseys all the time, during the games against rivals and CXC cliques. He was the leanest and fastest on the field. Very agile. He lives inside the projects and has a big CXC tattoo in Old English on his

forearm. One day I saw him take his shirt off, and across his entire back he had tattooed "Culver-Mar Vista Gardens-City."

This is the most intimate I've ever been with all these dudes.
And nobody's calling me names—no "new waver," "disco duck"
bullshit like back in the days. And these fools are planning hits,
right in front of me. I really can't believe my UCLA education
has led me to this. I guess I've been a Culver City boy all this
time.

9:30 p.m.

The twins, Wino and I walk to Wino's project unit. They basically let me shadow them, so long as I keep my mouth shut. It's
a reporter's dream in a way, to be all up in the mix like this. I just
roll with it. In his bedroom, Wino reaches underneath the bed for
a shoebox. All of us beaners keep shit in shoeboxes—for real. I
have one, too. For my Jack Purcell's. I have letters from this girl
that I was obsessed with in high school. The shoebox makes me
think about her and the old days. She was a senior when I was a
freshman, and she kicked it tough with the in-crowd. That Italian
dude, Rumble, was her boyfriend. And he was already like two
years older than her. I thought they were like the ultimate couple—like Destro and the Baroness from "G.I. Joe." And who was
I? Just some introverted and coy kid. A nobody. But at least she
and I exchanged letters, and she even flirted with me a little. That
meant something.

My mind shifts to Paulina. She's the only girl I think about
now. I wish I had a letter from her. We did more than just flirt.
Now that I think about it, I guess I actually *might* be able to compete with these dudes on the female level after all. Maybe because I'm educated and different. That's what girls have always
told me, that I'm different. Because I used to wear brothel creepers or something. Whatever works to your advantage, I guess. I
wonder if Raven or some other motherfuckers have letters and

pictures of Paulina. I'm starting to think that Wino might have some. But at least I have Paulina's underwear, and that great memory of her. Her bra is in my socks and underwear drawer, too. Nobody can take any of that away from me. Ever.

Wino pulls out a .22 pistol and loads a clip. I'm a little jumpy, like when Lurch took me for a ride in his BMW.

Leon sits on a nearby chair. Noel peers through a curtain. Nothing. Nobody there.

Leon says, "Let's go to a payphone and call this fool me and Lurch were talking about."

"Let's do this," Noel says. "We'll do it the way we took care of that *verga* a while back, *¿qué no?*"

The twins shake hands and smirk.

We all exit Wino's apartment and head up the block. I don't think I'm up for the task.

I pull Leon to the side. I say, "Hey, man. I'm just going to head home. I don't think I can be a part of all this."

Leon says, "In order for us to send a message to these outsiders, it has to be told by someone like us. That's where you come into play, Mikey. You have the rare opportunity to see some urban combat-type shit right in front of you. It's up to you how you wanna handle this."

I rub my face and my hair, and Leon says, "You've heard blasting and killing your whole life living here. Now you're just gonna get a little closer. It's your job now, isn't it? If it ain't you, then it's gonna be somebody else, like this fool we're about to blast—Scott Kidd."

The twins and Wino continue walking. Leon looks back at me. I think: Damn, I have a job now. To write about the neighborhood, right? To tell this story?

At the pay phone in front of the ARCO gas station, Leon pulls out a business card and punches numbers. They all look all over the place. Real conspicuous. Scott Kidd picks up Leon's call.

"Hey, Stan, it's Leon . . . from Culver City. We met at Vons . . . we got down at Bird's, remember? I wanted to apologize about the other day, man. I was way outta line, homeboy. *Dispensa*."

Stan probably tells him that it's not a problem. At least that's what I think he says, based on the twin's response.

Leon continues, "Well, my homeboys decided they want to talk to you, about the whole riot thing and your book. I guess they're into it, homes."

Stan responds with an excuse not to.

"*Chale*, dog, it has to be tonight. These fools are going away for a while, you know. They won't be available after tomorrow," Leon presses.

We all stand around, paused, waiting for Stan's response.

Leon asks him where he lives, testing him.

Stan tells him they can meet at the taco stand across from the ARCO gas station in about ten minutes. We know this because Leon repeats it, "'Across from the ARCO . . . ten minutes.'"

They hang up and the CXC boys post up in a hiding spot behind some parked cars.

About ten minutes later, Wino laughs and says, "That fool's not gonna show up, watch. Especially after you got down with him. We need another plan, dog."

"Let's roll to his apartment, fuck it," Noel says. "It'll be easier there, anyway. If he doesn't come out, we'll go inside. Light that motherfucker up in his living room. But if he opens the door, just start blasting. Or if he's outside, let's just walk right up to him, cap 'im in the dome."

When they arrive at Scott Kidd's apartment complex, he's standing outside smoking a cigarette. He's wearing house slippers and, just like Wino said, he most likely wasn't going to show up. He squints when he sees the Culver City boys because he doesn't have his glasses on. He drops the cigarette to the ground to put it out and hasn't even looked up yet when Wino pulls out his gun and fires—*pop, pop, pop.* My body jerks, the blasting is loud. The transplant throws his hands up. I close my eyes. I don't want to be a witness. Leon said that Scott Kidd wanted to know about this lifestyle, now he knows for sure.

Noel, at the corner keeping watch, yanks my shirt and tells me to leave and get an early start. I look back at Scott Kidd staggering up the stairs, screaming. Wino chases after him, I hear three more shots—*pop, pop, pop.* I'm pretty far away now, close to Slauson, but I can see that lights turn on in apartments and neighbors open doors.

10:45 p.m.

I got this story just as it happened.

Spy and Rumble were parked on Lucile Street in front of Playa del Rey Elementary School. Spy knew about a software programmer from Oklahoma, Chris McDonald, who lives at a house with Christmas lights on a backyard deck that circles around oak trees. Spy's girlfriend knows McDonald's girlfriend—they went to that house one night for a get-together. McDonald and Spy exchanged words about immigrants. McDonald suggested they deport all criminals and remove all street vendors from the entire city and county. Said they were all over the place, that it reminded him of a third world country. Spy felt disrespected, especially after what happened to that street vendor in Ballona Creek. Spy told him to go back to Oklahoma. Chris said, "This is America. This is our land."

Man, you can't disrespect the immigrant population to sons of immigrants and go all KKK on a gangster like that. But McDonald wouldn't know that, he's not from here. He doesn't know the street rules of Los Angeles. Or the repercussions. You accommodate to the gangs, not the other way around.

That's the social contract.

The gangsters recognized his house at once. They assessed the exits—so many. South toward Jefferson, which then goes west to the beach or toward the 405. East to the 90 freeway. North, back to the hood. The plan was: Whatever feels right. You'll know when the hit is executed. Rumble steps out of the car with a TEC-9 with a fastened silencer. Spy waits in the driver's seat. Spy could do the shooting, but he's lost the coin toss. Just like that, it's so easy for them to blast. Rumble gets to add another stripe to his jacket.

The streets are calmer in this part of Culver City. No dogs barking, no *paisas* hanging on the streets, no cars zipping by, no apartment complexes with hundreds of tenants stacked on top of each other and no gangsters posted up. It's cleaner: more white people than where we live. Their yards are manicured and there's plenty of parking on both sides of the street. They don't have burglar bars on the windows or around their yards to enclose dogs and such. The houses have more elbowroom, too. Probably can't smell the neighbors cooking or hear them fighting. Over here, the streets have stop signs and speed bumps because of the school. Not the case by Stoner Elementary on Braddock Drive.

Rumble pulls himself up over the backyard wall, which encircles a wood-deck patio, and he surveys the yard. He's spotted by a German shepherd that runs toward him and barks. Rumble backs off. He removes the TEC-9 that was tucked in his belt and with one hand he reaches over and squeezes the trigger. The dog gives out a sharp whimper and slumps over. Rumble confirms this when he hops back on the wall. Next, he darts through the patio toward the backdoor entrance. A light turns on in the kitchen. Rumble covers his head with his hoody. He's right there, just outside the door, near the Christmas lights, when McDonald opens the door. Rumble unloads a banana clip—a hail of bullets shatter the door and the window, and tears through the transplant's body. When he falls to the floor, Rumble storms back over the wall and dives right into the car. Spy speeds off south on Centinela Avenue, toward Inglewood.

NINETEEN
LURCH

October 24, 1999

Mine is the last hit of the night. I asked Mikey to stick around, but I think it was too much for him to handle. This gangster shit is above his pay grade, but there's something else. I haven't figured it out yet. I'm keeping a close eye on him, though.

Me and Stranger are two blocks from my pad and his. It's close enough for us to run home after it happens, close enough to not get caught. I chose this fool Stranger to go 'cause he's kinda weak.

Oh, Stranger . . . now there's a *vato* who should never have been from the hood, man, for real. His family is from San Antonio, Texas, like fifth generation Mexican American. His mom and dad moved to Culver City for a little while because one of their kids wanted to be an actor. That fool came out in some commercials and a few movies. They stayed for almost twenty years and raised the homie Stranger here. He came from a good family, had all the cool clothes and cool cars. But when his family went back to Texas, he stayed because the hood was all he knew. And he met a girl here, from Loyola Marymount. Said he wants to marry her. It's his way out.

We're sitting on the curb on the south side of Berryman Avenue, right on the corner of Braddock Drive. Behind parked cars. Mikey's missing out, this is like some pay-per-view shit. This is what I live for, like being front row at a concert or a football game. Or like ringside at a boxing match, where blood might spatter on your face or something. Gang-banging, in a way, is like a sport, I guess. Like being in a fight, or a rumble, or a prison riot. Or unloading a gun.

It's sort of quiet, but a dog barks here and there. An ambulance sounds in the distance. Maybe for the hit that Spy and them just busted. I tell Stranger to get up, and we walk to the dead end. On the way there, we stop in front of a house with a horizontal wooden fence, like Mark Stahl's. I peek inside through the spaces between the slats, but I don't see anything unusual. A few cats look at me and pause. We walk back to the corner to post up. A car drives down Braddock and bumps music. We duck. No enemy yet. Stranger's fidgety, I can see it in his face and hands.

I say, "Hey, fool, remember that one time that Thumper called you out at the park? Man, I never seen anyone do that. Strip down to his Timberland shoes and get down because he didn't want to get dirty. You's a fool, dog."

"What're you gonna do?" says Stranger. "I had a date that night with my fiancé. I even left my Texas Longhorns hat on." And he laughs, too.

I say, "Sorry, dog, I know some of the older homies have tripped on you. That ain't right. But you know how it is: some fools just have something to prove."

Stranger looks deep in thought, then he says, "Who's the target?"

"There's some fool that lives down the street . . . has a limo business," I say. "The neighbors told me he takes up all types of parking spots. And he acts all hard. The neighbor got into an argument with his wife, too. . . . Bitch was acting all tough, saying she was from New York and didn't take no bullshit or whatever. We'll see about that. If we see her, we'll smoke her, too. See how tough she really is. The husband put up that wooden fence where we stopped . . . trying to be all private 'n shit. Let's just post up here until he shows up, then we'll light him up."

I look around, inhale the smell of the sagebrush and the orange blossoms. I love this time of year, reminds me why I love Los Angeles. Stranger does the same. He's trying to seem normal. He looks nervous though, like he doesn't want to bust the hit. Maybe he's thinking about his girlfriend, maybe his parents. Or maybe about getting caught. He rubs his sweaty hands on his pants. He gets all giddy about squirrels chasing each other up the telephone pole. This is no place for him, he's better off with Mikey and them. Too late sucker.

ᏉᏋᏉ

After a few minutes, Stranger says, "Thanks for bringing me out tonight, Lurch. I'm glad you trust me."

"Don't trip, dog, just squeeze the trigger. The gun'll do the rest."

"A few weeks ago, I was thinking of getting jumped out of the hood and going back to San Antonio," Stranger says. "I don't know, I felt like turning my life around and going to college or something, you know? To study graphic design."

I look at him but I don't respond yet. He's weak. Shit like this will get us caught. After a while, I say, "Every man must face his demons on his own."

The dog barks a few more times and I say, "We're probably going to have to shoot that dog."

Stranger quickly changes the conversation. He knows I mean business. All weirded out, he says, "I'm just kind of nervous is all. My heart's beating outta my chest."

"It's normal. We all go through it. Every time you bust a hit, you go through it. It's part of the game, big dog. But you know what, just pretend like your the *carnal* in *American Me*. What was your brother's nickname in that movie?" I ask.

"Cheetah," Stranger says.

"Oh yeah, Cheetah. 'You're so cool, *ese*, you're so cool that I'm gonna call you *culo*.' That's my favorite line right there, straight up!" I laugh.

Stranger does too.

Then I say, "Damn, your brother played a gangster in a movie, and here you are about to kill someone. How does *that* feel? Maybe you *should've* gone back to San Antonio."

"Well you know my other brother is locked up in Texas, right? He's from the Texas Syndicate."

I stare into his eyes and say, "So you wanna be an actor or something? Instead of on the streets with us? A studio gangster?"

A few cars race down Braddock Drive, and I can hear cars whizzing down the 405.

Before Stranger answers, a car appears down the street. I shift my body up and look through a car window. "Oh shit, here comes that limo. It has an out-of-state license plate, too. Must be him."

"Wish me luck, dog," Stranger whispers.

"You'll be fine," I say.

The limo gets closer, and I say, "That's him. Get up."

Stranger stands up, but then he squats back down. As the limo turns on the street slowly, I run out through the middle of the street, tap the hood of the car and fall over as if I've been run over. I poke my head out and see the limo driver, a short and stocky white boy.

He hops out from behind the wheel and in a heavy East Coast accent says, "You all right, man? You all right? Yo, I didn't see you there."

As he stretches out his hand to help me, I shout, "Now!"

Stranger walks up right behind the transplant and shoots him twice. The fat limo driver falls forward. I get up from the ground. He has two bullets in his head, blood oozing out. The dog from down the street goes berserk. Me and Stranger bolt down Braddock Drive toward the projects, the limo stays like that, with the headlights on, shining on a dead transplant.

TWENTY

THE DOCTOR

October 25, 1999

I ask my wife, "What did all three victims have in common?"

"I don't know . . . they were all men?" She says it with sarcasm, rolling her eyes, resting a palm on her hip.

"Yes, that, but they were all outsiders, too. Transplants. Too many of them around here now, don't you think?"

"That doesn't sound right. It's wrong. It's murder."

She storms out of the living room. What a cunt. This is the most excited I've been in a long time. A triple-homicide of outsiders. The cops won't know how to connect the dots, and my wife can't see the grand scheme of things.

❧

Cecilia and I are in the living room watching local news. We're sitting on opposite ends of the sectional. She has a blanket wrapped around her and is holding a cup of tea. She looks troubled, I can feel her tension. I don't know why, though, that's the thing. When you're unhappily married, someone's always mad and you don't know why. Perhaps because I'm too excited about the murders. Maybe she thought I'd be bothered because of the proximity. It's not every day that three random white guys get killed in the neighborhood.

The sun is just breaking through. I feel like sitting outside and having my coffee while reading the newspaper. But I'm enjoying the TV news too much. My son is still asleep in the nursery. Numerous station vans, reporters and residents are in Culver City, where the shootings took place. I toggle back and forth between channels, since different channels are covering different shootings. I can see my wife getting irritated by me switching channels. Her body is going through changes. I like annoying her. I want to drive her mad.

One of the reporters mentions similar incidents in the Mission District of San Francisco that occurred two weeks ago, which left handfuls of people dead. The same thing is going on up there. People are resisting all these changes in various big cities. Notes were taped on some of the victims in the Bay Area that read, "Save the Mission—the plague is upon us! Fuck Silicon Valley!" I find it perfect, even romantic, and I feel like we should establish solidarity with whatever organization is taking credit for those killings. But we need to organize. Several of the victims up North had relocated to San Francisco and nearby to work in Silicon Valley, the way they are moving here to the 11th district and calling it Silicon Beach. There's the dotcom bubble over there, where tech companies failed and the situation forced an entire population to leave the region and search for new tech hubs and markets. To spread the industry around like a plague. And now they're here in Los Angeles.

I open the *Los Angeles Times* and I see an article in the Local section: "THE SPREAD OF SILICON" by Michael Bustamante. "How the tech industry made its way to Los Angeles."

He connected the Silicon Beach phenomenon back to one of the first outbreaks in 1984 in San Diego. He called it Orwellian, a dystopian nightmare that brought about the crack epidemic and the first silicon outbreak. The tone was alarming and conspiracy-like. The way Lurch and I have been dictating it to him. This place in San Diego was referred to as Silicon Beach, since it was near the sea. He wrote that there was also a very small disbursement in Claremont, in the colleges, but it never developed. The seed was planted in the Southland, nonetheless. He wrote about the methane in the Ballona Wetlands, the dotcom bubble and exodus of Silicon Valley and the mental health facilities in Mar Vista that connected all of it in Los Angeles. He said it was belting around the 11th District—around Santa Monica, to the 405, and looping around the 90. It was ingenious and philosophical . . . now we have someone on the inside that can help rattle things in our favor. I hop off the sofa and yell, "They have the Silicon Syndrome! That's what these transplants have!"

But I don't actually have an audience.

☙❧

I hear helicopter blades swiveling in the sky, right above the clinic, maybe above the projects. Sirens howl in the distance and they're getting closer. Maybe the triple homicide. I walk out of the clinic. Kimberly Vuong is outside too. Her eyes leap into mine. I grab her by the hand, and we scamper along toward Braddock Drive. We look toward an entrance to the projects, where LAPD squad cars, SWAT team personnel in navy blue uniforms, black helmets and semi-automatic weapons are pointing at people and at dwellings. The whole neighborhood is outside as well. We pause behind trees, poke our heads out and observe blue and red flashing lights, narc cars, government Suburbans, federal windbreakers and CRASH officers who look like civilians in jeans and short-sleeved button-ups. There are hundreds of law enforcement officials, like a task force. I can't help but stare at Kimberly's body right in front of me. I place my hand on her waist, taking a giant risk. She does nothing to resist. I keep it there and almost press my body up against hers. Just a little, just a hint. Her hair is in my face, a few strands in my mouth. Several Culver City boys and some regular-looking people are handcuffed on the curb. Some of the gang members are smirking and nodding their heads. Their naivety is great—we just have to politicize the leadership. The rest will follow suit. Some of these guys are face down on the concrete, and the cops have pistols and rifles pointed at their bodies. Dozens of other ones have their legs spread while the cops manhandle and search them. One Culver City boy dashes down Braddock without shoes, headed in our direction. A canine and a few officers are right behind him. The dog snaps at him, and a cop tackles him to the ground before he even crosses the street.

Kimberly turns around and throws herself into my arms. She says, "I can't see this anymore. Tell them to stop, tell them to stop it."

My heart rumbles and I keep her in my arms like that. I rub her back and her hair, and I wipe the tears from her eyes with my hand. We walk back to our businesses. I escort her, with my arm over her shoulder, into the pharmacy and tell her that things are going to be all right. When I try to back off a little, she pulls me toward her and tells me not to leave. I remove her lab coat from her shoulder, just slightly . . . to see how she'll respond. She does the same to my lab coat, but faster. We turn down the blinds of the entire pharmacy.

TWENTY-ONE

MIKEY

October 26, 1999

L urch called me last night, said I should go to the Santa Monica courthouse at like seven in the morning. I'm right here, keeping an eye out for anything unusual. He told me to wait for his homies. Something about a big court decision . . . part of the bigger picture, of the new world order. There's a cold chill circulating. I button up my parka and post up on the steps to the entrance near a bunch of scattered trees, where all these people are smoking cigarettes and drinking coffee. Well-dressed ones, thugs, women, whoever.

Little by little, I see Culver City boys show up. Exiting and trickling out of their cars like it's nothing. Some are cleaned up for the three-ring circus, wearing Timberland boots or shoes, pressed khakis or Dockers, and long-sleeved button-up shirts, with fades and short hair combed back. But others don't care, wearing baggy jeans, shorts with long white tube socks and sneakers, khakis, baseball hats. They walk through the parking lot and the front entrance together—a straight mob. They pass me up like a typical pedestrian, just one or two nod their heads at me. I wait for the last one and I trail behind them. They jam the elevators and go up to the third floor. I take the stairs.

There's a list of names posted up outside the district court; it's what the court is calling a "gang injunction." District Attorney Gil Garcetti and City Attorney James K. Hahn have filed a civil lawsuit against the Culver City boys. The injunction was granted by Santa Monica Superior Court Judge Patricia Collins, who agreed that the CXC boys are a threat to public safety. She identified at least 75 gang bangers in the order. Not Lurch though, he was too smart for that, too evasive to be identified for the list. All these fools named in the court order are supposed to be here, but only about half have showed up. They're all kicking it in the backrow benches, making tons of noise and talking and laughing like it wasn't something serious. I imagine that's how they are in the county jail: all crass and chaotic, but brotherly. I wait for them to sit down and, when they do, I sit on the opposite side. I'm not one of them. And they've made that very clear, too.

When the judge comes on the scene, she outlines a safety zone for the Culver City gang. She says they can't loiter between Venice, Jefferson and Sepulveda Boulevards, or Centinela Avenue. Within that squared area, these fools aren't allowed to associate, consume alcohol in public or carry weapons, pagers or spray paint. These dudes gesticulate and say shit that's inaudible—it's like a funhouse in here. I can't help but be amused. This guy Speedy stands up on a bench and says out loud, "Let them try to stop us!" and he laughs and some of the bangers shake his hand, but a cop comes over and cuffs him right there on the spot, followed by a bailiff who approaches and hauls him away. He's like, "What the fuck, get your hands off me, motherfucker!"

Then a bunch of CXC boys stand up and holler nonsense at the cops, which brings on a bunch of other cops who storm the court and cuff like half of them. Then the judge pounds the gavel and gets everything back in order and continues outlining the injunction. She sets a curfew of 10 p.m. to sunrise, and briefly says it includes Venice 13 and the Shorelines in Oakwood Park. Again, I'm amused because now I know there's a better way to remove people from the hood: through a civil lawsuit. Just straight up ban them from hanging out. And that's my next story, if my editor goes for it.

ᏮᎠᎧᏮᏬ

The doctor is in front of my house in his Mercedes Benz. He asks me to go with him to meet up with his business partner in Echo Park. In the car, he tells me that he respects my writing, that the "Silicon Syndrome" was brilliant. Just the right soundbite. He says I've coined a term. So now, he says, we're comrades and colleagues, and that I'm a great asset to the militia. I feel appreciated, for the first time in my life, like someone gets me.

We get off on Alvarado and circle around that little lake, the one that Lurch talked about at the meeting. There's a bunch of transplant-looking people on the streets. They're walking their stupid little dogs everywhere, pushing *paisas* and working-class people out of their way as if they don't exist. I think about Spaceland, I know it's close. Maybe Paulina is around. I think about going to her apartment in Highland Park, or to Eagle Rock? Somewhere over there. My heart picks up a beat as we drive down Sunset.

"I've never been to Echo Park before," I say as I look over the bridge at the palm trees like in Culver City. "It looks like our neighborhood."

"Well it's changing, that's for sure," the doctor says. "You see these houses that look like boxes? . . ."

I look around as he points.

"These were probably cottages or bungalows. Not anymore. These transplants have no sense of preservation. It's as if they want to give this whole place a makeover."

Next, we pass up a row of micro houses off North Benton Way. The doctor says, "Look at that right there. These goddam people. They're trying to return to a simpler life. They call themselves minimalists." He shakes his head from side to side.

"It's like decluttering," I say. "I get it. It's like getting rid of baggage."

"Yeah, it's a trend . . . they're marketing this idea of poverty and simple living to middle-class white people. It's the cultural appropriation of poverty. Pretend poverty. They're trying to appropriate how poor people have economized space. And they find it romantic."

Thus far, I've learned so much from this man . . . how he processes the social landscape and cultural phenomena . . . how he talks like a professor. My very own Mike Davis, *in vivo*. I just sit there and listen. Try to absorb what I can from the doctor.

"And then they turn around and ridicule our people who live in shanty towns, mobile homes and small houses. But when *they* choose to live like that, it's looked at as progressive."

I keep observing the streets. Echo Park is grimy and a lot of the businesses are typical barrio joints, but there's that one coffee shop or vegan restaurant that's packed full of transplants.

I point at one and also at a boxy house with large windows all around it.

"Look, there's a line for these places," he says. "These people clutter around like targets. If these gang members want to take them out, they just need to drive by with a high caliber weapon and mow them down. Just like that."

ⓒⱻⓒ

The doctor's colleague is going to meet us at a coffee shop on Sunset Boulevard, next door to their new clinic. So close to Spaceland, so close to Paulina. At the coffee shop entrance, there are cluttered plants sitting in various makeshift pots, like in bathroom sinks or old car tires. I guess that's new, being unconventional. The workers all have small scattered tattoos on their arms. They look like outsiders. One has a blue bandana wrapped around his head and a Dali mustache. I scan the rest of the workers and the patrons. Everyone seems so pretentious, like they're trying too hard to look trendy. Cool socks, cool mustaches, cool things on their heads, cool tattoos, cool ordering habits . . .

A waitress comes by and asks with a heavy accent what I want. I order orange juice. The doctor asks for black coffee. She turns to get our drinks, and the doctor says her accent is from Vermont or Rhode Island—where I was supposed to go. He says they talk like Canadians, but I've never spoken to them either, so what do I know?

Finally, in walks the doctor's partner, Igor Errazuriz, a public defender for the City of Los Angeles. He has a big nose, slick hair, and he's wearing thick-framed glasses, a driving cap and a corduroy blazer. He seems legit, looks like a Spanish anarchist or something.

Igor takes a seat at our table and right off says, "Plagues are similar to war. People die and they blame certain groups or a group. Like it's their fault. For us, the plague is the transplants coming to our neighborhoods. But to them, the gangs and illegal immigrants, or maybe just barrio folk, are the plague. Look around, these people are White Anglo-Saxon Protestants—WASPS. You and I, and this journalist," he points at me, "maybe we're their enemy. Like the Visigoths and the Moors."

"We're ready to mobilize the masses," the doctor says. "We just need an extra push. One last nudge."

"Most people are self-centered and they're weak," the lawyer says. He looks around and takes a sip of coffee. "They allow the government or law enforcement to think for them. But how do we encourage them to fight for the cause? What do our people love? More than anything else?"

"We love the neighborhood and community, that's for sure," the doctor answers.

The lawyer says, "If our people feel like that's being taken from them, then they'll fight. You'll see."

"What about the injunction?" the doctor brings up the sore subject. "What do we do about that?"

The lawyer looks around, waves his hand and says, "It's a good thing. Look around you. There's a whole bunch of people who are against all this, not just the gangs. The gangs are just the muscle. We need a charismatic personality to lead. That's how Hitler came to power."

"So, I need to look for a Hitler?" the doctor asks, looks at me and laughs out loud.

I laugh, too, although I don't know why.

"You need someone who can speak like Hitler," says the lawyer. "Someone people can respect and look up to. And fear." He places his hand on the doctor's shoulder. "It's you, my man. You're a well-respected physician. A role model."

The doctor's face goes blank. I'm surprised by this, too.

Then the lawyer hands him a letter and says, "They're increasing the rent at our new location. They've quadrupled the lease."

The doctor snatches the letter and reads it, then pounds his fist and screams out. People look at us. I get uncomfortable.

"I know you took out a second mortgage to expand," says the lawyer. "I'm sorry. You see? We have to do something about this, it's wrong." He sticks his hand out for the doctor to grab, like a gesture of solidarity, and says, "If you lead this, I will follow you. To the very end. *Hasta la victoria*. We'll do it together. Like Che Guevara and Fidel Castro. You're the radical medic, and I'm the radical lawyer."

The doctor looks at me and says, "And he'll be the writer reporting, like Hemingway." He laughs, all uncomfortable.

I get all weird and blush like a little schoolboy.

☙❧

Stan, Mark Stahl and I are at Prince O' Whales in Playa del Rey, having a few vodka tonics among the LMU crowd. I want to tell Stan about the doctor and the lawyer but I can't, not in front of Mark. I don't want to scare him, but I do consider warning him. I don't know what to do. How can I even justify what I know? What do I say, "A gang-banging militia is going to start a de-facto war against white transplants"? I haven't even officially thanked Mark for hooking me up at the *Argonaut*, which led to the *Los Angeles Times*. I kind of owe him.

I'm buzzed now and I thank him profusely.

"Nah, nah, man, that's on you," he says. "You have the skill and expertise and all that. You owe it to yourself. You don't owe me anything. You're a great writer, actually."

Then Stan starts talking about moving to Europe or Latin America because it didn't work out in Rhode Island. Then we start talking about expat living and all that.

"There's over a million expats living in Mexico right now," I say. "All along the beaches mostly, but I know there's a bunch in San Miguel de Allende, too. It's crazy."

I take a long drink from my glass.

"You been over there Mikey?" Stan asks. "With your mom or something?"

"Nah, I've just heard a lot about it. Read about it in college. In scholarly journals and comparative politics. But in a way, if you think about it, that's gentrification too. All those Americans and Canadians living over there and jacking up the real estate prices. You think those Mexicans can afford to live in those places now? Kind of like all these Australians or whoever moving over here to the hood."

I look away from Mark, don't want to embarrass him, or myself, or indirectly call him out.

Mark brushes his hair to the side and has the most surprised look on his face. He says, "Why? Why are there so many Americans living in Mexico?"

"Probably because of the climate and the cheap cost of living," I explain. "The services too. . . . Health care is cheaper over

there. And it's so close, you know, they can hop on a plane whenever and be back here in no time . . . in their real homes."
    I take another drink, but I'm a little irritated. Like I have to
justify the reason. It's not like I'm making this stuff up, I'm just
stating facts.
    "I don't believe you," Mark says. "Why would *Americans*
wanna live in Mexico? I just don't get it."
    Stan and I look at each other—we don't even have to say it
out loud. Some white privilege type shit written all over his con-
fusion. And I didn't even specify what type of Americans. But I
think we all know that I'm referring to older white ones, from
like the Midwest. Maybe his parents. Like the ones that took over
Santa Fe, New Mexico. Not like young Blacks or Asians or Latinos from urban areas. Oh no, not that.
    I tell Mark that I'm simply conveying what I've read, from
academics, journalists and statistics. I cross my arms even, and I
tell him if he wants to know why they go there, he should ask
them, not me. I take another drink.
    Mark says, "I can't even fathom how *any* American would
want to live in Mexico."
    He has this look on his face, like disgusted, like he needs to
wash his hands. Then he gets really quiet and runs his fingers
through his hair. Stan and I get serious too. It's very uncomfortable now, and I survey the college students instead. Looking for
a girl that's looking for me. Nothing. Stan's grinding his teeth
and starts biting his fingernails, like a fuckin' kid. Mark's just
staring down at his drink, nodding his head.
    I'm not sure what the fuck is wrong with this guy. I remem-
ber what the lawyer said about WASPS. Maybe he was right. Mark
Stahl from Nebraska probably never really looked at Stan and me
as equals and colleagues. We're his exotic Mexican friends or
something, dudes he can write about to his people on the farm
back home. But maybe this is all too real for him. After all, he's
never been around our people before, not in a small town in Ne-

braska, that's for sure. And right here, in Los Angeles . . . we speak up. We don't stay quiet. We don't roll over for anybody. I understand right then and there that *he* is the actual enemy. But not because he's white or a WASP or anything like that. It's not racial, at least I don't think it is for me. It's because he just doesn't get it. There are white people that get it, and there are those who don't. I used to think that Mark got it.

I excuse myself to use the bathroom. I can't look at Mark any longer. There isn't anything else to talk to him about, not anymore. When I traverse the other room of the bar, I see my old professor, Jaime Orozco, sitting at a table with a bunch of papers and folders. I wonder what he's doing in *this* dive bar. I'm buzzed and I mumble, "This motherfucker grades papers while he's drinking? No wonder I got an A in his class." I laugh hard.

I pull up on him. "Dr. Orozco, how're you?"

He looks up at me, his eyes are wide open and look astonished. "Michael Bustamante! Sit down, please. Sit down."

I look back toward the bar where Stan is. I no longer give a fuck about Mark Stahl. I just need to make sure my homie is all right. I don't want to leave him alone with that goon. Stan looks fine, though, talking to some white girl, like always. Looks like Mark is getting ready to split. Fuck him.

I ask Dr. Orozco what he's doing, and he slides a folder toward me. It reads: "Future Home of Playa Vista." He has my attention. He says that the development is going to ruin his view of the wetlands, the bluffs and the LMU sign.

I smirk as I leaf through papers, documents and brochures. It's weird that this professor's worried about his view and me and my mom are losing our house. But what do I know about having a view? One paper stands out: Brookfield Residential Properties. I ask him about it, and he says that it's the developer for Playa Vista and shows me the Playa Vista Masterplan. He points out the four-story condos, the business park, the yoga studios, the shopping centers, the satellite university campuses, the technology employers, the underground parking structures, the movie theatre, the health food stores and all the restaurants. They're going to sell homes there in the low millions. "What the heck?" I say. "This is bullshit. Pardon me. Who's gonna pay that? Over methane?"

"There's already a waiting list," the professor says. "Most of the units are already sold. It's going to increase traffic by about 50% around here. And basically, it's going to destroy the wetlands. This is now the gateway to Silicon Beach."

The professor looks depressed and lets out a long sigh. He rubs his head and shakes it. "You haven't even gotten to the good part yet."

He hands me an envelope with brochures and a printout of a Powerpoint presentation inside. It's a proposal to demolish the Mar Vista Gardens Housing Projects and revamp the area as luxury mixed-use residential. It will be the new home of Silicon Gardens. It's Lurch's premonition, his worst nightmare. The projects, CEXCE gang headquarters, have been identified for slum clearance and approved by the Los Angeles City Council. Scheduled date: November 22, 1999.

I think of the doctor and the lawyer. This is the last nudge that the community needs to propel it forward. Remove their homes and they have nothing. Like me and my mom.

☙❧

I'm startled by this noise—like a thump, like a knock. It's around three in the morning. I hear my mom's voice in the distance and I freak out. Who'd be at the door at this hour? I think it's either Lurch or Stan. I hop out of bed and dash to the living room. The door is open, and my mom's right there in her pajamas and robe, standing in front of Paulina. My heart literally collapses onto the carpet. I can see it there, pulsating. My mom gets all smiley. She moves to the side so I can see my girl. My dirty-blonde sweetheart in tight black pants and a short brown top that's pressing her tits all the way up to the sky, cut from below so you can see her entire belly button and stomach. She's just standing there, smiling and giggling. I get a boner just looking at her.

"Come in, come in," my mom invites her.

She must be proud of me, that I know a girl who looks like that and is looking for me. I remain glued to the hallway, too confused to move. Paulina glides toward me, the coconuts of her chest bouncing up and down as she nears me. As soon as my mom gets into her bedroom and closes the door, Paulina throws her arms around me.

"What are you doing here?" I ask.

"What, you don't wanna see me?"

Oh, her smile and her body and her smell. I just want to die right there. Don't care if I do, actually.

"Is this your room?" she asks and waltzes right in, grabs my hand and puts it around her so that my body pushes up against hers from behind. My stiff boner shoots up her ass, and I walk with her like that toward the bed.

"Why haven't you. . . ."

She shushes me and bends over on the bed. Just like that. She slides her pants off, her ass sticking out toward me. Then she ducks her head and pulls her hair over her shoulder. I run to the stereo and put music on, don't want my mom to hear any of this. Don't want to get a condom either. Fuck it, don't wanna ruin the moment. I play the Jesus and Mary Chain, "Just Like Honey," and I know "Head On" is next. She's just what I needed. A warm body. Paulina's body. I make love to her for as long as she lets me, just a few short hours before the sun returns. But it's not enough. I want more.

We lay there naked, her body tucked into mine, and nothing else in the world matters.

"I don't understand. What's going on between us?" I ask.

She puts her soft arm around me and says, "I like you, Mikey. Can't I like you?"

"What about Raven?" I say and twist my mouth. I also want to ask about Lurch, what she was doing at his house that night, but I don't. It's safer not to know.

"What about him? He's my boyfriend, but I like being with you. You're smart, educated, funny, attractive. You're different."

She places her lips against mine, runs her fingers through my hair, her arm still around my chest and over the pillow.

"What's the problem?" I say. "It's a dangerous game we're playing. What if he finds out? He'll kill me. I want something more than this. *I* can give you something different. You should be with me."

"Where? In Rhode Island? I'm a Cali girl. I'm not going anywhere. Besides, who's gonna tell him? You?"

I pull a blanket over my head and shift my body away from her. "I can give you more. Believe me. If you just let me."

"Well I can't. This is all you get. This is who I am. Take it or leave it."

TWENTY-TWO

LURCH

October 27, 1999

I'm rolling in Stranger's Monte Carlo with the homies: Wino, Stranger and Spy. It's been a few weeks since we busted those hits. I've been staying with my aunt in Mid-City. I don't know about these fools, though, where they've been. It doesn't matter. I just told everyone to lay low for a while. But the cops don't have shit on us, so we're back to our routine. They arrested all those people in the projects and did that gang sweep, and still . . . nothing. At this exact moment, it's past the gang curfew. So, we just can't be slipping like this on the streets. We're headed to this bitch's pad, all the way in Pacoima.

We stop at the ARCO gas station to fill up, bumping "Natural Born Killaz" by Dr. Dre and Ice Cube. It's dark all around here because we shot out the lights, like we did on Slauson Avenue. There's a tall brick wall flush with the alley. About five of the homies got murdered here in the early '90s. A handful of other ones got lit up. Everybody from around here knows not to go to this gas station at night. Not unless you want to die. Hopefully that meeting we had is gonna help unite the barrios. We gotta keep our neighborhoods intact now. If I gotta die for the cause, so be it. What good is it to die for the Culver City gang if they're

gonna wipe out the Mar Vista Gardens housing projects, the heart
of the hood?

I walk across the street to use the payphone, to let these
bitches know we're still going. I look back and I see a squad car
rolling up with its lights flashing. The pig turns right from Culver and parks directly in front of the Monte Carlo. I hide behind
some cars and peak to see what's going on through its windows.
They flash a light at the homies, who put their hands over their
eyes because of the glare. Damn, and these fools are strapped.
We all are. This is a street war, it's no longer a gang fight.
Stranger's pumping gas, and Spy is right next to him. Wino's
nearby in some bushes taking a piss. I hope he runs, but he does-
n't. He gets spotted too.

On a megaphone, a cop orders, "Get your asses over here.
Put your hands on the hood of the car! Now!"

Stranger stops pumping and walks quickly to the squad car.
He looks at me briefly. Hope he keeps his mouth shut—that
vato's weak. If anyone's gonna snitch, it's gonna be him. I smack
my teeth. Spy walks right behind Stranger and looks back at
Wino. Man, if the cops actually knew that each one of those fools
was involved in the triple homicide . . . I almost want to laugh.

One cop points a gun at Wino from inside the car and says,
"You, too, motherfucker . . . let's go."

The homies place their hands on the scorching hood of the
car. I can see their hands jerk back. The two cops proceed to step
out of the car, and in that short moment when they open their
doors, Wino starts capping—*bam, bam, bam, bam, bam!* It's like
what Psycho Realm said, "War between city blocks and cops."

I'm surprised as fuck, don't know why he did that. One pig
gets hit and falls back to hide behind the open door of the driver's side. I clap softly. The other cop shoots back through the
open window of the squad car—*praca, praca, praca*—and hits
Stranger twice in the head. That fool collapses, lands on his face.
I'm kind of relieved because now he won't snitch . . . but I got an-

other dead homie. Wino runs but he gets shot several times in the back—*praca, praca, praca, praca, praca!* He falls to the ground, convulses for like a few seconds, then his limbs and body are lifeless.

I feel like screaming, "That's one of my closest homies right there! Now he's gone."

You don't survive gun shots to the back. Spy is crouched by the cop's tire, his hands covering his ears and his face like from a horror movie. I feel sorry for him, wish I could help. Then he makes a run for it—*praca, praca, praca*—and one bullet smashes him right in the back. He falls over.

No, Spy, what'd you do? You should've stayed there, dog. He lies there face down. The cop loads another clip, creeps toward Spy with the weapon drawn and kicks him in the face. The other cop is all wounded 'n shit in the driver's side but is able to call it in. Spy turns over and he's like a cockroach on his back—arms and legs curled and whirling all over the place. But he's alive, thank God. The pig turns him over and cuffs him, presses on his back with his heel, probably where the bullet entered. Spy howls. The sound echoes. I just lost three more good homies.

October 27, 1999

I'm watching the news in my mom's living room because I got rid of my TV. Some reporter confirms the identity of the homies. I have a tequila bottle in my hand. The tears pour out of me. The reporter says that Spy is recovering at a nearby hospital. It's the same hospital where the cop *he* shot is, the reporter says. But he didn't shoot nobody. *Qué gacho,* they're gonna pin it on him. I hop off and yell at the monitor, "Motherfuckers! Arresting him for attempted murder on a police officer, when he didn't do shit." And I'm the only witness, for a fact. But you know how that goes, can't ever get involved. Damn Spy, they're putting you away for life, homie. Like Husky and Big Chato. It's all over for you now, my G. I pour some tequila for Stranger and Wino into the kitchen sink. "For the Culver City gang. For the Little Locos clique," I say.

◎◦◦◎

Everybody's at the ARCO gas station. A bunch of homies, relatives and friends of ours. They have flowers, candles, pictures and clothing articles. Mothers and aunts are crying, and everyone else is shouting at cops who aren't there. I'm like in a daze. Passersby honk their horns as they drive by the crime scene. Cincinnati Reds hats are all over the place, in the crowd and against the alley wall for remembrance. Taggers spray-paint on the blank wall in red: "187 on Pigs," "Fuck the Police," "RIP Stranger & Wino." When a squad car rolls up, a little homie hurls a bottle at the black and white that smashes into the windshield. The cop hops out of the front seat and billy-clubs him down to the concrete. The youngster shields himself with his hands while all the moms and *comadres* throw punches at the cop and strike him with their purses.

Hood rats in small shorts and low-cut blouses post up on the corner of Inglewood Boulevard, near the entrance of the church, and display posters that read: "Donations, Car Wash," "RIP Wino," "RIP Stranger." Across the street, others wash and scrub cars. Most of those fools aren't even from Culver City. Other barrios are here to help—Poserz, Criminals, Inglewood, Lennox, 18th Street, Helms, even some *vatos* from Venice—showing respect for the peace treaty and our dead homies.

The doctor stops by in his Benzo and shakes my hand, gives me a half hug. He says he's sorry for my loss. "Sun Tzu says: 'In the midst of chaos, there is also opportunity.'" He looks all around and says, "Everyone's united now, see. There is only *one* cause. They are martyrs in the war of the apocalypse." Then he bones out, just like that.

I'm still like a zombie and can't really process anything. Then I spot Wino's sister walking straight toward me. She looks tough: curly, dark, wet-looking hair, penciled-in eyeliner, hooded sweatshirt, blue jeans. Looks like she's all cried out. Her hands are shaky and cruddy.

All she says is, "Twelve times! In the back? He was running away! Anyone would run away from the cops if they're shooting at you!"

I don't know what to tell her. That he pulled a strap and shot first? That he's a hero? What do I say? I say nothing.

She cries nasty.

So I hug her, and her knees buckle but I hold her up. Her body trembles like I don't know what. I get teary-eyed all at once and just tell her that he's with God and that he's in a better place now.

◌ঌ৵৶

The ARCO gas station is super-packed now. Nobody can get us to leave. Everyone's wearing red, *everyone,* like a fuckin' 49ers game or something. Some taggers are doing a mural for the homies on that blank wall. They are painting portraits: Wino and Stranger, facing each other with praying hands between them. Relatives place flowers, pictures, letters and candles over the chalk-lined pattern on the ground where they fell. Signs are being held over people's heads: "Murderers," "Liars." Some people have pig puppets in police uniforms. One woman has a sign, "We Live Here Too." That one fucks with me a little. But that's what this is all about at the end of the day. Survival. Home.

Only I know the truth. Wino pulled out a strap and started blasting. The pigs had no choice. It was a righteous kill, even I know that.

I call Stranger's dad in Texas from a payphone and tell him what happened. That fool blames me, says that his son wanted to move to Texas to be with his family. I tell his dad that he told me the same thing, that I encouraged him to go, but he still stayed.

His dad's crying and yelling, says he wants his body flown to Texas, and all that. I feel bad, you know, because he was my homie, but I don't feel responsible. Not one bit. Stranger made his own decision to stay. He was his own man. Nobody would have tried to stop him if he left for San Antonio. We'd just consider him a punk. But he'd be alive. Now, he's dead, and he died for the hood and the cause. He'll be remembered like that. That's all. I can't do shit about it.

October 28, 1999

Wino's viewing before the funeral is at the Holy Cross Funeral Parlor on Slauson Avenue, next to Ladera Heights. The pamphlet says: **IN LOVING MEMORY OF ALVARO FERNANDEZ FEBRUARY 22, 1973—OCTOBER 26, 1999**

Today we think of you with love, but that's nothing new. We thought about you yesterday, and the days prior to that. We think about you in silence. We always say your name. All that remains are memories and framed pictures of you. We will never forget your face and all the memories we have of you. You are in God's care now, but you are in our hearts.

Parking is tight, the lot is super-packed. Like a car show. Everyone's here. Even *vatos* from other neighborhoods, like Lennox and Sotel, showing mad love. A gang of the homies are standing around the entrance, smoking *frajos* and cracking jokes. That's one thing I always hate about funerals: people joking around and laughing like someone didn't just die. I'm guilty of that shit too, but c'mon, have some respect, *¿qué no?* I walk toward the twins, they're with Wino's older brother, Crow. They're all wearing dark gangster locs, just like me. Good, because I can't look into anyone's eyes right now. Not today. I know that Crow's pissed off. I'd be too, shit, and he's gonna blame the hood, watch, like he never banged or nothing. I can feel his tension from a distance. I shake his hand and give him a hug. He shakes my hand like he wants to break it. That's it right there, he just called me out.

I say *dispensa* and all that and I walk to the bathroom. Just added a new enemy to the list. He's not gonna let this slide, and he's gonna keep blaming me for bringing the heat from the *jura*. I just know it. I'm gonna have to keep an eye on this fool, for real. Fuck, why can't shit just go smoothly? Especially with all these fools from other neighborhoods around, like those fools from 18th Street.

We literally just killed two of their homies recently. My man Knuckles did that hit. That's why he hasn't been around. Took off to Mexico for a little bit. And now I'm starting to wonder why God spared me and not those fools. Why Wino and Stranger and not me? Why is Spy busted and not me? But I guess that's the plan. Now I gotta own it—hardcore.

I look into the casket and see my little homie all pale and cold and stiff. With his eyes closed and gloves on his hands and a flannel shirt tucked into some jeans. People left pictures and other souvenirs in the casket. Rosaries and letters. I don't look at anything, though, it's none of my business. Instead, I recall this one time we overdosed on sherm behind the homie's pick-up truck, how Wino convulsed and bounced all over. I got all paranoid but not really, because I was on one too. I smile a bit, almost laugh out loud. It was just him and me smoking that night. I remember everybody was too busy partying and what not. But not Wino, he liked to get bombed up. At least at that time, because we went through a phase, you know what I'm saying? We started with booze, then weed, then sherm, then primos, then lines and then whoever went further got into heroin, crack, meth, speed and whatever else. Not me, though, that's when I started slanging. That's how I remember Wino: drinking, partying, doing drugs, having a good time. And that's how I remember he went out:

bouncing like that on the concrete of the ARCO. I can't believe he's never coming back.

◎◦◎

I'm sitting on a bench while the sermon's going, thinking about that paperwork that Mikey gave me about demolishing the projects and these punk-ass developers turning the whole complex into the Silicon Gardens. That bulldozer and the crane I saw in my premonitions . . . it's just around the corner. They want to bulldoze it, blow it up and burn it down to the ground. Where the fuck are all these people gonna go? Tents in the streets? Under the 405 or the 90? I don't think so, not on my watch, homie. I know for a fact, my man Wino and Stranger didn't die like that for nothing. And Spy's not in the joint just because. We gotta do it for them too, in their honor. I'm the one that influenced everybody to think about all this doomsday and Y2K shit. Damn, something tells me it should be me in that casket. If it wasn't for me. . . . Crow's right, if that's what he thinks. I got nothing to lose now, gotta go all out. Fuck it. But Wino *did* die for the movement: The Southernist Guard, as the doctor labeled it. In homage to the South Side and as a way to echo that we are protectors of the region. Of a way of life. Crow needs to understand that. I should reach out to him, make him understand. That's what Wino wanted, to go out like a soldier. Then I think that from here on out, we shouldn't even wear red anymore, it's too obvious. Especially because of all the homies on the injunction. We should wear all black instead—militant. Like we're in mourning for the death of the homies and the death of the neighborhood. We'll wear black shirts like those fools in Italy back in the days—fascists with combat boots and shaved heads. That can be us.

The priest is taking too long with the eulogy and I start to get fidgety. I pull out this thing that the doctor gave me—a communiqué, he called it—titled "Suburban Warfare." I had it folded in my back pocket. I'm reading it and I'm like, "What the fuck?"

Can't even concentrate on the funeral service because it's so deep. It's a call-to-arms against developers and urban planners, with an attempt to unite all the street gangs in Los Angeles, the working-class people, political activists, anarchists, liberals and whoever else. It's like a cross between *Behold a Pale Horse* and Psycho Realm's album. And it's deep and moving, and I cry a little, so like my tears are mixed for Wino *and* the movement. And the doctor pledges to get involved, all the way to the top. He's bringing other *soldados* with him, like lawyers and healthcare workers. I'm tripping out because I thought it was just a gang or street thing, but apparently it's not. So, I think about the people in the projects, like Wino's family. They're just like the rest of the residents: hard-working laborers that work all day for miserable pay and can't afford to teach their kids about a proper university education. Not like the doctor's parents who helped get him into USC. A gang of people in there don't care to be well-off or rich, they just want to survive. Some *paisas* only hope to save enough money to build a house in their small rural towns back home. But Los Angeles has this weird way of keeping people here. That's why these transplants wanna stay. Like you miss this place if you're somewhere else. It turns you into somebody when you're a nobody.

People in the projects, they live a simple life, not the competitive middle-class rat race. There's colleges around here—West Los Angeles College, Loyola Marymount University, Otis College of Art and Design, UCLA, Santa Monica College, National University, the RAND Corporation, USC, Antioch University and Pepperdine University—but none of us went. Are you stupid? That's on another level, homes. We can't even process the idea of getting in. Just the doctor, but he's a rare case. And Mikey and Rick. So that's what I want, for our people to do better. But with our help, to get them to do better than us. If they kick us out, then these transplants will be the ones with the access to a university education. They'll win. Not our people. They ain't gonna help us for shit. It's all on us.

Inside the projects, nobody is into indoor/outdoor living like what I've read in *Architecture Digest.* Yeah, I read that shit, I know what it's about. We don't decorate our homes with imported shit from Pacific Rim countries. I mean . . . I could. I could take my $300,000 and move to Brentwood or something. But I don't give a fuck about that. I care about the hood. On the contrary, our people live slow and slightly embarrassed. Our relatives back home in small towns expect us to be rich. Everyone in America is rich. If you go back home without money or gifts, or if you complain, then you're just a failure. So, *paisas* tough it out here. They stay to avoid ridicule. And as shitty as the projects are, or the neighborhood in general, it's our home, our community, and we have pride for the hood. The demolition of the projects will destroy thousands of lives. I can't sit back and do nothing. It's on against the cops now.

TWENTY-THREE

MIKEY

October 29, 1999

The streets are filled with soldiers getting ready for the demolition of the projects. It's still about a month away, but these people are planning a resistance. There's a bunch of black cargo vans lined up by the community center. Each has a driver, and the back doors are open and bursting with canned food, used military gear and water bottles. There are crates of weapons, too, like Lurch had in his backyard. As soon as the vans are emptied, a bunch of gangsters dressed in black hop inside. The van motors are running, and as soon as the back doors are shut, they scurry forward.

I ask Lurch about their destination, if we can go where they're headed.

He's like, "*Chale*, dog, stay right here and just keep documenting this scene. Where they're goin' is none of your business right now, homie."

But Stan and I decide to follow them anyway. This looks like it's gonna be good. Plus, this *is* my business, that's why I'm here . . . because they asked me to be here, and it's my job.

Nobody sees us slip out. We flee down Braddock on foot. My Jeep is parked on Inglewood Boulevard, right outside the projects on the corner, so I'm not tripping or anything like that. After the last van turns left, we follow the caravan at a safe distance. My hands are sweaty, like when I went to 18th Street hood, and my heart minces fast within my chest. Stan's all coked up, just so he's quiet, although his teeth are chattering and he's biting his fingernails every now and then. I don't care that he does drugs, just so long as he does his job. Some people work better when they're on something. You just gotta accept it. So long as he doesn't steal from me and get me caught up in some bullshit, I won't get in his way. I leave the radio off so that I can hear anything unusual, like sirens or helicopters or cars in high-speed pursuit. Gotta stay alert. Stan snaps photos of the Ballona wetlands. I can't wait to see what those images look like. It might be the last time we get to see that spot before Playa Vista pops up. Like the professor said, "They're going to ruin everyone's view."

The vans go down Jefferson Boulevard toward Playa Del Rey, then south toward South Bay. They park on Vista Del Mar near Dockweiler Beach. We park several cars away. Hopefully we weren't made. It's pitch black on the street, can't even tell that there's water down below. The militia hops out of the vans in stealth mode and runs down the cliffs toward the beach, struggling in the sand dunes. Stan tells me he wants to leave, that we shouldn't be here, but I tell him we'll only be like five minutes. Gotta see what these fools are up to. He says he can't even get good shots, though.

I brush Stan off, thinking he's more paranoid because of the dope. I still need to know.

The beach is empty. We walk down the hill on an adjacent rock path to get closer. We duck and hold the metal handrail without making a sound. There's no way anyone can know we're right here. In the distance, I spot the lawyer guiding the group in some sort of line formation. Then it occurs to me that they're in training, with this dude specifically, because he has like military experience from the Gulf War. They jog and do cardio and run with weights in their hands. Just five minutes is all I need, and we bounce quick-like. Nobody has seen us, so it's cool. Stan feels better.

꧁꧂

There's a crowd of people near the gymnasium. Stan and I have just returned and we elbow our way through to the front door. There's pallets of canned food and those wooden crates filled with rifles and other assault weapons. The goods are being distributed all over. These dudes are straight-up a real militia. This is the story, just what the *Los Angeles Times* readers need. Stan snaps pictures of all that, and I can see some people don't like that we're here or what we're doing. We're getting all sorts of uncomfortable stares. It's time to bounce. I elbow Stan and he understands.

Just then, Lurch steps in our faces and blocks our path. He's with Knuckles and Raven, and a small crowd forms behind them. Raven is mad-dogging me, pounding a fist hard. Oh shit, we fucked up. Or I fucked up, I don't know. My heart flies all over the sky, and I pray that whatever happens is expedient. We're just standing there in the middle of the crowd in panic-mode. I don't know what to do or what to say. Knuckles is adjusting his pants, and it looks like he's undoing his belt and I'm tripping. I have no clue what he's doing. It's all really weird.

"Did you follow the vans?" Lurch asks.

He has his fists balled and he looks fierce, his cold eyes staring at me without blinking. I've never seen him look at me like this before, not even when he caught me at his pad when he got out of County. I know he doesn't trust me the same way anymore. It's my fault. I fucked up. Should've just told him the truth.

I look over at Stan, then back at Lurch and say, "What vans?"

Knuckles has completely removed his belt now and he's adjusting his pants.

Lurch says, "What the fuck did I tell you, huh?" He seems all mad as he points at my chest.

I say, "What's the big deal?"

Now, Knuckles is holding his belt in one hand. Out of nowhere he strikes Stan—*wapush, wapush*—while holding his pants up with his other hand. The mob closes in on us, uttering things like, "Show 'em what time it is" and "Get 'em." Everyone's pissed, I don't know why. I thought it was about Paulina, but this is more serious, I guess. I just don't know with these people.

Stan shrieks and lifts his hands to protect his face and head while Knuckles keeps whipping him.

Lurch says, "I told you not to go! I told you!"

I say, "Isn't that why we're here, to tell your story? Isn't this what you guys wanted?"

Stan runs a little until he goes down. Knuckles whips him some more. It's so nasty looking at this. Just as Stan let's out a sharp howl, I jump on top of him, then—*wapush, wapush, wapush, wapush*—Knuckles thrashes me several times on the back. I lift Stan up so we can run out of there.

I'm screaming, "What the fuck, Lurch! What the fuck did I do wrong!"

Stan's smearing blood from his nose and licking it off his fingers. These fools see that and keep at a distance. Like Stan is Satan or something.

Then I spot Raven about a foot away, and I assume he knows about Paulina. He punches me in the face hard, harder than hard, and everything goes dark.

October 31, 1999

Around 11 PM, I hear a knock on the door. I'm in my room listening to "The Jesus and Mary Chain," when I hear the thudding. I should probably grab a kitchen knife, if there's one sharp enough to do damage. I don't trust anyone anymore—not Lurch, not Paulina, not the doctor . . . not even these goddamn trick-or-treaters. They've been around all night, can't take the hint of a dark porch. I haven't spoken to anybody since we got whipped. Not even Stan. I haven't left the house either. Good thing it's the weekend. I'm a grown-ass man, I shouldn't have to deal with this sort of thing. It's embarrassing. How am I gonna tell someone I got whipped? How can I go back to the projects, in front of all those people? Now, I definitely understand all the evil that Lurch is. He'll turn on anyone, regardless of who it is. If he can whip me and fuck Raven's girlfriend, he can do anything. Now that I understand this, oddly enough, I feel more composed. The fear and nervousness are gone. My hands don't feel sweaty, and there's no IBS in route. All I feel is hate. Now, I know what wanting revenge feels like. Revenge against Lurch for giving the order, Knuckles for carrying it out, Raven for sucker-punching me, Paulina for . . . everything. Nah, it's not gonna go down like that anymore. Whoever's at the door better have a good excuse. If it's Paulina, I'ma send her ass on her way. Fuck everybody, and like Psycho Realm said, "Fuck love."

I slightly scoot the curtain to the right and see Lurch and his broad smile.

He says, "What's up?"

I'm like, "Whatever." I think, "What a goddamn hypocrite."

The Crimson twins—Leon and Noel—are behind him, wearing dark beanies that drop below their eyes. I can see that they're both in good spirits, all smiley and giddy.

Through the door, I say, "What do you guys want?"

"I want to apologize, dog. *Serio pedo*. Open up, c'mon," Lurch says.

His words mean nothing to me. His apology means nothing. I look through the window again. I speak in a dull tone. "Apology accepted. Thanks." But I don't really give a shit. Fuck them fools.

"If you accept my apology," Lurch says, "then open up the door." His voice sounds stern now, not so much a plea anymore but a demand.

The nerve of this fool. Not gonna let him boss me around anymore. I'm done with them, for real. But then I think about the newspaper and my career, it depends on their movement. If I can use them instead of them using me, that'll turn this thing around. Damn, hadn't even seen it like that before.

I can't just leave them hanging outside like that. It's gonna make things worse. Fuck it. I turn the lock, open the door a crack. "What's going on?" I say it like it means absolutely nothing, like when someone introduces you to an unimportant stranger.

"Look, I'm sorry, for real," Lurch says. "But you can't miss this. Not tonight."

My eyes light up. "What's going on tonight?"

The twins smile and giggle like children at a playground, all weird.

"We're setting it off, right now. All over the city," he says. "This is the story, like you said, Mikey. . . . You gotta write about this. I'm serious, dog." He points at me. "You wanna tell the story, you gotta roll with us right now. Yes or no? I'm only gonna ask you this once."

My whole life is gonna come down to this decision. Like in the movie *Heat*, I have thirty seconds flat to decide, to walk away from my entire life or toward it. I stare into Lurch's eyes, then at the twins, then at the street. My eyes bounce back to the living room and the *Los Angeles Times* newspaper sitting on the coffee table. I have an article in there. People read my work. My writing is important. It's a sign from above.

I say, "Give me five minutes," and close the door behind me.

I hear Leon yell out, *Simón que sí,* fuckin' Mikey, you're an OG, homie, woop, woop!"

I become all giddy, like him and his brother outside. I know that this is it, this is the big moment. I just don't trust them, these backstabbing, murderous, gregarious, charming, charismatic, belt-whipping motherfuckers. My neighbors. My friends. My enemies.

We stop at stop at Lurch's house first. We're all wearing black boots, black pants, black sweaters or jackets, the twins with Navy peacoats. A black celebration. I'm like one of them now, and Lurch says so, too. It gives me goosebumps all over. I feel bubbly, like champagne.

They're wearing white 11th District arm bands. Noel says that they traded their red bandanas for these arm bands. We pick up a bunch of protest posters they've rolled up. Some of the posters have cartoons printed on them: typical working-class people are being trampled by fat cartoon tycoons and executives in suits and ties; some of them are sitting on top of condos and other buildings. In one of the posters, the Ballona Wetlands is chopped up and covered with FOR SALE signs. One poster says, "Mar Vista Gardens RIP 1954-1999" on a tombstone. We grab all this stuff, to paste it all over Culver City.

⟨∞⟩

We walk from Purdue Avenue to South Slauson Avenue. All those cargo vans are lined up right there. I pause when I see them. Leon elbows me and hands me a tall can. I take a long drink. I'm a little jumpy. I ask for some more.

His twin, Noel, creeps up behind me, grabs me by the shoulders and says, "Loosen up, dog, everything's gonna be *firme*. Don't think so much about the other night. That's just the way things are done. The homeboy Stranger, rest in peace, got whipped a few times, too. Nasty, dog, but he moved on too, you know? So should you, homie. You were just in the doghouse temporarily. Lurch likes you, for real."

He stretches out his arm and shakes my hand. I do actually loosen up. Maybe it's not all bad.

The twins spurt off, and I burp a few times. I look around with excitement. I'm happy again, pumped up. Lurch spins his hand around, like saying, "Let's roll." The mob is now about thirty or forty deep. They start boarding the vans.

"C'mon, Mikey, ride up here with me," Lurch says.

Knuckles is inside the van. He sticks out his hand for me to shake. I do, and no words are exchanged as I take a seat. I feel better.

It's quiet in the van. You can almost hear people breathing. Some dudes drink from flasks or beer bottles, a couple snort coke. Adrenaline is shooting through our veins. Lurch always said that you need to be sharp to do hits—sober. Being fucked up is for pussies. I don't want to be a pussy.

The van drives down Inglewood Boulevard, turns left on Venice and posts up at this business strip where Bird's tattoo parlor is.

Lurch points through the window and taps the glass. He says to me, "You see that, Mikey. It has to stop. Right now. I'm sick of these outsiders."

There's a gourmet bakery, a vegan restaurant and a coffee shop right there... all brand new. They kicked out the Oaxacan restaurant, the *panadería* and the *carnicería*. Our stuff for their stuff.

Reminds me of that drive through Echo Park with the doctor.

☙❧

Leon is the first on the scene. He tosses a Molotov cocktail into the vegan joint through a window he just shattered with a cylinder block. As he stretched out his arm to throw it, it felt like it would've been the photographic moment—missed it, too bad. Then Knuckles throws rustic bricks through the coffeeshop's window, and the glass splinters all over Mar Vista. Across the street, that dude Rumble torches a yoga studio. Noel and some other guys beat the bakery window in with bats. Lurch takes out a spray can and writes, "Not Welcome" and "Go Home" on the front of a boutique clothing store.

I can't figure out what sound to concentrate on: the breaking glass, the spray-painting or the laughter. I'm overly stimulated. I look at the fire for a second—so majestic, so glorious. It spreads to the tattoo parlor, probably what Leon was hoping all along.

We hear sirens all of a sudden, close by, not enough time for everyone to jump back into the vans. The ones who don't make it scatter in different directions. Like me, like Lurch. Everyone knows exactly what to do, but not me. I've never been in a situation like this, trying to evade the police. I bolt behind Lurch and all I can hear is my heavy breathing and the pounding on the pavement from my dirty boots.

Lurch cuts through Wasatch Avenue toward Pacific, toward the hood. He's stealthy and nimble, like he's been in training. I, on the other hand, slow down, can't keep up, have to catch my breath. I don't know what to do. I just think about survival. I stop to see if I can cut through someone's property or an apartment complex, but porch lights come on, and dogs bark and ram themselves into chain-link fences. I can see silhouettes behind apartment curtains. By the time I reach the Jack-In-The-Box on Washington Place, a helicopter is circling above and moving a beam of light around the vicinity.

When Lurch hits Centinela, he darts south, I can see that police cars are already near the Vons, the one where Leon works. I freeze up, my spinal column upright, almost like my entire body is cramped. Lurch is now headed back in my direction. What the fuck, there's no exit! His eyes are wide open and his mouth sealed. The cops must be just around the corner. I've never seen Lurch look so horrified. Not a good look for him. Makes me doubt his valor. His facial expression stays imprinted on my mind. He's just a regular man.

If he's horrified, I'm paralyzed with panic. My body shivers. Not like the IBS thing, but like . . . a I'm-going-to-die type of thing. As Lurch passes me up, probably to cut through property or something, he yells at me to run. A few seconds later, I'm on the corner of Mitchell Avenue and Centinela. A squad car's spotlight illuminates my face, and the helicopter's beam is just about to cover me. The chopper's tail is just wagging like a stupid dog. I run into the street, put my hands up. I have nowhere to go. I don't want to get smoked like those Culver City boys. I just want to write a story:

Neighborhoods Declare War on Gentrification

A bunch of police cars from opposite ends of the block roll up. It feels as if hundreds of flashing lights and beams are on me. I hear the helicopter rotor, the slamming doors of squad cars, cops shouting . . . my heart leaps out of my chest. Some big-ass white boy cop approaches me from behind and cuffs me. I turn to look at him, and he smacks the back of my head.

"Turn the fuck around!" he barks.

He pats me down and walks me toward a squad car. I feel so embarrassed. I wanna tell them I'm a college graduate with a 3.7 GPA and that I write for the *Times*. I'm just a cub reporter, but still, it should help, right? So much noise from the helicopter and the cops, I want it to stop. I want to take cover. I want to go home. And the noise does stop, when he pitches me into the backseat of a black and white.

ᏩᎠᏋᏦᏩ

At the police station, a cop escorts me to an interview room. It's so bright in the hallways that I have to squint the whole time. The cop handcuffs me to a chair, and I'm left alone for an eternity, but I'm thinking that it's really more like twenty minutes. I think about Lurch, and my mom, and Paulina. I wonder if the newspaper will fire me when they find out I've been arrested. Should I even tell them what I do? What if it makes it worse? I'm technically not on the job right now. I wanna cry. I just want to go home and get back to work. I didn't do anything, for real.

A detective in a well-pressed suit sits down in front of me. He's white and well groomed. I try not to look at him. He's not a friend. He talks to me real calm and calls me son and his voice is tranquil and soothing. Real smug type. He puts me at ease, like how you'd want your father to talk to you, without judgement, just facts. He asks me where I was going, where I was coming from and why I was running. I tell him I was at a friend's house on Louise Avenue—I'm thinking about Stan—but I forget that they got evicted. And then he asks for my friend's number, and my face sags because I just got caught up in a lie.

I simply say, "He doesn't have one."

The cop stands up, then he stands me up.

I say, "What's going on, where we going?"

He undoes my cuff from the chair and says, "To your friend's house. Since he doesn't have a phone, let's just go over there in person so he can corroborate your story. If he does, you're free to go. If not, we're going to charge you with breaking and entering, vandalism, arson, fleeing a crime scene, resisting arrest . . . should I continue?"

I close my eyes and hope it goes away. Like a bad nightmare. I hum "April Skies," a song from the Jesus and Mary Chain. I start singing it a little louder, and the cop tells me to shut up. No, it's not a dream. I'm literally fucked.

"Are you an anarchist or one of them black shirts?" he asks.

I look down at my clothes. I *am* dressed like the militia. I rest my head down on the table and want to sob, but I don't. I just keep saying, "I didn't do anything, I didn't do anything."

I can see that he doesn't believe me.

"Look . . . we've got a witness here at the station who gave us a statement . . . says you were trying to break into cars, too."

That is true to some extent . . . I was looking to see if someone left their keys inside or a door open so I could slide in and hide. But I don't tell him that. My IBS comes back and I have to get up, but he won't let me.

"Sir . . . I'm gonna piss in my pants. Please let me go to the bathroom. I'll confess to whatever, if you just let me relieve myself."

"Oh, all right, go ahead. I'll take you there."

And he does. I shit and piss and let out some built up gas. Now I'm ready for whatever. Fuck it, walk the gangplank.

When we return to the interrogation room, he shows me a printed statement and asks me to sign it. It says to confess to "malicious mischief." It'll be just a slap on the wrist, a misdemeanor. But I have to stay in the station until I present myself in court in a few days . . . unless I call my mom to bail me out. But how am I gonna get bailed out when we don't have any money and we're being foreclosed on?

TWENTY-FOUR

LURCH

November 1, 1999

Rumble, Raven and I are exiting the projects. I'm like trip-ping out, right, because this pig is right there on Inglewood Boulevard just waiting for us. Two *juras* approach my beamer with their guns out and tell everyone in the car to stick both our hands out the windows. We comply, we don't have no weapons in the car and we don't want to get smoked. It's nothing.

One cop says, "Any of you motherfuckers breathe, I'ma put one through each of your skulls."

Then he starts talking about shooting cops, about burning buildings and about killing innocent people. Like we give a fuck. Then he takes his flashlight and lights up the entire car. We're all just trying to move our hands to cover the beam in our face.

The other copper yells out, "Keep your motherfuckin' hands up! Where I can see them. Don't like the light? . . . well, close your fuckin' eyes."

These motherfuckers are straight tripping, dog. And that's good, I guess, 'cause we got them riled up, like back when we had the war with the Shorelines. They were scared back then, too. They take our IDs and keep them, just like that. Then they bone out. And as soon as I drive off, a narc car turns on its siren and rolls up behind us. We barely make it to Braddock Drive. I just turn right and stop the car. I'm literally like three minutes from my pad.

There's a handful of LAPD and FBI pigs. This shit is serious. They hop out of cars with flashlights and pistols and windbreakers n' shit. They're about to go postal on us. I look at Rumble, and then at Raven.

"Don't give them a reason to shoot," I tell them.

On a megaphone, a pig orders, "Everyone get out of the car! With your hands up."

So, we get out.

Then one of the pigs yanks me by the arm and pushes me up against a fence. He says, "Walk . . . you Frankenstein-looking motherfucker."

The others do the same to my homies. Neighbors turn on porch lights when they hear the commotion. Good, these fools can't shoot us like in a firing squad. Not with that many people around. And I can see that at least one neighbor has a video camera—he don't wanna miss another Rodney King thing.

Out of the corner of my eye, I see this one fool—big ears, light-skinned, maybe Latino, maybe white, maybe both—talk to someone in the backseat of a squad car. Like they have a witness or some shit. I immediately think of Mikey. He got busted last night during that whole crime scene and I haven't seen that *vato* since. If that's him, and he's snitching, I'm a kill that fool myself. I'll shoot him in the fuckin' mouth. Put the gun right inside of it, pull the trigger and place a mouse inside while blood is coming out. Like straight mafia or some narco-type shit. Don't do it, Mikey. Don't.

A few seconds later, that same *jura* walks toward the fence and says, "That's the one we've been looking for. That's Enrico Zanetti, AKA Rumble. Lift his shirt up."

Another pig lifts Rumble's shirt, and they examine his WS CULVER CITY tattoo in shaded Old English. The cop looks toward someone in charge and says, "This him?"

The one doing all the talking reaches for his nightstick and swings at Rumble's back. Bad, man. And as soon as the homie turns around to shield himself, other cops rush him. I jump in to help and get clobbered too, then get pushed up against the fence again. Raven tries to help, but gets smacked in the head and pepper-sprayed. He falls to the ground. Then a cop steps on his shit bag and it starts leaking. He covers his eyes and coughs as he rolls on the ground. The pigs keep spraying and swinging nightclubs at him. The smell is nasty.

All the while, I'm telling these fools, "Leave him alone! He's wounded. He's fuckin' wounded."

Just then, Rumble swings at one of the pigs and gets knocked out with the butt of a shotgun to the temple. The rest of the cavalry cock back their straps, and *now* it's a real firing squad. I pray that it's quick. Fuck it. Do what you gotta do, aim well. Another fool lifts Rumble up, but like in a chokehold, and slams him against a police car.

Witnesses shout like at the coliseum, like at a game or something, telling cops to ease up 'n shit. They start throwing rocks at them, and the cops start getting all mad and crazy, like they're gonna go even more cyclone. They retreat to their cars and drive off with Rumble, leaving me and Raven on the street like that. My little homie's all fucked up. I gotta drive him to the hospital.

November 3, 1999

I'm in the living room at the pad with my *jefita*. I hear a bunch of car doors slamming, a siren in the background. I think it's a raid. Oh shit. I look out the window. They're at Mikey's. I wipe the sweat off my forehead. Not LAPD, they're US Marshals. What the fuck? They got a weird emblem on the side of their cars, almost like a sheriff. They're talking to Mikey's mom, and she's going hysterical. This fool probably snitched, and they're putting them in protective custody or something. I'm fuckin' pissed like you can't believe. I just keep looking through the window. Maybe, just maybe, it's something else. Then, just like that, they take off. Mikey's mom is still outside, sitting on the porch, crying her ass off.

I got a strap on me, in case I gotta kill this fool and his mom. I roll up on her. She tells me that they came to remove her from the property because of the foreclosure. I think, "Foreclosure?" I have this huge sense of relief, dog, that Mikey's not a snitch. Lucky for me, lucky for him.

"How am I gonna get all this out in one hour?" she asks, not expecting an answer. "They gave me one hour. Where the heck is my son, huh? When I need him the most . . . ?"

I know where he is, but I don't wanna tell her. I feel guilty, you know. 'Cause it's like my fault that that fool's busted.

"Don't worry about it, Mrs. Bustamante," I say. "We'll help ya. We'll get everything out."

I go inside to make a call. Within minutes, a handful of the homies are here, and we're getting all their belongings out of the pad. I look up and see Mark Stahl walking in our direction.

"I want to help," he says. "Please let me help."

I feel embarrassed. I guess he's like a pretty cool dude.

November 6, 1999

When Rumble told me what that *jura* did to him, I wanted to smoke the pig myself. He almost threw my homie out of the squad car off the 90. He opened the door, pushed his head out and just kept beating him like it wasn't anything. All the way to Oakwood Park . . . just left him there without a shirt, in enemy territory. They wanted the Venice boys or the Shorelines to smoke him. They underestimated the gang truce, and some dude from the Dukes took him to the hospital. Even got the cop's name for him: Officer Henry Costa.

There's going to be a house party on South Slauson Avenue near the projects, at the dead end. In the parking structure of some apartments where my homie Knuckles lives. We put blue tarps everywhere, cover the whole place up so you can't see inside. Around 11 PM, we call the cops about the noise disturbance. We asked the DJ to put the music on loud as fuck. It's nothing, it's a decoy. There's only like twenty people in the back. None of us are back there, more like a bunch of teenagers and regulars, you know? More like a ditching party than anything.

My homie Rumble's on the front steps of an apartment complex down the street, right at the corner of Braddock, waiting for the pigs to show. Hopefully it's Costa, but if not, any fuckin' cop will do. Rumble moves quickly and in stealth mode as the cops drive up. He doesn't want help for this hit, he has his own plan. He asked me to keep watch. Got a strap on me, just in case.

One pig gets out at the dead end and walks toward the front door of the apartment, where the music's coming from. Rumble is across the street, like a ninja. The other cop steps out of the car and posts up on the lawn—it's Costa. Brave and stupid motherfucker. Rumble creeps in Costa's direction on foot, among the parked cars, closer and closer.

The DJ turns the volume down, and the cops walk back to the squad car. Rumble is pointing, waiting, and mad-dogging. Almost homie, almost. When the cops drive off, the music comes back on full blast. The cops don't even drive a hundred feet when they stop the car and put it in reverse. Costa's partner steps out first and walks quickly toward the front door again. He even has his hand on his holstered gun. Costa stays in the car and says something into the radio receiver. The driver's side window is all the way down. Rumble is like one car away. The music is still banging, and I'm getting nervous just watching this shit.

Rumble grabs the rosary around his neck, squeezes it, gives it a kiss and looks up at the sky. He says something to God, cocks back his Glock 9mm, walks up to the car window and blasts the pig—*boom, boom, boom!* Costa slumps over. Rumble spits on the dead cop, just like that, then bones the fuck out through the creek.

PART II

TWENTY-FIVE

MIKEY

November 12, 1999

L ike Psycho Realm's song says, "War between city blocks and cops." And like Raymond Chandler once wrote, "The streets were darker with something more than night."

This is our new reality. There's a battle zone in Culver City and it's spreading to other parts of Los Angeles.

ᎾᏉᏐᏋᎾᏉ

There's a neighborhood council meeting, everybody's here, but it's not like the other meetings I've been to inside the gymnasium. There are more transplants here than not, but also a bunch of working-class Mexicans, some elderly Asians and a handful of Blacks. It's disproportionate to the demographic of the community. All the white people came out like a mob. You can tell because the parking lot is filled with Foresters, Outbacks and electric cars with license plates from places like Idaho, Minnesota, New York and Oregon.

I walk in through the front entrance of the facility. I notice that several of the guys are wearing Keen hiking boots and North Face fleece jackets. Many have beards, and the girls look like they don't wear make-up or comb their hair. They look "natural."

However, there's a bunch of people that look like the type I see at concerts, like they listen to Belle and Sebastian and Death Cab for Cutie. They're wearing Asics and New Balance sneakers, torn jeans and band t-shirts, vintage dress shoes, checkered flannels, cardigan sweaters and thrift store dresses. They look like me, or I look like them. They're friendly—all smiles and warm greetings. They probably think I'm one of them, minus the color of my skin. Cheese, grapes, crackers and wine are at a little table by the entrance. Spoiled fucks. I sit down in the back row to be inconspicuous. I turn on my tape recorder, see if I can eavesdrop on people's conversations before the meeting starts.

This dude is telling some other guy that when he first moved here from Indiana, he liked the idea of living around working-class Mexicans and Mexican Americans. It was something new, something different. Says he loved the lunch trucks on the corners and the music our people played at parties: Mariachi followed by gangster rap or oldies. He even brought his mom out once, and they actually *walked* down Inglewood Boulevard to El Abajeño. They took pictures and everything. The other guy says he enjoyed the thrill of living dangerously, near exotic people.

He didn't live like that back in Montana, so it was exciting to live on the edge. They both like eating burritos after late nights at bars or clubs, or the bacon-wrapped hotdogs outside of venues. Montana says that these little dark and brown people from Mexico and Central America seemed harmless, but he doesn't treat them the same as white people. If he saw one and his family was crossing a street, he wouldn't wait until they reached the other side of the curb if he was driving. He'd drive before they finished crossing. Indiana says, Dude, I do the same thing.

"O-M-G, I thought I was the only one!"

They laugh like hyenas, and then Indiana says, "They're kind of like a burden, actually. Especially the gardeners and contractors. . . . I always price them down."

Montana jumps in and says that he threatens them with deportation.

"Well, at least, at least"—with his hands up like a plea or something–"they're not Black." The other guy agrees.

It makes me think about this one time at the Manhattan Beach Olive Garden, when I saw a large family of dark-skinned Latinos. Oily hair, third-world dress style. They didn't speak Spanish when they asked for a table. The white server told them that they were at capacity and didn't have room. It was a weekday afternoon and plenty of tables were open. The family walked away with their heads hung low. The server looked satisfied and high-fived a co-worker. It stung me like I don't know what. Like right now. I wanted to say something then, but I didn't have the courage to stand up for my people. I was embarrassed for myself. As I'm embarrassed now.

I do know that a lot of these transplants are poor as well. Even with their white privilege and all that, they're still working-class or below poverty level. What's *their* excuse, huh? We at least have a whole colonial history. But these poor transplants, they send emails, letters and pictures to their friends and relatives back home, and they help boost the region. Bragging about the beach or complaining about the traffic or commenting on whatever, like they know this place. What I'm saying is, they behave just like immigrants, conveying good times, success and abundance, even if they don't have shit. If they return to their hideous towns or backward-ass cities without anything to show for it, they're failures. That's why these people don't go home, even to visit their parents. Not even if there's a war against them.

I'm thinking all this, when Montana says, "This place is too hood for my taste. I'm outta here."

As he's walking out, Mark Stahl walks in. He looks all around, trying to figure out where he's going to sit. It's like he examines the division and feels it. He goes right ahead and crosses the barrier, like he makes it a point of building a bridge. I slouch a little, don't want him to see. My eyes get a little watery for him.

ᔪᔪᔪᔪ

The meeting starts. A transplant steps up to the podium and says, "When we moved here, it seemed like a decent place to live. The food was great, and the sunshine made it worthwhile . . . and, of course, the cheap rent. But now, with all the shootings. . . . I don't know how these people live like this. They're like animals. This is just backwards."

A transplant in the audience says, "We moved here from Venice because the Blacks and Mexicans were always shooting at each other. That's why we bought a little house over here instead. We even lived in the Mission District in San Francisco for a while, and it wasn't as violent as it is here. We're going to have to move again. You can't raise children here."

An old Cuban lady, who can hardly stand, says she's been living in a tiny bungalow for 55 years, and her new landlord gave her one month to move out. She can't afford to relocate with her fixed $900-a-month income from Social Security. She doesn't know what to do. Now, all her belongings are out at the curb, including her old toilet and bathroom sink . . . her old life.

An 85-year-old Chinese lady who retired at eighty says she also has a fixed income and got an eviction notice taped to her door. A translator is speaking for her, says that most of the people on her block are in their eighties and nineties and they don't know how to go about finding a new place to live. They don't use the internet. A lot of them now live in tents at the 90 freeway underpass off Centinela and . . .

A guy with long hair talks over her, says, "This is supposed to be an up-and-coming community. That's why I moved here from Vermont. I skate all over . . . to my job at Trader Joe's, and I make skater videos. I mind my own business, but I got shot at last week just down the street. It looks like I gotta move again!"

A Mexican man with a heavy accent says that he lives with his wife and two-year-old in a four-unit and that the owner was pressuring him to sign a document to vacate voluntarily. The four tenants got together and refused to sign, so the landlord paid each out with $5,000 relocation expenses after months of negotiations. The man said he agreed to move because the money would go a long way, that he only brings in like $700 a month.

One Hispanic lady says that she got an eviction notice, based on an unlawful retainer filing, even though she has Western Union receipts that confirm she pays rent in a timely manner. Several other Latino residents share how they've contacted attorneys and tried to fight eviction notices in court, but the judges only encouraged them to move because it's too costly and time-consuming to take their cases to trial. They're shit out of luck.

The president of the neighborhood council, Jonathan Newman, finally pipes up: "I'm happy to say, the developers are working on Playa Vista. We have turned into a YIMBY organization— Yes in My Back Yard. We want Playa Vista. The projects are getting demolished next week. Once Silicon Beach takes off, it will be a renewal of the region. You'll see. Just hang in there, folks," he says flapping his hands toward the audience as if begging for patience.

He continues, "In the meantime, we have to keep putting pressure on the city council and law enforcement. These gang injunctions work. Every time you see these thugs out there, you have to call the police. We have to stand up to juvenile delinquency. There were more LAPD officers killed in the line-of-duty in 1999 than in any other year in the city of Los Angeles. And I'm a retired police officer. We can't just sit back and do nothing about it."

Next, a surgeon from Westwood stands up and says he bought a twenty-unit apartment building with good bones, but that the electric wiring and plumbing were a disaster. It should've been gutted decades ago. He says, "I don't know how people live like that, it's not civilized. My firm's goal is to turn this building into an upper-level apartment complex. But to do that, we have to relocate these poor tenants. We try to be humane, we even hired a property management company to help them with a program called 'Cash for Keys.' We give them forty-five days to vacate and $1250 for moving expenses. I mean . . . how much time do they need? How much money do they want?"

A Filipino lady says that her ten-year-old daughter was dragged out of their front door by the US Marshals after her foreclosure and . . .

A white guy jumps up and interrupts, speaks right over her. He's tall, has long wavy hair, a beard and a military hat with a star in the middle. He's wearing skinny pants and has a bunch of tattoos. Like he's in a rock 'n roll band. Then it occurs to me: it's the guy Lurch was talking about all along! I can feel it in my gut. The anti-Christ. It has to be him. He has an accent, a clean one. Scandinavian, I'm almost certain. Says he's a ceramicist, a sculptor and a painter. But those are just his hobbies, he says, his real job is as a venture capitalist and developer. He says he owns the land where the Northgate Market, the WIC program, the pharmacy and the clinic are located. The doctor's clinic.

"It was really peaceful when I moved here," he adds. "It was this beautiful industrial enclave that no one seemed to know existed. It was like a secret when *I* found it, but now there's this new thriving, creative community here. And it's only gonna get better with time, especially with Playa Vista. I'm part of the Silicon Beach development. We can't give up just like that."

He continues, "It's my duty as an artist to make the world a more interesting, complex and weird place. That's why we have to stay in Del Rey and help transform this region into another Silicon Valley. This business strip, with the clinic and the grocery store—I'm converting it into a Whole Foods Market. It'll be the 50th store they open."

Mark stands up noisily and stomps out of the meeting. All eyes are on him. Then some Latinos, trailed by some white people, follow suit. This sends a direct message to the current speaker. I see in his face the wound it inflicts. It breaks up the synergy. I get up from my seat and run after Mark.

TWENTY-SIX
LURCH

November 22, 1999

At 6:00 a.m., Department of Water and Power workers, construction trucks and politicos show up at the front entrance of the projects. The trucks honk and rumble and wake up some of our people. Many of us are already there, waiting for them. I can see neighbors across the street on Inglewood Boulevard on their porches and at their windows, waiting to see what's going down. We're paused, waiting to strike at the right moment.

Right there on Allin Street, a handful of workers put up a small billboard that reads, "Silicon Gardens, Coming Soon!" I wanna smoke those fools just for doing that, but I can't, not yet.

For months, the City of Los Angeles Housing Authority has sent letters to Mar Vista Gardens residents, promising to relocate them to another housing project or Section 8 placement. Where? To South Central with the Blacks in Jordan Downs and Nickerson Gardens? *Chale*, dog, not gonna happen. Not on my watch. This is their home. A bunch of the residents were like, "Fuck that, they want to deport us or bust us . . . put us in some concentration camp with FEMA or something." Those are the ones who split. But most residents stayed, and we're here now, ready to fight back. This is all we got.

These outsiders don't even know what's coming. They can't see that the militia is running in a straight-line formation toward the front entrance. The sound of our boots on the ground is like an orchestra. And these government people can't hear the pounding hammers that are nailing plywood over the windows. They can't see that we're adding extra deadbolts and exterior sheathings to doors and adding longer screws to the hinges and installing steel rods around the locks. They haven't noticed that we barred all the doors to prevent the battering rams from smashing through. They haven't checked the crew that's adding thick plastic films over window glass. And they damn sure haven't seen that each of the buildings in here has a wooden cross at the peak of the roof.

We have Uzis slung over are shoulders, ski-masks and bandanas over our faces, bulletproof vests over our clothes, replacement cartridges strapped all over our bodies, and we have hundreds of SKS assault rifles. The twins are posted up inside the security kiosk, with AK-47s sticking out of the open windows. I can't believe they don't see any of this madness. They're too busy putting up that stupid billboard.

Then a bulldozer makes a beeping sound as it tries to enter Allin Street off Inglewood Boulevard. We shoot its tires out and hit the driver once in the arm. It's just a warning shot, just to make him stop.

Now they get it. They're stuck, looking all over the place, all confused. Some workers even take off their construction hats. Bad move, homie. But we don't wanna kill anyone unless we have to. Another shot is fired, another warning.

They listen, they scream and they run, all up and down Inglewood Boulevard. But five of them don't make it. The doctor's idea: We capture and escort them into the management office, the closest and most roomy building in the projects, at the corner of Allin Street and Inglewood. We order them to lie face-down on the ground, hands over their heads. Tears in their eyes, they can't believe what's happening to them. Like they're about to shit in their pants.

I spray-paint over the Silicon Gardens billboard in white block letters: "The Southernist Guard." I tape red bandanas around the posts. It reminds me of a Nazi flag because of the colors, but we ain't no fuckin' Nazis, homie.

Then we start laying out barbed wire backed by plywood panels. We drill small holes here and there so we can see through the plywood. The lawyer and a crew are setting up a bunker at the front entrance, piling cylinder blocks all around it. They stack sand bags near the kiosk to protect the heavy artillery.

We hear lots of sirens coming from I don't know where, and helicopters start flying over. When the cops appear, they hop out of their squad cars with weapons drawn. We have a platoon to meet them, all lined up right there at the entrance. The pigs are behind their cars now, the militia behind our barriers. Both sides point weapons at each other.

Then a cop walks toward the front entrance with his hands up. He's a middle-aged white dude wearing an FBI windbreaker.

"I just want to talk to whoever's in charge. Just talk, that's it," he announces.

Everyone has the fed in the line of fire.

I walk toward him with a mini-14 rifle in my hands. The lawyer and the doctor are with me. We're all covered up in ski masks.

The doctor says, "We're shutting the gate, and we're not coming out. This is our home."

The FBI guy says, "Release the hostages, and we'll give you whatever you want. It's not too late. This is just a misunderstanding."

The doctor says, "We want the developer to stop construction on Playa Vista and here. Can you do that?"

"You're asking for the impossible," the FBI man says. "This is out of our hands, sir."

"Then you don't get the hostages," the doctor says.

We look back at the management office, where the 11th District Councilmember Cindy Miscikowski has a pistol pointed at her temple. Everyone can see this through the open blinds.

"You try anything, she dies," says the doctor.

We walk backwards and shut the gate.

TWENTY-SEVEN

MIKEY

November 22, 1999

You're either in or out. Those are your only options. If you quit the projects, you can't return. I beg Lurch to let me out . . . to fetch Stan, to advise my mom. Lurch gives me one hour to come back, tells me to join the stampede that's exiting through the front entrance. Two guards post up there, and they surveil all border movement. The *paisas* and project refugees carry packed suitcases as they flee in haste to cars, bus stops and down Inglewood Boulevard to wherever.

I run down the Ballona Creek bike path at a steady pace to where my Jeep is parked at the Purdue Avenue dead end. I keep thinking, "I still live there." But when our house got foreclosed on and we had to move, my mom put all my clothes and personal belongings in the Jeep. I wasn't even there when it happened. It was when I was in jail for that thing that went down on Halloween. Lurch helped her move. So embarrassing. He said that even Mark Stahl helped. I thanked him, and he said I could park my Jeep in his driveway until I figured things out. Mark even said I could stay in his garage, and the only thing I kept thinking was, "Why is this dude so fuckin' cool?" But I decided not to stay with him.

Now my mom and me don't talk. She moved to Inglewood with a friend. I slept in the Jeep for a few days when I got out of jail, but then my sister told me to stay with her until I found my own place. I sleep and shower there and that's it. But I keep parking over here, thinking that somehow I'm gonna get the house back. I'm like that old lady that said she kept going back to her apartment until they gutted it and threw out the toilet and sink.

I pass down South Slauson Avenue and look left: nothing. I get to Coolidge Avenue and turn in the same direction: nothing. Then I look toward Berryman Avenue before I get to my block and, after catching my breath and placing my hands on my knees . . . still nothing. No sign of Stan anywhere. I haven't talked to him since we got whipped. Sometimes he goes on drug binges and disappears. I just keep thinking I'm gonna see him on the street somewhere, where he liked to skate. I get to my Jeep, turn on the ignition and just sit there. I could drive off and never return to the projects. That's an option.

༺⚬༻

I pack a duffel bag with clothes and some toiletries, then proceed on foot down Purdue Avenue. And right there underneath the 405 overpass, where it intersects with Ballona Creek, Stan is walking with some girl, holding her hand. I can't believe he's right in front of me. The girl is thin and frail-looking, has scattered tattoos on her arms, frizzy hair, loud make-up and dark skin. I've never in my entire life seen him with a girl like that. I run to catch up to them and call out his name.

They stop dead in their tracks. He turns, and there's a smile on his face.

"What are you doing here?" I ask. "I don't even know where to find you. You don't carry a pager, and I know your house phone is disconnected."

Stan points and says, "I live here now. This is my pad."

I see a blue tarp with a tent underneath it. It has three pallets posted up around it like a wall. Clothes hang on a wire. My face hits the pavement.

"What the fuck, Stan? What happened?"

He lets his girl's hand drop for a second as he nears me and says, "They sold the duplex . . . an all cash offer. The new owner gave us two weeks to move out. Two weeks, bro. You know what I did?"

"What?"

"I broke all of the windows. Took a bat and whacked all of them, that's what I did." He laughs and adds, "The cops are probably looking for me. Pretty gnarly, huh?"

I point at my Jeep and confess, "Well, I live in there. We lost the house too."

He gives me an empathetic look. We agree that now we're just some homeless bums and laugh to hide our pain. I tell him about what's going down inside the projects. I tell him about the quarantine and put my arm around Stan's shoulder.

"You still got your camera, Stan?"

"Yeah . . . but . . . I'm bummed out by what happened with Knuckles and Lurch."

"Well, they apologized to me. . . . It's cool. They know I came back for you. . . . They've got an apartment ready for us at the projects . . . bed, shower, kitchen. . . ."

His girl perks up at the mention of shelter, and he finally introduces her as Patty. I notice she has a slight gut, I don't say anything.

☙❧

I keep thinking that Lurch's gonna make a big deal about Patty being there with Stan. They all make awkward faces at each other when we step through the front gate of the projects . . . like they all know something that I don't. Patty harbors a half-smile, and Stan looks to the ground and bites his nails. Lurch communicates smugness with a smirk and a wink. I think, "Lurch fucked Patty, for sure, and Stan probably knows it." Nobody's going to bring it up.

We enter our abandoned unit—11950—our temporary home for the next . . . whatever. We take it like we have squatters' rights. Stan sinks into a sofa in the front room, and Patty hits the shower. I put my duffel bag in a room and go straight toward the front door. I want to see what the empty world looks like.

I make a mental note of the buildings' set up: a bunch of horizontal bungalows painted two-tone; the first floor blue, the second grey. I count the units: 62 rows of bungalows arranged in a U-shape. Soldiers and barracks and checkpoints have popped up all over the facility. There are guards all around the management building where the hostages are being kept. It's right next door to our unit.

Nearby there's an outdoor table and chairs. Children, women and elderly folk are huddled together, writing postcards, scribbling things like *"Dios primero"* and "I'll come find you when this is over. I love you." Others are writing letters to friends, inmates and relatives. Some of the *paisas* have calling cards in their hands and are dialing their *pueblitos* in Mexico or Central America, telling their families not to worry. Several people are standing at their doorways or leaning out of their windows, and I can hear their phone conversations as I glide around the buildings. Toward the middle of the projects, I see some women pulling weeds in their yards or spraying lawns. A few people in training gear run around buildings and jump over obstacles. Other people simply grill meat outdoors, clutch beers and joke around, as if everything is normal.

TWENTY-EIGHT
THE DOCTOR

November 22, 1999

Iset up a medical clinic in the middle of the projects, inside the Boys and Girls Club. That location was the most strategic because it will be accessible to patients and wounded comrades when the fighting starts. I brought all the equipment from my Echo Park office. When I heard about the plans to turn my site in Del Rey into a Whole Foods Market, it was the final straw. I felt that it was payback—the owner is Georgina Tweedy's husband. That entire incident with her came back to haunt me. I should have serviced her. Instead, everything came tumbling down. This is all happening for a reason. We'll take that developer down, along with all his plans.

I brought over all the surgical gloves and masks, gauze pads, syringes, medical supplies and over-the-counter medicines I could muster. I even brought some nurses with me who have been there since I first opened. I also brought Kimberly Vuong. After we started seeing each other, we learned that we shared the same radical ideas. She pledged to fight by my side. I do actually love her, too. I never thought I'd find love again. I forgot what it feels like to need the simple touch from a person. I keep singing that song from Billy Joel, "The Longest Time." I know it's cheesy, but that's where I am at this exact moment. Love for the movement, love for a new woman.

The hardest thing was leaving my son. Before leaving, I rocked him in my arms for almost thirty minutes before he fell asleep. A thin blanket was wrapped around him, his body resting on my forearms, his face settling flush against my shoulder. I looked wistfully at the picture of the three of us—his mother, he and I—hanging on the wall. I stared down at my son's eyelids and at his face as it swayed with each breath. I felt my eyes soften. The tears ran down my cheeks to my top lip. My chest caved in. I kissed him all over his face and held him closer to me. He moved a bit in his sleep, and my heart sank further and further. I almost changed my mind and stayed. But I don't want my son to grow up in a world where people like him and me are considered substandard. He has more of my DNA than my wife's, and he's sure to encounter so many obstacles just because of his skin color. It isn't fair. After I put him down, I wrote my wife a letter explaining my choices, and left her instructions on how to access and handle monies. They will be okay, and if I die in this struggle, then it was written. The life insurance policy and liquid assets will provide for them.

We have to make strategic decisions here at the projects. No US Postal Service delivery. We cannot trust government employees. We shot out the tires of the USPS truck the other morning and warned the letter carrier to cease distribution and to ask for a transfer. When the telephone lines were shut down and the cell tower was disengaged, some anarchist hackers in here illegally tapped into the city's power source.

A resident surrendered a couple of house phones and some office furniture and, before we knew it, we had a cybercafe, with guards all around. We established a schedule: 9 a.m. to 5 p.m. Mondays, Wednesdays and Fridays for regular business. And we urged people to use the computers and phones only for essential communication: marriages, births, deaths, court dates and so forth.

We're on the world stage now. This isn't just a simple hostage crisis. It's a revolution.

TWENTY-NINE

LURCH

November 22, 1999

The quarantine is making us more disciplined. For the most part, all I cared about before this was being a player and making money . . . and representing for the hood. That's basically it. A lot of the homies were like that too. But now, I have this sense of loyalty . . . for the community, for Los Angeles, for our people. I know others feel it too. I see *paisas* and anarchists chilling, ex-gangsters from different hoods sharing experiences and some *vatos* even bringing their righteous ol' ladies here. Deadbeat husbands are chillin' with their wives. Neglectful parents are spending time with their kids, throwing a ball around, actually talking. They're little things that really count. Friends and neighbors are learning about each other. People are exercising and getting into shape. We've become heroes to the outside world—that's what the media said. Our little garden village is now the face of the resistance. Our West Side militia is now the Southernist Guard.

We're learning to appreciate things we might have taken for granted in the past. For example, yesterday, when the sun shot through the projects, everyone came out and went for a walk. We grilled *carne asada* in the yards all afternoon. I swear to God, man, every person in here was outdoors having a good time, like it was summer. I even brought some plates to the hostages in the management office. They were all grateful and happy, and the city councilwoman asked if she could talk to me one-on-one, or with the doctor or the lawyer, but the twins told her to back off.

I'm tripping out too, because Mikey and Stan are in here, with that hood rat Patty of all people. I knew Stan was a sucker, but damn, that fool is straight dumb. To be with a girl like Patty, who has five kids, who smoked rock during every pregnancy. . . . Man, I wonder where those kids are right now . . . probably in foster care 'n shit. I really wanted Mikey to move to Rhode Island or wherever he was gonna go. I really expected more from him. Something's different about that guy now. Ever since he started writing, and more since he got busted on Halloween. Like he's trying to play me or something. I'm keeping a sharp eye on him. Can't trust anybody, especially with all these hoods in here.

Fuck it, I go and check up on these dudes. See what Mikey's reporting. The door is kind of open, and I push it forward. No need to knock. These fools can't keep secrets in here. Not from me. Plus, I gave them that unit. And last I checked, Mikey and Stan were both homeless.

Stan and Patty are at the dining table. Mikey's on the sofa. I'm standing in the door frame. I ask how they're holding up, and Stan says that it's cool and simple, that they're home.

I'm offended, you know, 'cause there isn't anything simple about any of this. We're all taking the biggest risk of our lives for this cause. I left my son. We kidnapped government employees. What the fuck is so simple about that?

Stan bites his nails all stupid.

"What's simple about it, homes?" I challenge him. "These people haven't gone to work or the grocery store, or done whatever else they normally do. Most of the people fighting for this place don't even live here, dog. If they would've left the projects when the government asked them to, they'd be *homeless* right now."

Mikey says, "We're all in the same boat, man. Being away from home is hard. Period. Even when it's so close. There are days when I just want to walk to my pad. There are little things that people miss. I miss my records and my bathroom. What about you guys?"

"Cash rules everything around me, son—dollar bills, y'all," I say. "I miss making money."

I pound my fist and stare into Mikey's eyes. Oh shit, now I know why this fool was at my pad that one night. I finally put two and two together, dog. This motherfucker! It just occurred to me, just like that. I got no proof, though. But that's how things are in the joint also, everything's based on speculation. And this right here is basically like being locked up.

As I'm thinking about all this, I say, "If the world ends, it won't matter anyway . . . all that money lost for nothing."

I'm looking straight into Mikey's eyes, waiting for a reaction. I need him to understand that I know something he doesn't. His eyes bounce all over the place, he's nervous. I got this fool. Oh man, I just know it. He's not gonna get caught up in a crossfire like I had pictured after all. I'ma handle that fool in here myself, when I get the real story out of him.

THIRTY

MIKEY

November 24, 1999

Day three of the quarantine. I establish a routine. I started with intermittent fasting and shrank my eating window to eight hours, from 9 a.m. to 5 p.m. This means I fast for sixteen hours in the evening and overnight. I write and journal as soon as I wake up, since I'm allowed to work in quarantine and check in with the boss via email. I jog in the evenings for about an hour and a half, then have dinner at 6 p.m. Then I read and formulate my thoughts.

I decide to write a letter to Paulina. I mean, I know her address and all, but I don't know how I can get it out to her. USPS hasn't come by, and I know there's a way to smuggle it out, like a manuscript during wartime hysteria or pandemonium. I think there's something going on in the sewer . . . in the underground tunnel, but it's all very hush-hush. Just like with the hostages. Nobody's telling me shit about that. I'm basically just a war correspondent. Hopefully, I don't get caught up in any crossfire.

I keep thinking about the letter to Paulina. Back in high school, the best part about writing a letter was waiting for a response. It came randomly. Weeks, days, hours or never. Personal letters had a special touch, not like email. The penmanship, the color of the writing tool, the color of the paper, the font, the envelope (if any), and how it was folded. Some stationary even had scents. Email made letter-writing standard, drab. Same font, for the most part. It's all part of Y2K and the millennial change. Everything is getting easier and duller. No need to be resourceful like before.

I wonder what Paulina would think of me now . . . a combat correspondent for the militia and the *Los Angeles Times* in the housing projects. I can't think of a cooler job—she'd be impressed, I think. I just have an introduction to her thus far: "Dear Paulina, the first time I saw you, you were wearing . . ." and I detail it like in that song, "Late Night, Maudlin Street." But mine is "Late Night, Purdue Avenue." I think about that time I saved her at my pad. And I imagine her being with me when the house got foreclosed on. I conjure up this fake world with her and me as a couple, playing tennis or something, in all-white Fred Perry gear. And all these white people talking to me like I belong.

෧෩෧

In the evenings, the helicopters circle above, shine spotlights inside here and make announcements to the hostages that they will get rescued soon. I pray that we lose all electrical power in here. Then I'll have an excuse to quit and I'll abandon the cause and go back to sleeping in my Jeep.

Patty and Stan already get on my nerves. We're like cellmates. I know how Stan walks around the house late. I recognize the sound of his footsteps—lengthy and quick. He wakes up early and folds all his clothes. He and Patty only fuck in the twilight hours, and her moans are low and intense. She pisses around six in the morning, and after that she makes coffee. Stan skips breakfast, and he walks out of the shower without a shirt, having tossed it near the damp towel on the floor. They seem happy. They have each other, I have nobody. I'm Mr. Lonely. It makes me jealous. I'm the third wheel. I feel a slight sting in my spleen. It makes me think about Paulina more: where and how and with whom she sleeps. And what she thinks of at night and what keeps her up as she tosses and swivels in *her* loneliness. "Where do you go to, my lovely? When you're all alone?"

⬥⬥⬥

I'm walking briskly to exit the projects, at the furthest end of Allin Street. I've never even bothered to come in this direction, since it's basically like the easternmost and our unit is in the westernmost location. Here is where the bungalows push up against Marionwood Drive, adjacent to the run-off that's part of Ballona Creek. You can see South Slauson Avenue from here.

I can't fuckin' believe it! There's Paulina. My heart sinks down to my small intestine and spills onto the ground, flowing down to that little flood control channel. Her dirty blonde hair and her green eyes, and her freckles . . . she's so goddamn gorgeous. I can't imagine why she's here. I look around for Raven—nothing. Paulina's standing in front of a large group of women who are sitting in chairs, like she's teaching them something. She looks like a straight-up action figure, Scarlet or something from "G.I. Joe." She's majestic! When she starts to look in my direction, I scoot and I hide behind a tree. But I think she saw me, even though I'm wearing my parka and the hood over my head.

Paulina's holding a megaphone and says, "What do we want?"

The crowd says, "Justice!"

Paulina responds, "When do we want it?"

"Now!" they shout.

In Spanish she says, "*El pueblo, unido, ¡jamás será vencido!*"

She's carrying a speaker box on her left hip, and it amplifies the chants. She looks different with her beanie, scarf and heavy coat. No make-up on either. Simple and regal. Not like the times I saw her out partying or when she came to my house flashing cleavage and wearing tightened wraparounds that heightened her curves. Nah, she looks like someone's wife or a teacher or a counselor. Someone who'd be married. Someone I could marry. She leads her mob around one of the bungalows, like they're practicing for a protest. My heart beats quicker than ever.

THIRTY-ONE

LURCH

November 24, 1999

A delivery truck shows up at the front entrance with Gateway written on the side in its cow-print logo. Three employees unload computers from the back of the truck and swivel pallet jacks around. The employees in the front seat have their hands up and out of the windows. They know best. The driver has a letter in an envelope. We tell that fool to toss it on the ground.

Everyone inside the projects has guns pointed at the truck. Some of our guns have infrared scopes. Red dots are all over the Gateway workers. The twins and Knuckles walk outside the front gate. They're G'd up, Uzis strapped around their shoulders. Knuckles has a flamethrower pack over his shoulders and hops in the back of the truck. He squeezes a nozzle that spits a stream of flammable liquid. The twins point the guns at the employees and ask them to bounce, quick-like, but not before they scoop up the letter. The Gateway employees run south on Inglewood Boulevard toward Playa Vista, faster when someone shoots in the air. The back of the truck lights up and the homies run back inside the projects. The Gateway truck is just sitting there at the front entrance, up in flames, and then its tires become hot and explode—*boom, boom.* A couple of dudes think they're gun shots, and a couple of dudes blast before they figure out what has happened. We're ready for whatever.

The twins hand me the letter. It's from Mapchat, a tech firm, and is addressed to *The Southernist Guard*. Mapchat does GPS inside cars. It says that they want to integrate into the community and not change or erase our history. But I know these fuckin' punks snatched up houses, warehouses and entire blocks with cash offers in Venice, and they bought some land in Playa Vista. Now they want to donate computer equipment and cellphones to us?! Fuck, we don't need 'em. They're not welcome in the West Side. Go home. I burn the letter with my lighter, and we leave the truck right there on the street, in flames.

THIRTY-TWO

MIKEY

November 25, 1999

Thanksgiving morning. Nothing's different, nothing's out of place. The sun is out and its hovering high, creating a crispness and warmth. It's the type of weather that allows you to wear a light jacket or shorts and skate around the neighborhood . . . like Stan used to.

I look out the window. A gang of Culver City boys are headed somewhere, to the gym, I think. I grab Stan and we head out to the field behind the gym. Everyone is posting up all over the bleachers. Some people are wearing white Culver City High football jerseys, shorts and cleats, and they're tossing a football around. The gear is much spritelier than all the black-shirt attire of the past few weeks. On the opposite end of the bleachers, others from the militia, the ones that aren't from the hood, are setting up shop. They aren't as excited as the CEXCE 13 boys, but they're running scrimmages or something. One of the Culver City boys has a boombox blasting out "Maggie May" from Rod Stewart. The whole thing reminds me of the Cuban revolutionaries, the Barbudos, when they were in the Sierra Maestra playing baseball in their down time. Hemingway was right there with Castro smoking cigars. The doctor said I was like Hemingway, because of my sparse and economic writing. I'll take it.

Stan takes pictures. These images are what'll make the militia look normal—All-American.

Everyone's warmed up, the bleachers are packed. Lurch walks to the middle of the field and blows a whistle. Two members from each side are near him when Lurch tosses a coin. At last, something thrilling during all this madness. I've wanted to see the CXC boys play football since forever. After the '93 peace treaty, they played against Venice, Santa Monica, Sotel and Lennox on the regular. The hood always won. They were champions of the West Side.

Right from the get-go, it's on! Straight up. And I don't even like football. Stan and I are sitting on the grass in the middle of the field, away from everyone. Stan has his camera locked and loaded in anticipation.

At halftime, Raven walks up on us. I literally get a heart attack. Stan has one for me too.

Raven says, "So, what up, bad dudes, you wanna play or what?" He laughs at his own joke.

"Nah, we're good, we're not really into sports."

"What are you into, then?" He looks all around behind him.

"Music and the arts, I guess," Stan says. "And movies. Oh, and skating."

Raven does the rock 'n roll hand sign and in a dumb voice says, "Skate or die, bro!" Again, he lets out a goofy laugh and says, "Some fag shit, no?"

"It's not . . ." I start to say.

"I know, I know," he interrupts. "I'm just fuckin' with you." And he slaps me a little on the shoulder, playfully. "I know it's not fag shit. I'm into that stuff, too. I listen to Wu-Tang and watch the "Godfather" as much as the next motherfucker. I know about Diego Rivera or whatever. So, who do you think's gonna win, huh?"

"I'll place my bets on you guys," Stan says. "This game is freakin' gnarly!"

"That's for sure, homie," Raven agrees. "Gnarly is right. You know how we do. This is The Culver City gang! MVG for life, big dog."

"How's your stomach, man?" I ask. "How you holding up?" Raven looks away from us and says, "Ain't no thang but a chicken wang. Just some stupid wound. You'll see me in action tonight, though. I'ma light up any pig that rolls up through here, you know what I'm saying? He lifts up his white t-shirt and shows us a 9mm handle sticking out of his belt, right next to his shit bag.

☙❧

At six in the afternoon, I hear an alarm coming from the watchtower near the front entrance. The sun is ducking behind the ocean, and the sound of boots rumbling on the ground gives me goosebumps. Stan and I are sitting in front of our unit on two rattan chairs, looking out into the projects and the street. Patty's inside . . . probably smoking crack or something.

The resistance soldiers up. A squadron sinks into the battle station behind the sandbags. The doctor and his staff lock themselves in their medical unit. The medical team sets up a bivouac post with blue tarps behind their facility, in case they can't attend to all patients. I see the twins through their unit's window untying the hostages' hands and having them sit at the dinner table like it's a Thanksgiving feast or something. Lurch's there too.

In the next minute, Lurch is outside the management office. A Ruger Mini-14 rifle strapped over his shoulder, he walks across the lawn toward us to hand us two Glocks.

"This is for your safety," he says. "You don't have to use them. Keep 'em handy, just in case."

"Thanks, man," I say. "I don't think that'll be necessary." I put my hands up to reject it. But not Stan, he accepts one of the guns and slides it down his pants pocket.

"Mikey, remember," Lurch says, "you can leave whenever you want. I'll open the gate myself. Right now even, if you prefer, *vato loco*. This is where the shit hits the fan. When they come in here for us, like really come, I'll kill the hostages. I won't hesitate. They'll be the first to go. There's no way out of this."

"I want to stay, man . . . for real," I say. "It's my job. I gotta represent for the hood, too, you know? If this is the end, I'm glad to be standing here with you all."

I reach out to shake Lurch's hand. He takes it, then Lurch purses his lips and walks off.

Suddenly, he turns back and says, "You're pretty down, Mikey."

～∞∞～

I feel a chill run through my body. I don't have anything to say, though. I just look at Lurch. That's the closest I've gotten to some real acknowledgement from him. Feels weird . . . awkward. I thought these gang members were all hard and cold, but Lurch just showed a warmer side. Can he actually have a heart and show empathy and understanding? I guess that's why he's part of all this, because he feels so much about this place. He has mad love inside of him. Love for the hood, for the region, for our people, for the militia. I realize for the first time that maybe I love the neighborhood, too, and I'm here because I am also willing to sacrifice something. All this time I'd been wanting to leave the neighborhood, but it turns out that maybe I love Culver City, Del Rey and Los Angeles, and maybe for some of the same reasons that Lurch does. I recall several memories of what my life consisted of up until now: the crashing water on the Palos Verdes cliffs and along Playa Del Rey—tower 14. The weekend lunch get-togethers at the San Pedro Ports o' Call waterfront, surrounded by gangsters, *paisas*, and hoodrats. Culver City High and walking around campus. The taco joints on Inglewood Boulevard. The hikes throughout the metropolis— Santa Monica and Malibu. The ghetto restaurants in Huntington Park. The bicycle trips on the strand—from Playa Del Rey to Santa Monica, or in the opposite direction to Redondo Beach. UCLA. The bookstore visits to Torrance and Manhattan Beach, and especially Midnight Special at 3rd Street Promenade, or going to Soundsations in Westchester for CD's and films. The concerts, movie theaters and cruising spots in Hollywood, the nightclubs and bars in Silver Lake, Hermosa Beach and West Hollywood, the backyard house parties, and being with relatives during holidays. I picture infrastructure and the metro, traffic jams and airplanes, Mediterranean-revival homes and modernist ones, native cactus—it's all worth fighting for. The militia is right: it's ours. Silicon Beach is gonna change Los Angeles, but we don't want it to change. Fuck Silicon Beach.

☾☯☽

It's nightfall, the militia is positioned all around the projects. They're in the trees, rooftops, near dumpsters, behind cars, in the playground and around certain bungalows. An announcement is made to turn off televisions, lights and candles by 8 p.m. Everyone in the projects turns out the lights. The silence is profound. Stan and I are on the porch, Patty's in bed. We just sit here and wait, whisper to each other here and there. The quietude is harder than expected. Boring and scary. Lurch said it was like being in prison.

I wonder what Paulina is doing. How she and Raven get through the night. I picture what a conversation with her might sound like in this situation. Maybe we'd talk about college or music . . . or about clothing styles. In my head, I sing songs from bands to kill time. Stan drinks coffee and smokes cigarettes in the bathroom, on the down low. I think about my childhood and my mom. And books. For a little while, I think about Raven, and I picture him fucking Paulina. It hurts so bad. I wonder if Raven has PTSD because he was shot. Maybe I have it too, especially after that night. Or after we got whipped. Maybe it was a good thing that Lurch gave me that strap. I take it out, grip the handle and cock it back.

I yawn every few minutes. My head tilts back periodically and jolts my entire body, which wakes me up. It's cold, I wrap a blanket around my arms tightly. I tap the ground with my feet. Stan tells me to take a quick nap, just for a little while. And I do, fuck it. But when I wake up, it's already morning. No raid occurred during the night.

THIRTY-THREE

THE DOCTOR

November 26, 1999

They've started calling the industrial area of Culver City the Arts District. Software and technology businesses have been repurposing old warehouses and storage facilities, and developers are setting up lofts, condos and restaurants. The metro is expanding this way too, so that people can commute to downtown Los Angeles. Ragged homeless people, many who have been displaced, are pouring over and pushing shopping carts along Rodeo and Jefferson and putting up tents in the flood-control creek channel. They wash their clothes and bathe in the toxic, methane-infused sewer water where the street vendor died. The creek is now bloated with old syringes, used condoms, trash, human feces, old tires, disease-carrying rats and all types of other disgusting waste. There's a new name for it, too: Silicon Creek. Everything is being rebranded. There's even an attempt to sell South Central as South Los Angeles. It's the erasure of the twentieth century. Goodbye, West Side.

They're building a high-speed bullet train through the creek underground, that will start in Playa Del Rey and shuttle you all over the region. I saw a map and a brochure online. Our district is the new gritty and cool place to be. Homes along the creek are being promoted by real estate agents as riverfront property, even though the rail yards and warehouses block the view of the murky, trickling water in the concrete flood-control channel. We sent the developers and the urban planning department a letter:

1. Culver City is under attack in the form of neo-colonization and therefore must be defended.
2. In doing this, we commit ourselves to protecting our community by any means necessary, which means that outsiders should not feel safe.

THIRTY-FOUR

LURCH

November 26, 1999

There's an Oldsmobile parked on Allin Street and Inglewood Boulevard in front of the projects. A gangster car. Looks like the one that shot up Raven at Mikey's pad. It's honking its horn and flashing its headlights, all stupid 'n shit. A few of our guards have these fools in their line of fire.

Some dude gets out the car and yells out, "Culver City gang! Culver City! Open the damn gate, motherfuckers!"

The guard in the watchtower centers a light on him. It's the homie, Crow, Wino's brother. He's drunk, dancing all around like a *vato loco* with his arms winged out and knuckles tapping each other, periodically throwing up two C's with his hands and crossing them—CXC.

My homie Knuckles points an SKS rifle at him, looks to me to give him the sign. I climb up the watchtower and through a megaphone I ask Crow what he wants. He calls me a fuckin' pussy. I try to be all cordial 'n shit, but I've known since the homie's funeral that this *vato* was gonna trip hard someday.

"Hey, Crow, who's with you in the *ranfla*?" I ask nicely.

He doesn't answer, just keeps talking shit.

"Hey, Crow, just walk on by . . . take off, man."

"Look, Lurch, I fuckin' started the Little Locos clique. I jumped all you *mocosos* in. Now you little motherfuckers think you're better than me. Fuck you, Lurch, you got my brother killed."

That's what I wanted to hear. I just wanted him to say it. Show his true colors. But now, there's no room for this type of betrayal. We gotta be solid. I think about that car and Peter Ramírez from 18th Street—Pelón from County. And I remember what Stimey said, "Can't trust anyone from that shady-ass gang." I gotta think about them during this military campaign, these traitors.

Crow throws a beer bottle at the gate. It smashes all over the entrance. The doctor and the lawyer are looking to me to make a move, to stop this three-ring circus.

I warn Crow, "You have ten seconds to leave, big dog. Or else, *ya sabes. . . .*"

When I get to three, Crow reaches into his waistband. I give Knuckles the greenlight and he fires several shots, striking Crow all over his body with precision. Then he shoots up the Oldsmobile as it speeds off, burning rubber. Crow lays in a lump at the entrance. It didn't have to end this way, with the death of one of our own. Wino's brother, nonetheless. I'm going straight to hell.

Two guards open the gate and storm the dead homie. They look in all directions, check his pulse. They go through his pockets and take his wallet and whatever else is on his person. They find an FBI business card.

THIRTY-FIVE

MIKEY

November 27, 1999

It's the weekend, and nothing has gone down yet. A gusty blanket of feverish wind is sweeping through the Southland. The timing of the winds is different every year in Southern California. In 1999, the Santa Ana Winds, also called the Devil's Winds, come in late November, fanning the wildfires in the deserts and valleys and pushing the ashes and dust toward the coast. Palm trees swing violently in the projects, and one crashes down on the recreational center next to the gymnasium. No major damage. A few eucalyptus trees break in half and smash two cars, the front windshields and hoods of both cars sink with the impact. Instead of cleaning the area up, we use it as a battle station. The militia forms a small bunker around the fallen trees.

We haven't received much rain throughout California either, and the governor has declared a state of emergency because of the drought. We don't care. We have vegetable gardens and an herb patch to maintain, to feed the militia. Nobody stays outside for long, because the debris, ash and wind affect eyesight and exacerbate allergies. Along the coast, the smell of salt water and seaweed creeps into open windows. The sea-spray from the wind-tossed ocean also affects our breathing. I've been sneezing all week and I have a bad cough.

Another type of plague is coming. Some of the quarantined walk around the bungalows with sunglasses and red railroad handkerchiefs wrapped around their mouths and noses. Others wear surgical masks. Y2K is just around the corner. It's almost over, although I don't know if people can handle another month of this. We put a stop to demolishing the projects . . . the job is over, right?

Stan and I are posted up in the living room. He says, "You know, I was supposed to go to Costa Rica this month to surf. I'd been planning it all year . . . till they evicted us."

I look at him with droopy eyes. "I didn't know that, man. I'm sorry. This whole thing's a mess. It's put everyone's lives on pause. I was planning a trip Argentina . . . to Buenos Aires. Can't afford anything anymore. Couldn't prevent my mom's foreclosure either. I'm going to have to look for somewhere to live when all this is over . . . unless we die in here. That'll be my new priority."

"We're not gonna die, homie," Stan says. "You can stay with me and Patty right there, under the bridge."

We both laugh hard. He even slaps the sofa a few times.

"*Ay*, but for real . . ." he adds. "You talk to that girl Paulina yet? I know you've seen her in here. I have."

My heart collapses. "Nah, it hasn't been the right moment, bro. Plus, Raven's here . . . so you know how that goes. It's too dangerous."

His eyes pierce my soul. "You really like her, huh?"

"I do, bro. I really do. But, she's not into me like that."

"Of course she is, don't be stupid. You're a good catch. You're educated, smart, and you're a good dude. And kinda all right looking." He winks at me. "I mean . . . you're no Stan Corona, but you're decent. All you gotta do is get rid of Raven."

"I can't compete with a gangster. Same as junior high, same as high school."

"*Ay*, Mikey, thanks for bringing me here. For real. It's the best thing that could've happened to me and Patty. You know she's pregnant, right? Can't have a baby under the bridge." He stares at the floor and starts biting his nails.

I just stare at Stan confused, mostly because they drink and smoke on the regular, like nothing. I can't believe it. I look at him and nod my head. He doesn't notice.

December 23, 1999

Around the end of the year, people pull out their Christmas decorations. The projects are adorned in typical holiday regalia. As in Anytown, USA, families take Christmas lights out of storage and string them around trees, on dumpsters and bushes, and they encircle everything with green and red ribbon. Aluminum foil is wrapped around posts, stockings are hung. The entire projects are lit up . . . it's almost beautiful in here—All-American.

At twilight, Stan, Patty and I sit outside our unit with a bottle of vodka. Lurch gave me a thermal shirt and pants and a sweater a few days ago. I'm warm and I'm buzzed. The Devil's Winds are still strong, ushering in the winter chill. Someone brought leftover military gear from the surplus store on Venice Boulevard, and Stan and I grabbed Russian-style ushanka hats, wool blankets and aluminum cups. We look like Soviets.

"So, what do you think's gonna happen on New Year's?" Stan asks. "You think we'll still be here?"

"Hopefully we can go home sooner," Patty says.

I look at her and can't help but say, "You have no home, and you're pregnant. You shouldn't even be here to begin with."

I don't know if it's the vodka buzz or the chill, but neither Stan nor Patty react to that. What the hell?

Stan says, "Do you actually think something is going to happen?"

"No, yes, I don't know. I don't really think anything's gonna happen . . ." I say.

"We're gonna leave in a few weeks, no matter what," Stan says, ". . . maybe before New Year's."

"Yeah," Patty's on the same page. "I spoke to my mom . . . she said we could go stay with her in Wilmington whenever we're ready. We need a place ASAP, especially for the baby." She squeezes Stan's hand and says, "We can leave before Christmas. Can we, please?"

I look at her stomach and I say, "You guys are really having this baby?"

Stan looks puzzled. "Of course we are. What d'ya mean?"

I don't clarify anything, I'm lit.

"Nothin', Stan . . . just give me a cigarette."

But I really want him to stay. I can't do this quarantine alone. Especially since Lurch said they'll hold the line until the New Year.

"You really believe in all this, Mikey?" Patty asks.

Annoyed, I shoot back, "I understand what they're fighting for . . . what we're fighting for. This is all going to get taken from us. We're gonna have nothin'."

"Well, what's yours, anyway?" she asks.

I stare at her, then stare at Stan. I light the cigarette. "The soul of the city is ours, that's what. It's going to vanish, just like that."

I puff smoke, offer Patty a hit from the cigarette, but she turns it down. I don't believe her.

Stan shifts forward on his chair and says, "Let's just pack our shit and get out of here in the morning. Just leave . . . c'mon, Mikey. This is over, man. Nothing happened on Thanksgiving, and nothing's gonna happen on Christmas or any other day. Let's celebrate the New Year outside of this goddam quarantine. Not in here with these psychopaths."

"You do what you want, but I'm gonna stay right here," I say, pointing downward. "Let me get another cigarette before you leave."

Stan reaches for a box of American Spirits from inside his coat pocket. He sparks one and hands me another and his lighter. He says, "Here. I'm not going to leave yet, Mikey, but I'm getting really close. I'm just letting you know."

I don't say anything. I'm just annoyed. What I really want to say is, "Get this crackhead out of the pad." I can't stand Patty, for real. She's just a piece of shit. Drinking and smoking and doing drugs while pregnant. What kind of . . .

Stan interrupts my thoughts, lifts his glass and faces me. "A toast! To the end of the world."

He clicks his glass against mine and smiles widely. Patty smiles too. My frown turns upside down.

I laugh and say, "Cheers!" It's the most normal I'd felt since we've been on lockdown. Like the good ol' days. Hanging out, drinking and smoking, talking shit. Damn.

"I miss music," Stan says. "I miss spinning records and CD's, and dancing northern soul. What about you?"

"My family. My sisters," Patty says.

I look all around me and wonder what an aerial shot of the projects looks like at this exact moment. It must be a stunning sight, the bushes and dumpsters lit up. I don't think a housing project ever looked so beautiful. Like that neighborhood in Torrance that gets all those visitors for the Christmas lights.

Stan's and Patty's words make me think about my life. I have nobody to return to. *They* are gonna start a family and *they* are returning to one. My mom told me not to look for her. We didn't leave on the best of terms. I just split without saying anything. And my dad, haven't seen that dude since right before I graduated from UCLA. He didn't go to my graduation either, fucker.

"I miss The Jesus and Mary Chain," I say.

"Ooh, choose one . . ." Stan says, ". . . The Cure, The Smiths or Depeche Mode?"

I say, "The Smiths, no doubt about it."

"I always liked The Cure the best," he says. "And guess what? They're playing in a few days at Irvine Meadows. Mark Stahl's going. He sent me an email about it a while back. I think he has extra tickets. Wanna go?"

Damn, I forgot about Mark. He's been nothing but the best, more than what these CXC boys have been to Stan and me our whole lives.

"Are you serious?" I say. "Let's go then. Let's fuckin' go. Fuck the plague. . . . It's all about The Cure, motherfuckers!"

We toast hard and laugh hard.

Then Stan says, "Merry Quarantine, man, I love you." And his eyes get watery.

❧

Fire and smoke are rising from somewhere south of the projects, near the freeway entrance.

"What the fuck is that?" I say, hopping up from my chair. "Look, some palm trees are on fire too!"

People come out of their units and point south.

I announce to Stan and Patty, "This is it, this is the big fire. The locusts are coming!"

I must be buzzed. I pull the hood of my parka over my head, grab the Glock that Lurch gave me and cock it back. I down my vodka, serve myself another one real quick and down it too.

"Fuck it, let's do this! Let's go over there with Lurch and them," I say.

But Stan and Patty freeze up. They're not up for it.

I go out to the street and look south as ambulances whiz down Inglewood Boulevard in front of the projects. I can see down Jefferson Boulevard. Near the 405, small offices and other business are catching flames. There are also flames near the wetlands, where Playa Vista is being built.

The militia run toward their battle stations. The alarm on the watchtower squawks. A unit near ours has a television set outside. Lurch and Knuckles are there with a bunch of other people. We gather around it, too. I look toward where the hostages are—nothing. I think it's time to let them go. A news channel shows images of people looting the grocery store, like in the '92 Riots. More fires are set in apartment complexes and houses near the main intersection. On the TV screen all we see are small fires on rooftops and trees catching the flames.

A running looter dressed in black military fatigues pauses to talk to a reporter. Out of breath, he says, "We're . . . burning the houses . . . and apartments because . . . we're killing off the gentrification . . . plague. All these apartments have for sale signs . . . they'd be sold to transplants, not us. *¡Viva la revolución!*"

There's a roar inside the projects. Lurch says that the city has our back, and that the bombings in Guernica, Munich and Tokyo unified residents. Like now. He high-fives some gangsters. A bunch of them cheer him on.

I point the pistol at the police helicopter that buzzes over the projects and say, "Fuck the police!"

Before I can pull the trigger, Paulina places her soft hand over mine. I hadn't even seen her in the crowd. She just rolled up on me, just like that. My eyes light up.

Lurch's all pissed, asks Stan if I'm drunk. Stan indicates that I am, but Paulina defends me, says that I'm getting ready for the big finale. I'll be going out with a bang.

Paulina takes the gun out of my hand and pulls out the clip. She looks inside the gun to make sure there isn't a bullet lodged inside the chamber. Lurch looks at me kind of weird and tells Stan to take me inside to sober up.

As Stan hauls me off, I yell out, "Paulina! Come back! Paulina! *Ay*, Lurch, sorry, dog. *Dispensa*."

Stan and Patty drag me away. I slur and stumble and say, "Did you see her freckles? Did you, huh, did you? She's gorgeous, huh? I fuckin' love her. I fuckin' love you too, man. Go tell her to come back, c'mon, Stan. Paulina! Tell her that I love her, man."

All of a sudden I see Raven coming out the unit where the hostages are kept. His eyes leap toward me, land right on my chin. I forgot about that dude with the shit bag.

I look at Stan and say, "Fuck that fool. Lemme fight him. C'mon. Take me to him, Stan. Take me."

THIRTY-SIX

LURCH

December 30, 1999

I got another dead homie on my hands—this time it's Knuckles. They just left him right there on top of the manhole to the underground tunnel. His guts and intestines were sticking out all over the goddamn place. One of the anarchists found him lying there all cut up.

We've been using that tunnel for emergencies, an' like for food 'n shit like that. Only a few people know about it, and it's how we're gonna escape this fuckin' place when the shit hits the fan. But now it might be compromised. They found my homie like at three in the morning. Probably went to see his lady and his kid and got caught on the way back. Didn't tell anyone he was going.

Who'd wanna take him out like that? That's what I'm tripping off of. This ain't the cops. They would've lit him up like the other homies. Nah, this was personal. Someone stabbed him a bunch of times and carved out his insides. We had to drag his body in here like that. And now we have to bury him inside the projects, not out there. People won't get it, they'll say it's blasphemous, but it has to be done this way. He has to stay with us, like they do in real wars.

Nobody's outside their bungalow today. Not for nothing. It's like a ghost town in here. Ashes from burnt trees and buildings are all up in this piece. I can still see the damage from here, like little clusters of black smoke. The residue lands all over me, and I can taste that shit in my mouth. I write "The Plague" with my index finger on a car window that's pasty and dirty. I spot like two or three people walking around looking blank and pale, and they have stone faces. Just like me.

Mayor Richard Riordan declared martial law in the City of Los Angeles last night. He held a news conference in front of City Hall. He called us "wolfpacks." The doctor told me that's what the American media called the Nazis back in the day. He said they're trying to compare us to Nazis so they can storm this place and kill us all. Fuck it, you *vatos* wanna do this, it's on.

Hundreds of people post up around the backside of the gym for the burial. We don't need to wait for a coroner or mortician or anything like that. Outside the project gates, a whole bunch of people show up too. Women, children, guys, girls carrying flowers, glass candles and rosaries. They grip the burglar bars and peek inside.

We built Knuckles a coffin out of plywood and dug him a hole. Two *cholas* with teased hair and thinly smeared eyeliner, apply make-up to his face. They wear black sweaters with the words, "Rest in Peace Knuckles" in white Old English iron-on letters. I get up close to see his stiffened body. He looks intact. You can still see all his freckles. He still looks like the homie.

I'm standing way in front at the ceremony, my hands blocking my eyes, nose and mouth. This is too hard, homes. I pull a rosary and some pictures out of my pocket and drop them inside the coffin. The doctor pats me on the back. We shake hands, and he hugs me.

I say out loud, "My *carnal*, Cisco . . . Knuckles, was the life of the party. He was well-loved by everyone. He loved all of you here. And he had that smile, you know? Always smiling and clowning around. Always having a good time. You'll be missed, homeboy."

I look up to the clouds, interlock my hands and then close the casket. I cry and my body jerks.

Some *paisas*—men and women—drop to their knees and pray. They chant words together and make the sign of the cross on their chests and forehead. Some of the homies lower Knuckles into the earth and begin to shovel dirt over the coffin. And just like that, he's gone.

A boombox plays Antonio Aguilar's version of *"Un Puño de Tierra,"* and some people sing along. I fall to the ground.

THIRTY-SEVEN

MIKEY

December 31, 1999

There's something different about Stan, I can't figure it out. Moments, literally just moments after he told me that Knuckles was murdered, he got all weird. Even smirked. And now he's being all sneaky, taking off in the dark like a crackhead. I ask him where Patty is, and he just ignores me, says he's gonna go by the gym with some dudes from Poserz. But he said I can't go with him, and he's all mad at me. He doesn't even look at me. I don't understand what the fuck.

I hop off the sofa and peer through the cracked blind. Stan walks fast with his head cowed. Every now and then he looks behind him. I throw on my parka and in stealth mode go after him. I hide behind trees, duck behind cars, halt behind dumpsters.

He meets with some dudes at the playground. I don't recognize them. A couple sit on the swings, some stand. Two of them wear Pittsburgh Pirates hats, like Poserz dudes do. There's a dim lamp post, and I can faintly see their profiles. Stan shakes their hands, and one of them hands him a beer and something else. Money and some dope, I think. I look closer. . . . It's Pelón from 18th Street, the one that hit me and Stan up. I'm vexed.

Stan laughs a little, and it's like they know each other. Stan stuffs the large roll of money in his pocket and downs the beer in seconds. Their conversation is inaudible from where I'm standing. My heart races like a speedway. I really don't understand what's going on. I jet through the parking area and make my way to the gymnasium parking lot, where all the Culver City guys are gathered in memory of Knuckles.

There's a bunch of people there. I slow my pace when I spot everyone. I'm out of breath when I reach them, and I bend over and grab my knees. Some people stare at me, but they dismiss me right away. Lurch and the twins are there too. I haven't seen much of the twins since this thing started, and they don't pay me any attention either. It's the first time since the quarantine began that I feel like I don't belong. Like I'm invisible. These people are all congregated in cliques and they're telling stories. I don't have anything to contribute, and I don't have a clique to join. Then a light turns on in my head: that's why Stan smirked. I want the night to end and I want to know what Stan's involved in. At that exact moment, I'm on the outside looking in.

I see a girl I went to middle school with: Leslie Gomez. Looks like she gained weight. Her hair color is different, lighter. She looks at me and smiles.

"Leslie, how are you? Do you live here in the projects?" I ask.

"Oh my God, Mikey! I haven't seen you in ages. What are you doing here?"

We hug and I tell her that I'm a war correspondent for the *LA Times*. A journalist.

"Wow, I always knew you were going to do something interesting in life."

"Whatever. . . . What about you? Are you married? Have kids?" I ask.

"I have two . . . and I'm divorced, on my second marriage," she says with a little laugh. "I came down alone for the funeral, though."

I don't know whether to congratulate her or offer my apologies. I say nothing.

She lives in Vegas now, says that Knuckles was her next-door neighbor, and they were best friends.

"I'm sorry for your loss," I say.

Just then, Paulina walks in our direction. My heart beats a lot faster. She's wearing a black military jacket, jeans and heels. I've never seen her dress like that, action figure-like. Her hair's combed in a way that clouds her face. She's looking around a little nervous, it seems. Is she hiding from Raven?

Paulina comes up to us, and Leslie introduces her to me. Paulina and I act like we don't know each other.

"I'm trying to avoid people recognizing me," Paulina says.

"Yeah, let's get outta here," Leslie suggests. "These guys are gonna drink and party and get fucked up all night."

I look toward the Culver City boys as they gather near parked cars. Their group is growing larger by the minute. They're taking pictures and posing, throwing gang signs. Leslie invites me to move on with the two of them. I'm not sure where to, but I go.

☙❧

In one of the units, Paulina slides onto the sofa. I squeeze in next to her. I'm nervous as fuck. Leslie sits to my right so I'm in the middle. When my arm brushes up against Paulina's, I feel renewed, alive. I forget about the funeral and the insurgency all together.

For the first time since the quarantine, I think about the possibility of real love. New love is different than existing love. The latter needs to be protected. For example, when the doctor left his wife and son to join the movement, that was love that needed protection. Or when husbands send their wives to live with relatives while the husbands stay and fight for the militia. Another type of love is what the Culver City boys are doing right now in the parking structure: remembering their dead homies. But none of those loves matter to me because all I can think about is romantic love, for Paulina. She and I could die together in here and I would find it pleasurable. I really would. It's like "Head On" by the Jesus and Mary Chain. I know there's a strong possibility we won't make it out of this. Not because of the militia, but because of Raven. I've taken a huge risk by coming into the housing projects and can easily get struck by a stray bullet . . . or get my stomach slit, like Knuckles . . . or get buried in here, whatever.

Leslie appears with mixed drinks for the three of us.

"You should learn how to handle a weapon before you get hurt," Paulina says to me and smirks.

I remember when she disarmed me a few nights ago. "I'll just stick to writing," I say.

"Well, you're here now," she says. "You can take weapons training with any one of the guys."

I get bolder. "Can I take weapons training with you?"

Paulina rolls her eyes and looks at Leslie.

Leslie smiles.

Paulina says, "I miss Knuckles already. I wonder what's going to happen to his kids."

Leslie sobs a little and says, "He was my best friend. He protected me from assholes when my brothers weren't around."

"How many kids did he have?" I ask.

Leslie lifts two fingers.

At that moment, like an opportunist, I sweep through and ask Paulina how she got involved in all of this.

She looks at Leslie. "Is he serious? This guy!"

Leslie laughs and purses her lips, then nods her head.

I'm confused, like I said something wrong.

"Paulina's one of the biggest union organizers in L.A. She helped organize the residents."

"Okay, so how was I supposed to know that?" I ask.

"That's okay, Mikey," Paulina says. "You wouldn't know because you've only been interviewing men and dismissing the women's role in the movement."

"Whoa! Like . . . like . . . I'm not sexist or anything," I defend myself.

"Any man who says, 'I'm not sexist or anything,' is sexist," Paulina comes back at me.

⚭⚭⚭

We are all looser now and I find myself massaging Paulina's ankle. I don't know how I got this confident.

"If you want to shoot somebody, you can shoot Raven," Paulina tells me.

That's the second person who's told me I should get rid of him. She and Leslie laugh like whistles.

I think about it and then say, "I'm a lover, not a fighter. If I die pursuing a story, then so be it. I love telling a good story."

Paulina claps and says, "Wow, you're so full of yourself. Can you be any more pretentious?"

Now, I'm kind of pissed, you know? Because she comes off like she has this hard exterior, but it's probably all a front.

"Look at your eyes," I say. "You're so insecure. You can't even look at me. What are you afraid of, huh? Does she know about us?" I point at Leslie.

Paulina laughs, like nothing can faze her. "What, are you a psychologist now? You're the insecure one. You don't know me. I'll give you some free advice. Mind your own freakin' business, and don't try to analyze other people. You don't know anything about me, Mikey."

She emphasizes my name, it's so belittling.

Leslie screeches and gets up to use the bathroom. "Oh my god, you guys are so stupid. You were meant for each other."

We're alone now, and I squeeze in closer to her, facing her. I place my arm over her shoulder and gaze into her eyes. I know she won't back down.

"It's almost morning. Shouldn't we be out there or something?" I say.

"You wanna go, go," she says, blushing.

It's the first time I actually see her let her guard down. I stand up and grab her hand. She gets to her feet and my chest starts to throb, my teeth chatter. I squeeze her hand as we walk down the hallway. She's down for whatever—my girl. We look into each other's eyes. Now I know that there's a strong possibility that a future of love can exist between us. I want to take her out to lunch tomorrow, somewhere in Beverly Hills. Outside of this goddamn quarantine. Away from Raven and all these fools. Stan and Patty were right: I want to hold Paulina's hand in public and go to a movie or that Cure concert. Maybe this thing hasn't extinguished all hope. Many people who are quarantined have given up something personal to be here. What did Paulina leave behind?

I try to kiss her. She pushes me back.

I back off and say, "What the fuck?"

"Be quiet. Listen," she whispers.

We hear gunshots all around. The sounds are near and far, and the guns pop and zap and boom. Some pops sound like fireworks. Are these fools celebrating already? Dogs bark with fury. I start to back away, but she pulls me closer to her.

"It sounds beautiful, doesn't it? This is the only place I want to be, Mikey . . . with you."

PART III

THIRTY-EIGHT
THE DOCTOR

January 1, 2000 12:40 a.m.

It's shortly after midnight when I spot Lurch alone. He looks exhausted. The flame is sucked out of his face. His eyes are opaque. He's hiding behind a dumpster smoking a cigarette. I ask him for one. The collar on his navy peacoat is flared up. He's shaved his mustache. He looks different, like a perplexed gentleman looking for an out. Like he's about to go underground. We don't talk, we're both out of sorts. I look at others walking by, their heads hanging low and their feet dragging. We are all going nowhere. The mood in the projects has shifted.

The computers didn't turn on us on Y2K, robots didn't declare war, no locusts swarmed, the anti-Christ didn't arrive with the four horsemen of the apocalypse, the Devil's Winds didn't blow us away into the inferno and the cops or military didn't blitzkrieg the projects. The only outcome has been just a little over a month of quarantine and self-reflection.

A couple skips and hops and looks cheery. Countless people are outside and they don't have guns strapped over their shoulders anymore. They seem less preoccupied. They seem relieved to have survived the quarantine and Y2K. The people I see aren't wearing their black shirts anymore. We've lost momentum. As Kimberly walks briskly toward me, someone tells her, "Great night for a stroll, young lady." As Mikey passes us up in haste, I try to talk to him, but he just walks on by. Kimberly embraces me and says, "Happy new year," but I'm not happy.

MIKEY
January 1, 2000 1:00 a.m.

Stan and Patty didn't leave. Neither did I. We stayed until new year's to ride this out. I find Stan slumped on a sofa near a dumpster. His clothes are disheveled, and his eyes are bloodshot. Saliva is trickling from the corner of his mouth, and he clears the phlegm in his throat repeatedly. He looks brittle, seems thinner. At least his camera is still wrapped around his neck.

Before the quarantine, he was hardcore into indie fashion and hygiene, but not anymore. His military jacket has coffee stains on the tips of the sleeves, and he's wearing fingerless gloves. A few buttons on his shirt are missing. His black khakis look like they've been worn without ever having been washed and they have paint and dirt stains. His work boots are no longer polished, and one lace is undone and ragged. It's evident he does not change his clothes anymore—he's worn that outfit for at least two weeks. It looks like he does live under a bridge now. He's sitting slouched on that sofa with an empty vodka bottle at his side and a newspaper reclining against his elbow, like a true street bum.

I ask him about Pelón from 18th Street. He tells me it's none of my business, that I'm being too judgmental standing over him all high and mighty, looking down at him. I just keep asking over and over until he says that he was involved in Knuckles' murder and begins to laugh really hard.

THE DOCTOR
January 1, 2000 1:27 a.m.

I'm untying the tent and tarps around the bivouac station. It's time to surrender. Mikey comes by, dismayed. He says it's all my fault. He's yelling and causing a scene. I ignore him, but I ball my fists. I'll beat this dude down if I have to.

"Everyone dies, Mikey. Just be happy you lived through all this," I tell him. "It was worth it. We're still here, and the world is listening, at least for now."

Mikey gets in my face, almost in a fighting stance. I jab him in the temple and he falls to the ground and blacks out for several seconds. When he comes to, his vision is blurry and he tries to adjust his sight. I stretch out my hand to help this little punk up, but he pulls out a pistol from his waistband and points it straight at my chest.

"Back the fuck up!" he yells. "Fuck you!"

Kimberly appears at the back door of the unit, and he turns to point the gun at her too, gestures her to stay back. This motherfucker is going postal.

"Take it easy, Mikey, put the gun down."

"You fuckin' murderer," he grunts. "You're no doctor, you don't help people. All this bullshit is your fault."

Kimberly's screaming is making it hard to think. "Calm down, Kim, please sit down," I suggest to her.

We have a small audience now.

"If Lurch and them hear you," I say to Mikey, "they're going to shoot you. Let's just talk. Can I sit down?" I have my eyes on a blue milk crate. He says, "Okay, sit down."

I take a seat on the crate and pull out a cigarette. I laugh a little and I say, "You're just like me. I see you, Mikey. I used to be shy and nervous just like you. Until I got to USC."

His demeanor changes slightly.

I laugh and say, "I got a free ride. . . . It wasn't Harvard or Yale, but it was a good fit. Then I screwed up. I sold cocaine and weed at parties to rich white kids."

"Why'd you stop?"

"I got popped. . . . The cops pulled me over one night and found an 8-ball of dope in the gas tank, a pistol in the dashboard and saw the VIN number had been tampered with. The car was stolen and chopped. I was arrested and sent to County. They charged me with transporting an illegal substance, carrying a loaded firearm and grand theft auto."

"I knew it," Mikey says. "You are a fuckin' criminal, just like the rest of them. You don't believe in any movement. This wasn't for our people."

I shoot him a look of annoyance. If he didn't have that pistol in his hand, I'd strike him again. "On my court date, the judge offered me a five-year suspension, instead of the seven years that the prosecutor was pushing for. The judge released me, but he said that if I got arrested for anything, like anything, within the next five years, I'd do a mandatory seven years in state prison. Just like that. 'And I want you to re-enroll in the university, to finish your degree.'"

Mikey stares at me blankly while I take a drag of the cigarette, then asks, "Well, what happened?"

"I went back to school, that's what. But before I got released from County, I got stabbed by a Nazi lowrider during a riot, from my cheek to my throat. That's how I got this damn scar. Lurch saved my life in there. Did you know that?"

"Lurch. . . . Lurch?!!"

"Yes, and Lurch influenced me to finish my degree. I eventually graduated with honors. Then I got into Princeton and USC for medical school, then I did my residency. I became a doctor."

"So what? You want a pat on the back?"

"Mikey, you chose a righteous path and stuck it out . . . even when things got rough. Now, you've got a promising career in

journalism. The writing you've done on the whole Y2K thing and
this quarantine phenomenon . . . that's award-winning material.
And I'm not flattering you, I really believe it."

I can see that I have his attention now, and he's letting his
guard down. In a few hours it'll be morning and I'll convince
Lurch to let the hostages go. And this will all be over. I keep
thinking about Cecilia, how she took care of me on the inside.
How she waited for me and stuck by me. All the visits. Damn, I
messed my whole marriage up . . . and my son? . . . I wonder if
it's too late to get back to them.

"Wait, there's more," I continue. "You'll like this. After I did
my residency, I couldn't get DEA clearance to practice medicine
because the medical board investigators claimed I wasn't suit-
able for a license. It tore my whole insides apart. I didn't leave the
house and cried for days. I thought it was over. But after a few
months, I got myself together, and at a private hearing I addressed
the DEA, the Medical Board of California, the District Attorney,
the FBI and a few other medical organizations. I expressed my
commitment to the medical profession and the need to minister
to people in underserved communities. I acknowledged my past
mistakes and told them that I had learned my lesson. I was gen-
uine. A few months later, they gave me my license."

I'm teary-eyed as I look at Kimberly. She rubs her nose and
mouth. I've never told her that.

"Then I worked in Del Rey and here inside the projects. People didn't judge me or ask about my scar. Everyone trusted me. I
never had that before. People at USC expected me to sell drugs,
you know, or be a fuck up, because I was the only Mexican in
my program. Some classmates made me feel unwelcome, they
looked at me like a janitor. It was all about privilege there. That's
why I opened a facility here, to help *our* people. And now *those*
people—transplants and gatekeepers and fascists who tried to
keep me out of academia—want to kick us out of the projects and
the rest of *our* neighborhoods? I don't think so, Mikey. Some-

body had to make a stand. It was my social duty, and maybe it was yours, too. Because you have an actual voice. But it's all over now. We lost the war. And now, I'll probably go to prison."

LURCH
January 1, 2000 1:47 a.m.

Fuck it, the twins and I decide to have a party, like it's 1999. Everybody's outside anyway, drinking and bullshitting or whatever. We're all still alive, so I think the dead homies would've wanted us to celebrate this way, *¿qué no?* In their memory 'n shit. Besides, there's a lotta gangsters here from other barrios, so it'll be a West Side party, like back in the day. Nothing changed when the clock turned to 2000 A.D., so I think we're gonna call it a day with this militia thing. The people are restless, they've lost their will to fight. I can see it all over their faces. Maybe I have too. I don't want another homie's blood on my hands. But let's just have this last party *y ya estuvo*.

The speakers, turntables, light and sound equipment arrive through the front double-door entrance of the gym. The DJ hauls in record crates. I plan on getting fucked up until I drop and won't wake up for like five days. Fuck everything, man. For real.

ॐ

The base booms out the speakers, "When I Hear Music" by Debbie Deb. Damn, the crowd goes wild. Takes us back to the 80s and the 90s. It's 2000 now, I can't believe it. Gang signs and hands are in the air. The crowd rolls up from all the housing units, from everywhere. Kids, moms, *paisas*, anarchists, hood rats, gangsters and of course the CEXCE gang—the CC Riders. The homies are flamed up in Cincinnati Reds hats, red railroad handkerchiefs, red shoelaces, red and black football jerseys. The twins are wearing fedoras with red rags around their throats and shoulder holsters over their Falcons football jerseys. Some of the *paisa* women show up with trays of *tamales* and *empanadas* and that sort of thing. We're back to our old ways. Everyone has pitched in with whatever alcohol they had at their pads. The gym is jam-packed to capacity and LED lights bounce off the walls. The DJ spins "Play at Your Own Risk" by Planet Patrol, and the crowd roars like at a horserace. It's beautiful, man. We're back in the mix! No time to think about the demolition of the projects. The quarantine is over, son! My only thought is to release the hostages, and I will, soon.

The DJ throws on an instrumental, "My Mind's Playing Tricks on Me" by the Ghetto Boys. Oh shit, I know what's coming next. The homie Jon-Boy gets on the mic and starts rapping, hard as fuck. He busts the homie Spy's line: *"West Side, Culver City Little Loco, I ain't drunk, that's my homeboy Wino. In the 'hood it's just straight up ballin', any disrespect your ass'll be fallin'."*

The DJ switches to an instrumental of "Float On" by the Floaters, and this dude from Lennox grabs the mic: *Here I go again just busting rhymes, evil ass youngster never dropping dimes, a straight young-ass gangster from the big Lennox, fuck with us get sent home in a box."* Sneaky from Venice raps next: *"In the West Side of Los you live your life in the fast lane, mostly gang banging and selling that cocaine. . . ."*

Man, it's wild up in this piece, and I can't stop the tears from coming down from my eyes. I'm ecstatic and angry all at once, you know what I'm saying?

Then the party lights go out.

What the fuck? So does the music. Like in a second. It's straight black in here, so people run in opposite directions like in a stampede and they bottleneck at the exits. When the lights come back on, Jon-Boy is spread out on the floor, blood pouring out of him . . . a red puddle around his chest. My eyes pop out. He's still breathing, though, gasping for air. I take my jacket off, put it under his neck and hold him in place. Out of nowhere, as I'm looking around for the twins or the doctor or anyone to help, I spot that fool Pelón from 18th Street peeking from behind a crowd. He's grinning. He's with Mikey's friend, Stan. They bone out amid the commotion when they catch me looking. I elbow my way through the crowd to follow them, screaming, "It's them, get 'em! It's them!" Nobody's paying attention. My shouts are drowned out by the screaming. I keep running toward the exit where I saw those fools. "I'm gonna kill 'em so bad," I feel like screaming out to the world! I'm holding the Mini-14 in my hands as I run, careful that it doesn't accidentally go off and kill an innocent person. There's so many people running in different directions, it's like chaos. I can't believe this. I'm so fuckin' pissed. Stupid, stupid, stupid. I stop in my tracks. I don't see these fools, but I know they must be heading toward the exit. It's the only way out. Sure enough, I spot Stan from a distance. They're almost at the front gate. I run faster, but they're gone with the wind, just like that.

MIKEY
January 1, 2000 2:13 a.m.

There's people running all over the place, something went down at the gymnasium. It's like a madhouse. I'm looking out the window toward the management office. There's only one guard there with the hostages: Raven. I don't know where the twins or Lurch are. If I'm gonna make a move, it has to be now. The doctor said that the quarantine was over, so the hostages should be released. That's all I can think of now. The front gate exit is just a few feet away. There's nobody at the bottom of the watchtower, just one dude on top. I pack my duffel bag, grab the pistol.

THE DOCTOR
January 1, 2000 2:14 a.m.

This Culver City boy, Jon-Boy, is dead. Someone in here punctured him in the heart. I couldn't do anything for him.

There's no room in a revolution for factions or treachery. These people have now turned on each other. Now, we have to release the hostages, no matter what. I have to find the lawyer and Kimberly. A nurse tells me that the lawyer's near the front entrance by the barracks. I gallop in that direction.

I hear the megaphone from the watchtower. The guard is shouting at someone walking on Inglewood Boulevard, aiming a rifle at him. I look through a peephole in the plywood and spot a young white kid and an Asian girl walking hand-in-hand near the front entrance of the projects, going south toward Ballona Creek. The white kid looks special needs, flapping his hands and walking like he has a limp. I look at the time on my wristwatch. I don't know why they're outside so late. They turn left and walk east, toward the flood control channel. I wonder where they're headed. The guard advises them that they are approaching an off-limits site. He's doing his job. A crowd of young Black Shirts approach the couple. They're young militants from inside the projects that crept out to regulate the neighborhood. Also doing their job.

MIKEY
January 1, 2000 2:14 a.m.

Raven grabs a beer from the refrigerator and downs it while pacing in the management office. He's getting buzzed. Gonna have to make my move soon. My heart races around a track. I cock the Glock back—*shik, shik*—and swing the duffel bag over my shoulder.

THE DOCTOR
January 1, 2000 2:15 a.m.

Some of the young militants are wearing ski masks, others have handkerchiefs and two sport gas masks. The group surrounds the couple, and a self-appointed spokesperson in the crowd says, "Get the fuck out of our neighborhood."

The white kid, who can't even make eye contact with them says, "Get the fuck outta here!" and laughs with vengeance.

I know for a fact that he's sick, autistic perhaps. He proceeds forward in their direction, claps twice and flails his arms. He's now all up in their faces. They look around confused. They didn't expect this response. I need to stop this, but part of me just lets it happen.

The spokesperson says, "Calm down, you crazy psycho. You know who the fuck we are?"

"Fuck you, fuck you! You're crazy. You're crazy," says the kid and he continues laughing.

The girl tries to grab him, and only then do I realize she's wearing a name tag, like she's his therapist at a clinic.

She grabs it and pushes it up from her breast and says, "He has a mental health condition, he's in my care! Leave him alone!"

MIKEY
January 1, 2000 2:16 a.m.

Raven spills beer on the floor but doesn't clean it up. Instead he laughs. He's buzzed for sure—vulnerable. He's alone and starts dancing in this cool gangster style, with his elbows folded into his chest and his knuckles touching each other at the tips. Fuck it, here goes nothing. I look at the Glock one last time before stuffing it down my pants. I store the duffel bag under the rattan chair on the porch. All I can think of is Stan. He said he had something to do with Knuckles' murder, and he told me to take out Raven. So did Paulina. Here's my chance. I feel compelled to do the right thing. Put things back in order. Even if it's the last thing I do.

I creep toward the back of the management unit behind cars and trees. There's loud noise and distractions everywhere. Like the doctor said, "Where there's chaos, there's opportunity." My heart thumps, and I look up at the watchtower. The guard is facing Ballona Creek. Something's going on over there, too. The

two soldiers behind the bunker also face that side, so nobody has
their eyes on the most important facility. My palms are sweaty as
I move closer toward the back exit. I'm only a few feet away now.

THE DOCTOR
January 1, 2000 2:16 a.m.

One of the boys in the group pulls a knife from his belt clip
and lunges at the kid. The young thug catches him in the forearm
as the kid moves to shield his face. With the other arm, the kid
yanks the knife from the aggressor, pulls his arm toward him and
slits his throat.

A girl with a gas mask whacks the kid on the head with a
baton, and the boy falls over the first aggressor. The therapist tries
to run but a girl wrenches her by the hair and drops her to the cement. Another young girl takes a boulder and drops it on her face,
smashing her brain instantly. A stream of blood makes its way
down the channel. The rest of the militants push her lifeless body
down the embankment. It rolls evenly, lands on shrubbery and
used trash bags.

At the same time, the rest of the aggressors beat the kid with
batons until they run out of energy. His skull and face have been
smashed to the point that he'll need a closed casket at his funeral.
The boys push the body down the embankment next to the girl.
And then they push their comrade down, without thinking about
the repercussions, perhaps. Three teenage bodies dead in a matter of seconds . . . for our stupid cause.

MIKEY
January 1, 2000 2:18 a.m.

Raven staggers out of the back door, laughing, and stumbles
on the grass. He proceeds to take a piss on the bushes while
singing along to an oldies jam, "Hello Stranger" by Barbara
Lewis. I love that track too! I slither in through the back door. It

leads to the kitchen. I glance in all directions. I look up and see the hostages—four men and the councilwoman—sitting in a makeshift cage. They're dressed in business clothes, perhaps what they had on when they got captured. They smell foul, like they haven't showered in weeks. Their mouths are gagged with red handkerchiefs, and their hands are tied with rope to chairs and bars. I want to cover my nose but think it might be offensive to them. I lift my finger to my lips instead, and the councilwoman starts crying. I walk right past them and whisper, "I'm going to get you guys out of here."

I hear the backdoor shut. I bolt down the hallway toward a room and slide under a bed I find there.

THE DOCTOR
January 1, 2000 2:19 a.m.

The teenagers don't know what to do about their deceased comrade. They huddle around each other and consider their options. Some do the benediction sign. A couple cry. One has his hands up. The others are terrified. One kid says that it's self-defense, and they decide to do nothing more. Bringing him back up is out of the question. They agree that they have to tell Lurch or some other leader.

They return to the projects near building 20. I hide behind trees so that they won't see me. They set fire to some papers and branches in a trashcan. Some are still crying. One of the kids goes to look for Lurch or someone else in charge. It's my cue to leave. I have to go back to the bivouac station, get Kimberly and the nurses and let the hostages go. Then turn myself in.

MIKEY
January 1, 2000 2:24 a.m.

I wait for Raven to go take a piss again or do something else. I don't know what. I just wait for footsteps in the distance or a door to open or close. All I can see is grey carpet in the dim light and some white sneakers underneath the bed. My hands are sweatier than shit. I feel like I'm going to have a stroke. I place my right hand over my chest and close my eyes. I count to one hundred and then hop up to my feet. I take the pistol out of my waistband and hold it out in front of me. I creep closer to the door and poke my head out. I don't see Raven anywhere. I tip-toe closer to where the hostages are. I see Raven walk by their cage. He stops near a stereo and I jerk back a little. He looks through tapes, and I recognize a four-unit compilation called "Book of Love" by Art Laboe. My sister has one too. He reads the back matter, where the songs are listed. I approach him in stealth mode and whack him in the back of the head with the gun. He falls to the floor without having a chance to look back at me. I hit him one more time as he slumps over. I really wanna shoot him, and I probably would if the hostages weren't around. I step on his shit bag though—that might cause some damage. It happens so quickly that I don't even realize what I've actually done.

LURCH
January 1, 2000 2:29 a.m.

This fool finds me near the gym and tells me he needs to show me something, *de volada*. I don't wanna leave Jon-Boy like that, just laying there. But something tells me this is really important. I run with him to a playground, thinking it's another dead homie. Or Stan or some *putos* from 18th Street.

The kid says to me, "It's my fault. . . . It was all my idea. I'll take the blame, swear to God."

A girl in their crew says, "No, it was all of us. It's not fair. We all played a part."

Another kid says, "We don't know what to do. We're sorry about this, Big Lurch." Then he cries like a little bitch.

I'm like, "What the fuck? What'd you guys do? Fuckin' say it already."

They take me to a fence, and through a peephole in the plywood they show me where three bodies lay. I spot the victims slumped in the creek. I can't believe what these kids have done. And they're trying to take the blame for each other, trying to do the right thing, like some real soldiers. But they're all just innocent kids that have made a terrible mistake. They got caught up in all this bullshit. Something in my gut tells me I should take the blame instead. This can all be over now, and these kids might get the chance to live a normal life. *I* have the chance to do right by them.

But right before I say this out loud, sirens blast all over the place and a ghetto bird hovers over us. A bright light shines inside the projects and bounces around from unit to unit.

MIKEY
January 1, 2000 2:29 a.m.

As I grab a knife from a drawer, I hear sirens howling. I see the bright light skipping inside the unit and all over the cage. I freeze and drop the knife. I think it's coming from the watchtower. Then I think that it's the big LAPD raid, or the FEMA one that Lurch always talks about. I dash through the back door as the watchtower sounds the panic alarm.

The masses are outside of their units making tons of noise. I run over to where some TVs are set up. The news is reporting on the murder of an autistic boy and his therapist along Ballona Creek. The boy's parents are holding a conference. The dad's a fireman, the mom a district attorney. We're royally fucked. But I'm not thinking about the dead kid, I'm thinking about Raven. My heart is still pounding and I feel I might have left something behind. Maybe a pencil or a ball of paper fell out of my pocket. Something. I wonder if he saw me, or if he's awake by now. On television, the D.A. pleas for her son's killers to come forward. She says that her son had autism and that his in-home physical therapist took him for a walk because he couldn't sleep with all the fireworks going off. They walked all the way from the Culver City side. Just a nightly stroll through the neighborhood, like it wasn't dangerous.

The mom says, "If you turn yourselves in now, you may get a lighter sentence. If you wait, justice will be long and brutal. I promise you that."

The crowd around the television gets bigger. I keep my eye on Lurch. The twins are there, and so is the lawyer and the doctor. The CXC boys are huddled and they look up at the management office where the hostages are. Something doesn't seem right to them, and I'm not close enough to make out their dialogue. My heart races. I'm thinking about Stan and Knuckles. Lurch and the twins march to the front door of the management office, and I hear someone scream . . . maybe one of the hostages. The crowd shifts toward them, and through the window I see Noel picking up Raven. The sirens are calmer, and the helicopter's light is illuminating the crime scene just outside the projects. It's like we've all forgotten about that already. Lurch picks up a knife from the floor, and the twins help their cousin to his feet. Blood oozes down his neck, and someone calls for the doctor. Noel and some other people take Raven to the medical unit. The doctor bones out behind them.

LURCH
January 1, 2000 2:41 a.m.

I grab the councilwoman by the back of her neck and say, "Who did it, huh? Who the fuck was it?"

But she keeps her head down, crying out of control. The other hostages mumble some bullshit, and I remove one of the guy's handkerchiefs from his mouth. He laughs and says, "Your days are numbered."

I think about what he says, for like five seconds. Then I point the Mini-14 with a silencer at him and spray him in the chest, in front of everyone. Just like that, I don't give a fuck. *Boom, boom, boom.* Blood splatters on the wall behind him and on the faces of the other hostages. They scream like they're on a rollercoaster ride. My heart leaps out of my chest, too. But the good kind, the I-will-kill-all-you-motherfuckers kind. Everyone respects the gun. Straight up.

I yell out, "This place is on lockdown! There's a fuckin' *rata* up in this piece!" I know just like that, more people are gonna die . . . until I find the traitor.

I look in the direction of Mikey's unit, across the way. I'ma start right there. Stan for sure, Mikey too—for bringing him here.

MIKEY
January 1, 2000 2:44 a.m.

There's a knock on the front door of my unit. I freeze up and squeeze a pillow on the sofa. I know it's Lurch and them.

The knock gets harder.

Leon orders, "Open up, Mikey, c'mon. We know you're in there."

I run to the front door and open it. "What's going on?" I ask, trying to keep a normal face.

Lurch looks at me sternly. "That your bag there? You planning on going somewhere?"

I look under the rattan chair at my duffel bag. Noel picks it up and throws it inside the living room. They all have guns, not pointed at me, but not pointing away either. It's weird, you know?

Lurch asks about Stan, where he is, and I tell him that he and Patty split because she's pregnant.

"I'm only going to ask you this once." Lurch says. "Was it Stan?"

"Was it Stan what?" I ask.

"I told you I was only going to ask you once," he says, and tells Leon to open my bag and see what's in there.

Lurch looks back at me and says, "This is considered high treason, homie. I didn't think it'd end like this."

I squeeze the pistol's grip inside my parka pocket. If these fools point a strap directly at me, I'm going out blasting. I fucked up anyway. Whatever happens, happens. Right before Noel opens the bag, the front door sways open. Some anarchists storm the living room and say, "There's an emergency! The doctor needs you at Raven's place! He's not breathing."

As they turn to bolt out the door, Lurch yanks my parka sleeve and says, "C'mon, Mikey, you're going too, *ese*. This ain't over."

☙❧

When we arrive at the unit, there's already a mob outside. They want blood.

The doctor says, "He's all right. It was a close call. He just suffered a concussion."

Lurch says, "Don't trip doc, I know who did it. And I'ma handle that *pedo* right now. Then he looks at me and says, "Let's go, upstairs."

The twins and Lurch all go back to their stern look toward me, but the twins bone out. It's like Lurch just communicated something solely with his eyes.

Upstairs, Lurch says, "You know something, Mikey. I recognize that duffel bag from somewhere. I just realized it right now. From that night you were at my pad, when I got out of County. Remember?"

I swallow spit and I brush my hair to the side. I say, "What do you want to know, man? I'll tell you everything. For real, Lurch. I'm . . ."

Lurch says, "I know you fucked Paulina. She told me that night. She told me how you asked her for a relationship and all that. How you're like all in love with her."

My face gets ruddy, and I get like this stab wound sensation in my stomach. I say, "What? What are you talking about? Paulina . . . nah, man."

Lurch laughs like a madman. He says, "You've been lying to me since the beginning . . . about everything, homie. What do you think Raven's gonna do to you when he finds out about this? And when I tell him about what you just did to him? I know it was you, motherfucker."

I almost have a heart attack. I don't know what to say. The words that come out are, "Don't you think this quarantine has gone too far?"

Lurch laughs. "I killed a hostage—yeah, now it's gone too far. I'ma kill the rest in a minute, and then I'm gonna kill you, slowly but surely. You know, homes, I gave you a gang of chances to leave, dog. I never knew why you wanted to stay. But now, it makes sense."

"I'm with *you*, Lurch. I've known you practically my whole life," I say.

Lurch says, "There's only one way out of this. *You* get to kill the next hostage."

My heart drops and my eyes widen. I can't even really process what he's saying to me. I only hear soundbites and random words: "Stan . . . that's why you got a whipping . . . Knuckles got killed, Jon-Boy did too . . . you tried to kill my homeboy . . . Raven."

It's all like in slow motion, like I'm on drugs.

The last thing he says is, "I can't let that slide. Gonna need some dirt on you, you know what I mean? You're gonna kill the councilwoman, and then I'ma let Raven handle you."

My IBS comes back, in full fury. I'm trembling hardcore now. Feel like shit is immediately gonna shoot out of my asshole.

I thought Lurch was just gonna put one in my head and it'd be over. This is worse, all the anticipation and all the talk. But I remember I have a pistol too. Inside my parka's pocket, I place my finger on the trigger. Lurch stares at me, but he doesn't say anything. He just looks at me, disappointed. I blink and lower my head. I look in a different direction. He doesn't know what I'm doing with my hand. Maybe I can get the drop on this dude. I say, "We don't have to do this. I'm not going to kill a hostage. This is all over. Even the doctor said so."

Lurch looks confused, like it came as a shock to him, and he says, "Fuck it, any last words?"

Lurch points the gun toward me and his eyes light up. I start to raise the Glock in my hand, in my parka, then we hear a bunch of sirens and inaudible talk on a megaphone coming from outside. Lights bounce around everywhere too. Lurch darts toward the window. He looks out, forgets about me completely. I pull out the gun and point, and when Lurch turns around, I shoot him in the face. A spray of blood streams out of his temple and his body collapses, just like that. Blood oozes out of his head onto the carpet. I make a run for it.

◎✲◎

On the streets inside the housing projects, there's a thunder of activity—gunfire, sirens, screams, voices, helicopters. I run in a zigzagging pattern and slide and maneuver behind cars and trees toward the management office. I see gangsters and anarchists falling over from bullet wounds, some of them are running for cover. No doctor or medical team attending the wounded. Bullets fly right past me and I arch my back and duck, even shield my head with my arms. My heart is beating so fast. I pray to God that I don't get shot in my back. Or get paralyzed.

I make it to the unit in one piece and the door is unlocked. I look toward Inglewood Boulevard and I see that the SWAT team is prying the gates open and shooting their way in. They're taking heavy fire from the militia and neither side backs down. A nearby helicopter shoots out the watchtower and it collapses onto the front gate. The guard falls from the tower and lands on shrubbery. It sparks a small fire—when the tower falls—and it crushes a portion of the barred gate. Officers swarm Allin Street behind the flames and take advantage of the smoke screen. The SWAT team rushes several units at once, including mine, with weapons drawn and with night vision goggles strapped over their eyes. They have infrared scopes too.

I run inside the unit. The hostages are on the floor of the cage, lying on their stomachs. They're kicking and struggling and trying to scream through their gagged mouths. I grab a knife from a kitchen drawer and proceed to untie the first person.

When I remove the bandana from his mouth and cut the cable ties from his wrists, he says, "They ran down there! Through the tunnel."

I don't know what tunnel he's talking about, but I move a rug to the side near the dining table where he pointed, and there's a big hole in the tile and there's a ladder that drops down below. My heart beats fast and I can hear footsteps on the roof and windows shattering near and far. The city councilwoman is the only hostage missing. I toss the untied hostage the knife and I climb down the ladder. He wishes me luck.

I smell gunpowder all over. There's piled dirt, and I slip a few times as I descend. I'm tripping out because I didn't know these fools built a goddamn tunnel into the sewer line, and it's sophisticated as fuck. Probably why I didn't see the twins the whole time I've been in quarantine. And now Noel and Leon, or whoever, have boned out with the politician. I have to get her, it's not right that she's a hostage.

It's muggy and tight until I reach the ground. I run and step on mud and water in the sewer. The walls are concrete and the ceilings are high and circular. I rub my hand against a wall. It's full of ridges. It's kind of dark down here, but those fools installed a power line with Christmas lights to create a visible walkway. There's graffiti everywhere. A lot if it is block letters by the Culver City boys, but there's a lot of stoner gang stuff too. One section has anarchy signs and "Black Sabbath #1" in heavy metal font. I try to read all the writing, looking for clues.

THE DOCTOR
January 1, 2000 3:55 a.m.

The militia, packed with revolvers, Uzis and M-14s shoots at the cops on the rooftops. Helicopters circle above and drop personnel on top of buildings, but the resistance guns some of them down.

The lawyer gave the order to attack, I didn't have time to tell him to stand down. The Southernist Guard toss pipe bombs and Molotov cocktails into the management office, hoping to kill the hostages, but they are being corralled through the backdoor to safety. Some of the bombs land on cars and ignite them. They explode. The hostages are safe now, just outside the front gate, so the SWAT team flings tear gas canisters all over and everyone covers their eyes because of our burning tears. Some anarchists roll around on the ground. A handful of soldiers run with unfiltered cigarettes up their noses to prevent the gas from entering through their nostrils. More cops invade the projects by the dozens and handcuff numerous wounded resistance fighters, but the shootout is still steadfast.

I strap an SKS rifle over my shoulder and run to the top floor of the medical unit. I'm in my doctor scrubs and I have a helmet. I picture myself like Salvador Allende, right before the coup in Santiago de Chile. Kimberly asks me what to do, and I tell her to run, to turn herself in. She grabs my hand, expecting me to go with her, but I shoo her away. I tell her to just run and to not look back. She listens. I go up to the top floor. Some fighters are with me. I tell them to shoot through the windows.

A shooter posts up across the street in another unit and exchanges fire with us for over one minute. A bullet grazes my forehead, and I feel a warm liquid slide down my face. I duck and crawl to another window. I spot the lawyer and a squadron maintaining a section of the projects from behind the bunker with the sandbags, near the kiosk. He's still holding it down. Then I see a parade of bullets take him from behind.

The guards that are with me take shots to their heads. I think a sniper did it. The victims fall, and some of their blood squirts onto my face. I get up and shoot like crazy out the window while tears spray out of my eyes. A barrage of bullets enters the windows and my body. I can hear heavy stomps of boots on the roof and on the staircase. I just keep on shooting and holding on until it all goes dark.

MIKEY
January 1, 2000 4:05 a.m.

The sewer doesn't seem to end. It's just like this labyrinth—branching passageways to different areas. It's humid and steamy and it smells like shit everywhere. I keep stepping in numerous puddles of rippling water and I see giant rats running and crawling all around. I'm so disgusted, and my body is itchy all over. I feel like I'm breaking out in hives or something. Finally, in the distance, I can see a few people in dark clothes running, splashing water as they go. They aren't that far ahead, and I run faster to catch up. I spot one person on a drainpipe, and when he climbs back down, I see that it's Leon. He signals something to the others, and they follow him up. There's at least ten people with him. And then I see Paulina. She's nudging the councilwoman up the ladder. I have to stop them. My heart pounds like crazy. I love her for sure and hate her at the same time. I picture Raven and Lurch fucking her, and it tears me apart for like a second. Until I remember I just killed Lurch.

I increase my speed and yell out, "Paulina! Paulina!"

When I make it out of the sewer line through the drainpipe, I hear a bombardment of bullets. The slugs hit the cement, throwing sparks everywhere. Those fools are shooting at me! Something rips through my chest and my right arm. I feel like it's burning. Bullet fragments bounce off walls, and shotgun pellets hit me all over. Then I feel a flame-type of thing on my right leg, then a silky wetness slides down below my knee cap. My body gives out. I collapse.

❧

When I wake up, I'm literally handcuffed to a hospital bed. I'm in a nightgown and have a sheet over my body, up to my neck. The room is cold and small with a curtain halfway open. A television monitor is on, showing images of the housing projects on fire. Clips of police attacking Mar Vista Gardens and people being pulled out on stretchers and body bags are constant.

I'm in shock still, really, more than anything else. I try to move but I'm strapped in pretty tight. I look at a nearby chair and see my raggedy and bloody clothes.

A nurse inside my room says, "You lost a lot of blood, young man. But you're going to be just fine." She pats me on the head.

"Where are we? What happened?" I ask.

"UCLA—on Washington. You got shot a few times, but nothing major. They found you on National by Ballona Creek."

"Who found me?" I ask.

"I don't know. You were passed out, from the bullet wounds, I guess. They were mostly fragments that struck you all over though. Your right leg received the most tissue damage. You'll be on crutches for a few days. That's it. Oh, and there's some people outside that want to see you. They've been waiting for a few hours."

The nurse steps outside and slides a curtain open. Through a window I recognize the hostages crowding around the room entrance. They're with children and women, and I assume they're with their families. I'm horrified that they're here. What the fuck do they want? Oh shit! My dad's out there too, with my sister and her kids. And Stan, my mom, Mark Stahl, Rick. It's like a madhouse. What the fuck!

A cop comes in first and uncuffs me. He has a newspaper in his hand and says, "Can you sign this for me?"

"What's this?" I ask.

"One of your articles. It's about the quarantine. My wife and I have been following your stories since this whole thing started. I'm honored," he says.

I don't know what to think. I'm irritated more than anything. I sign it, although I wrinkle my forehead and squint. Am I a somebody now?

"Should I let them in now?" he asks.

My father runs in first and hugs me with a warmth that I've never experienced from him. He says, "I'm so proud of you, son. I'm so glad you're alive."

And I'm like, "The fuck do you want, hypocrite?"

Other people stroll in and I hear "Congratulations" and "Thank you" and all types of other awkward shit. Stan snaps photographs with flashes and I cover my face. I wanna punch that fool more than anything.

Stan gets really close and whispers, "You did it, man. You did it. You're like the gnarliest dude in all of Los Angeles right now."

January 3, 2000

It's the rescheduled date for the Mar Vista Gardens housing projects demolition. The sun is out strong to bear witness on the ceremony. It's been frosty and grey all week, and suddenly—*bam*—the bluest sky covers the West Side in a tarp of cool breeze and brilliant light, unusual for mid-January. I've seen the climate

change from the bedroom window since I've been bedridden—
to recover, but I really hoped that this day would never come.

I smell burnt chili peppers, tomato sauce and a hint of onion
all the way from the room in my sister's apartment. I walk with
crutches to the kitchen. My dad is reading a newspaper at the
table. I don't even know why the fuck he's there. He's wearing
reading glasses and has a cup of coffee in front of him. My mom
is there, too. She's wearing an apron as she mashes refried beans
in a saucepan and flips crisp and burnt tortilla chips. There's a
slab of *queso fresco* nearby and cracked egg shells in a box. My
sister pours a glass of orange juice and takes a seat between my
dad and her daughter, who's in a high chair. I'm tripping out, because we haven't been together like this for a long time.

Slightly sarcastic, I say, "Did someone die, or what?"

My mom says, "I'm glad you're awake, we can all eat together now."

She hugs me. I don't reciprocate.

My dad says, "You're a hero, son. It says so right here. It says
you were the only one who tried to free those hostages. I knew I
raised a good son."

My sister says, "Proud of you, bro," but she doesn't look at
me while feeding her kid. Like it just slides out of her.

I don't know how to process all this phony familial stuff.
However, Lurch had indirectly taught me that family is everything. That it was up to me to try. Am I getting a second chance?
At least they're here, making the effort for the first time. It has to
count for something, I guess. But it's weird and I just make fool-
ish facial expressions. They don't know what our resistance went
through during the quarantine. They don't ask either because it
doesn't matter anymore. I'm alive and that's all that's important
to them. I tried to help the hostages. The newspaper said so, and
there were numerous articles that I wrote, and that means something to my family. My sister kept every newspaper where an article of mine was published. They're stashed in her closet.

She says to me, "Everyone I know asked for your autograph. You're famous, little bro."

There are stacks of mail for me on the countertop, apparently fan mail. There are also envelopes from the *LA Weekly, Los Angeles Magazine, The San Francisco Chronicle* and a whole bunch of other local and state publications. Some from as far away as the Pacific Northwest. They express their condolences and offer job opportunities as a staff reporter or as a regular contributor. *The Los Angeles Magazine* asks if I want to write a long-form piece about gangs. There's two letters from actual book publishers—interested in a memoir or non-fiction book about my experience.

I'm like, "What the fuck is all this? None of it makes sense, you know?"

I harbored and protected murderers, kidnappers and arsonists, and I killed Lurch. Shit, I killed Lurch. What did I do?

A letter from my editor says that they submitted my pieces for a prize in journalism for investigative reporting. I should be ecstatic, but all I can think of is Paulina and the councilwoman.

And Lurch. Oh, and . . . Stan, and Knuckles, Wino, Spy, Rumble, the twins, Jon-Boy—the whole quarantine crew and the resistance in general. It matters more to me than I actually thought. Should've tried to stop it sooner. I have flashes of Lurch's face exploding and blood streaming out of his temple. And that look on Raven's face when he was on the floor, and Knuckles in a casket. And the doctor and the lawyer all geared up, ready to give up everything.

I can't be at the house anymore. I ask my sister to take me to the demolition ceremony on Allin Street and Inglewood Boulevard. It's more comfortable to wear shorts because of my wound. I throw on some black corduroy house slippers that only gangsters wear in public. But I kinda feel like a gangster, you know? I have a stripe now. I throw on a ballcap and dark sunglasses. I hope nobody recognizes me. Perhaps I need a haircut and a shave too.

My mom asks why I didn't eat. I tell her that I'm not hungry and what I really need is just fresh air and to see the outside world. My dad tells me he loves me, and I'm like whatever. If my parents are getting back together and being all weird and fake, then I'm out.

I tell my sister to go down the old block. We pass up Lurch's house, his mom while sisters and a few relatives are outside. His mom is weeping while two of the daughters console her. I stare at them and scan their bodies draped in black as my sister drives on slowly. They don't look up at us—they don't acknowledge that the world exists. I killed Lurch. I feel a cold wind inside me.

The metal bars on the houses on our block and on Braddock Drive that were fortified last month came down, and the crosses on some of the rooftops are gone. White artsy-looking people are walking down our old streets with a sense of normalcy. There's a white lady and her two daughters sitting and playing with some *paisa* ladies that are posted up on a corner with clothes thrown all over the yard. Like they're having a yard sale. White people are just right there, like nothing, making friends or some shit. And the little white girls are just playing like *paisa* kids. I cringe. The front entrance of the projects on Allin Street is full of bulldozers, Department of Water & Power vehicles, LAPD squad cars, people in suits, the media and civilian observers. A bunch of cameras and news vans are posted up on Inglewood Boulevard. Some of the project units have already been burned down to rubble. Plywood and metal bars and glass are all over the goddamn place. The management office is completely gone, just like two studs remain. There's a gang of commercial construction and debris dumpsters hitched on big rigs, lined up outside.

I say to my sister, "Just drop me off right here. I'll be okay."

She says, "But you can't walk so well. The doctor said you can't be on your feet for too long. And what about the gang members, huh? You're not safe here."

"I'll call you in a bit. I'll be okay, I swear to God. Don't tell mom and dad, though. I need to be here."

She wants to stay with me, but I need to be alone. She leaves me there by the crowd.

I elbow my way through the mob and make it all the way to the front row. The councilwoman, the hostage—Cindy Miscikowski—is right there with the mayor and the police chief. LAPD officers and secret service types guard them. There's even a white ribbon in front of them to cut. I assumed that that was only for an opening ceremony or some shit like that. I didn't know Miscikowski had been released. I have the widest smile, and she notices me from afar. She runs toward me and squeezes me tightly. She holds that position for a long time. The media snaps photographs like crazy, and I get teary-eyed. I'm full of joy and anger and fear.

She whispers in my ear, "That young woman let me go because of you. She said it was because of you."

Paulina, my girl.

The councilwoman cuts the ribbon, and the mayor blows a whistle. The bulldozers make beeping sounds as they move forward and smash right through the bars and run over buildings. Stucco walls are mowed down. I look below at the cement carvings Stan loved so much. I see a broken piece of cement. It reads: "Culver City Little Locos." It's cracked and disconnected from the pavement. A high school marching band plays military marches, and people dance and celebrate.

And then I see Wino's and Knuckles' relatives, and Lurch's, and the doctor's, and they're crying and screaming, preparing for a life of bereavement. Lurch's mom looks at me. I sob and cover my face. I wonder if she knows. I can't even look in their direction anymore. All I can see are flashes of Lurch laughing and talking. I feel weird. And then I see some *paisa*-looking people and some youngsters running toward the barely-standing project entrance. The cops tackle them, slam them down on the sidewalk and cuff them as they yell. Their pained roars echo through my entire body.

The projects come down hard. It sounds like the 4th of July. All that is left are pieces of stucco and windows that are about to sink into the abyss. The handcuffed people and others, the CXC boys' families call out to their homeland—their ruins, the only place they longed to return to. It reminds me of Knuckles' funeral. My eyes get moist.

The projects are being liberated after being strangled by poverty and crime for so long. All the memories and friendships of the projects are dying at that exact moment.

THIRTY-NINE

MIKEY

June 3, 2000

The Jesus and Mary Chain announced an outdoor set at the Hollywood Park Casino and Racetrack near the Inglewood Forum. There's never been a concert here, but with Silicon Beach sweeping the West Side, everyone wants in on renovation and re-branding. The Forum had recently closed due to low sales be-cause of the constant shootouts between Bloods and Crips, and whoever else. And it was total madness during basketball games and rap shows, but now the city is doing this arts district thing in the industrial zone and they have the Inglewood Open Studios program for the artists over here. Even the band's management thought it was a weird but unique venue to play, since they are scheduled to go on after the last horse race. It's their last tour be-fore they break up or take a hiatus, so I had to come, no matter what. They're my band, all day every day.

I don't live in the West Side anymore. My friend from down the street, Rick, and myself, are renting a two-bedroom house with a swimming pool in the Holy Glen neighborhood of Hawthorne—South Bay. It's a bachelor pad, so we invite friends over on a regular basis. Rick has to be close to the Air Force base in El Segundo because he got stationed over here after New Mexico, and I had to get away from Culver City. I couldn't be around the remnants of the Culver City boys, the projects, the quarantine, my family, or the 11ᵗʰ District anymore. The Silicon Gardens complex is almost finished and the Silicon Beach crowd took over the region. It felt like our whole past was stolen and white-washed. Our neighborhood used to be filled with regular and common people who did common people things, but these new transplants are too cool for school.

They walk down our streets without any concern and they snap photos of everything. Hawthorne is still normal, but the plague is coming this way. I can feel it.

⊚✺⊚

A bunch of our friends are at the pad before the concert. Stan and Mark Stahl are here too, and a bunch of our friends and acquaintances from high school and college that play in bands and do artsy stuff. We drink vodka tonics in the living room and play 80s and 90s new wave and postpunk songs to get in the mood. Rick does some bad ass moves—like the lead singer of Midnight Oil in the "Beds Are Burning" video—to "Sex Dwarf" by Soft Cell. We catch him on camera and he looks like a silhouette moving his hands and arms through a shadow play effect. I remember he did the same thing the night I had sex with Paulina for the first time. And I get really depressed.

The parking lot entrance at Hollywood Park is crowded, never seen it like this before. Mostly white people and Latinos, and a visible-looking Asian and Black person here and there. There's a lot of cool, stylish people, like from the old scene, you know? My friends and I are dressed in classic post-punk—Doc Martens, brothel creepers, band T-shirts, cardigans, jeans, that sort of thing. I'm wearing black Docs, black Levi's, and a navy blue Harrington Fred Perry jacket. I shaved my head, too and let my sideburns grow like mutton chops, like Stan, so I look more like a skinhead now. I guess there's a new scene. Mark Stahl says that a lot of these scenesters live in Echo Park and Silver Lake where he spins records. I wonder where these people go to dance on weekends, or if they go to venues that we frequent. I bet you they go to Tower Records for album release parties and acoustic shows, but they probably don't go near Soundsations in Westchester or Fais Do-Do in Mid-City. Or house parties in our neighborhoods. I guess I don't really like that they are here in Inglewood.

We sneak in our flasks with straight vodka and we buy cheap beer that they serve in red plastic cups. Pabst Blue Ribbon or some shit like that. We post up in a spot close to the stage, but not too close because that's uncool. That's desperate.

During the "Blues from a Gun" song, Rick and Stan sing the chorus while their heads are close together and they face opposite directions. I don't know why that gesture has such an effect on me but I think it's just a picture-perfect moment and I want to live in that for a long time, you know? Like our entire past is wrapped up in that gesture. Then the band plays "Head On" and I imagine Paulina and Lurch and my eyes get super-watery and I just can't take it.

We go get beer and Stan and I are talking about the band and Rick's trying to pick up on a white girl in line. I can't hear their conversation but then Rick says, "Hey Mikey, this girl says there's no gangs in Santa Monica or Venice. She doesn't believe me."

I look at her and say, "Yeah there are. Santa Monica is one of the oldest gangs in the West Side. They used to call them tomato gangs during the Depression because they used to have food fights with produce. That's how they started."

With attitude she says, "What are you, like the gang expert? I've never seen any around there."

Rick says, "He's a journalist—he survived that quarantine in the Culver City projects. Mikey here is a real live gang expert."

She says, "There aren't any projects in Culver City. Aren't those like in South Central or East Los Angeles?"

I remember what Lurch once said, "One day people will say that Culver City boys used to live there." But at that moment, I realize it is much worse than that. I wave my hand at them to dismiss her and me and Stan walk to another line. I can't listen to that kind of talk anymore. Can't be around ignorant, white-entitled, arrogant bullshit.

In another beer line, Stan and I overhear these two white girls talking.

One says, "Oh, did you hear? They're gonna build outlets right there in Hawthorne."

"Where is that?" the other asks.

"I think it's around here somewhere. Inglewood—Hawthorne, same thing. I'm surprised we're even here. I never leave Playa Vista, especially to go South to a ghetto place like this."

The other girl says, "Yeah, I stay in the upper West Side of Silicon Beach—Malibu."

And they both squawk and take a drink from their cups. My blood boils and Stan puts his hand on my wrist. He nods his head.

One of the white girls says, "Yeah, like after the Hawthorne Mall got looted during the 1992 riots or something, that place was abandoned and it's been like that ever since. And it's like, seriously, you gotta do something there."

"Yeah, we won't have to go all the way to Camarillo to those other ones," says the friend.

The other says, "Well, when they open in Hawthorne, I'll never go. I'd rather go to Camarillo or Cabazon. Those people there, it's like, 'No, I don't think so.'"

And I walk away again and Stan follows me. He catches up and says, "Why didn't you say something? You could've defended our people and our neighborhoods, you know. They're talking about people like us."

I say, "Why didn't you? Besides, they're not our neighborhoods anymore."